DESIRE

BOOK ONE IN THE TWISTED HEARTS DUET

MAX HENRY

DESIRE
Copyright © 2018 Max Henry
Published by Max Henry

Cover Image: Mr.Big Photography
Cover Design and Interior Formatting: Cover Story Designs
Editing: Hot Tree Editing

Four simple rules when you're a man on parole:

1. Don't lust after your best friend's daughter.
2. Don't get into a physical fight over her.
3. Definitely don't f*ck her.
4. And whatever you do, don't fall in love.

I have a bad habit of breaking rules.

FOREWORD

DESIRE is set in a fictional town in New Zealand, and as such I have written in my native tongue and used NZ English spelling and some slang terms.

Also, the legal age of consent in New Zealand is sixteen years old. Please bear this in mind when following Zeus and Belle's journey.

Much love,

xox Max

PROLOGUE

Belle (Age 7)

We made him cry before he gave in and said why he hadn't been at school for a month. Marley Anderson's mum was killed in a car accident. As soon as he told us, I remembered. Dad was quiet that day when he picked me up from school. The news story had been on the radio, and all over the papers that get delivered to our letterbox for at least a week.

A big truck lost control and squashed her car against the barrier. She didn't have a chance at making it; that's what Dad said when I asked him about it. Right before Mum stole the newspaper and told me, "Little girls shouldn't be interested in depressing shit like this."

I wish it was her. I wish it was her car that had been squashed against the concrete, not Marley's mum's.

Marley's mum was nice. She was at the parents' day, helping him with the activities our teacher set up. She helped me ice my cookie because my mum didn't come.

My mum never comes. She'd rather stay home and drink. At least she won't be home anymore now that she's leaving.

Marley told me it's not fair, that his mum died. Said he missed his mum and that she wasn't supposed to leave him. I said life isn't fair; my mother tells me that a lot, although I never really believed her until today.

My favourite boots scrape across the dry ground as I swing back and forth under the big branch, the rope creaking overhead with my weight. Mum makes Dad sad; that's why I hate her the most. I don't mind when she makes me sad, because I don't love her. But Dad loves her, and I love Dad. Life isn't fair, and neither is Mum.

The branches of the tree above me sway with the wind. The dark clouds in the sky tell me we'll get rain, especially when I can hear thunder in the distance. I like storms. Mum says it because they're miserable, like me. But I don't think that's right. Storms are powerful, proud. They're strong, and I'm not strong. So, they're not like me.

"I've tried everything, given you everything, and yet here we are doing the same fucking dance. I'm done. Had it."

If I was strong, I wouldn't cry when my dad raises his voice. I wouldn't cry because it means that he'll be sad after, when Mum is drunk and asleep. I hate it when he's sad because I can't do anything to make him happy. He cuddles me, wipes my tears and tells me he loves me. But I wish he didn't love her too. If I was strong enough, he wouldn't need to love her too. He only loves Mum because I can't make him happy.

"What are you doing out here, dove?"

I smile at Zeus as he walks across the yard. He's Dad's best friend. They've known each other since they were kids like me, I think. He's nice. He makes Dad happy, just not how Mum should.

"They're fighting again."

"It'll be the last time, I promise." He lifts my coat, holding it out for me.

I hop off the rope swing and walk over to him, slipping my arms inside. It's warm because he held it against him on the way out here. It smells like him.

"Who is that man?" The stranger turned up before Mum and Dad started fighting again. It must be his fault.

"Nobody." Zeus looks sad. Maybe Mum makes him sad, too?

"Why is he here?"

"Your mum is going to live with him." He squints a little. "Didn't your dad tell you?"

"I thought it was just a story."

I like Zeus. He's big, and big people make me feel safe.

"It's not a story." He sits on the side of the deck and pats the wood beside him.

I climb up and tuck myself in next to him. He blocks the wind, and I feel warm. I like being warm, especially with Zeus.

"Will she come back?"

"Do you want her to?"

"No." My answer upsets Zeus for some reason. He frowns at me, putting his strong arm around me and pulling me in tight.

"Dove...."

"Will Dad be happy now?"

"I hope so." He stares across the yard as the cool breeze kicks up the dead leaves.

"Do I have to go inside?" I don't like the man in the business suit. He's strange. I don't know any men who wear those kinds of suits—not in real life. Dad wears coveralls, and Zeus wears bright yellow shirts that are always covered in mud.

Those are the kinds of men I trust. Men like Dad and Zeus.

"I don't think so." Zeus smiles at me. He's handsome. I heard my mum say it once to a friend, but she made it sound like a bad thing. I don't think it's bad. "How about I keep you company out here until he's gone?"

"Okay."

"What should we do?" he asks. "It might rain soon, so we might have to go in anyway."

"I can swing until then. You can push me."

"Okay." He lifts me by my waist and sets me on the ground so I can go to the swing.

I climb onto where the rope knots around the piece of wood, balancing just right so that I don't fall off. Zeus stays close just in case I do anyway. He likes to keep me safe, unlike Mum.

I got a ride home from a policeman once. Mum came to get me from school because Dad had to stay at work. She never comes to get me, so I don't think she knew she couldn't drink that day. It scared me a little when she hit the road sign, but the policeman said it could have been worse. He was glad it wasn't.

Mum slept through dinner that night. I think that's why she didn't argue with Dad. He did everything for me. Made my favourite. It was weird when he sat in my room while I slept, but I think he was just happy that I was okay. I made him happy that day.

I overheard him tell Zeus, *"The bitch could have killed her."* I think the bitch was Mum.

Normally Mum goes on holiday when her drinking is too bad, but she didn't this time. Maybe she got enough rest at home? She slept a lot.

Marley said he wishes his mum was just asleep. I do too. Then she could wake up and make Marley happy again.

I wish my mum would go to sleep and never wake up.

Maybe then Dad and I would be happy too?

"Ready?"

I smile at Zeus and nod. "Yep."

At least we have him. Zeus makes us both happy. Maybe one day Zeus can live with us instead. I think that would make Dad happy. It would make me happy too.

Zeus plucks a dandelion flower as I kick my legs, and hands it to me when I swing near to him.

"Make a wish, dove. Make it a good one."

I lift the stem to my lips, knowing exactly what I want as I watch him come and go beside me.

I want for everyone to be happy.

I pull in a deep breath and blow; the fluffy pieces get whipped away on the wind. *Perfect.*

"What did you wish for?" Zeus asks as the first spots of rain tickle my face.

"It's a secret." If I tell him, it might not come true. And I want it to come true.

I want Zeus to make us all happy.

One day.

ONE

Belle (Now)

The sun is out in full force today, which means half the school first fifteen play an off-season game of rugby on the green, shirtless. Naturally my best friend Kate and I have set ourselves up under the trees that border the field, making the most of the goods on display.

I'm riding a high that only the last full day of high school brings. Final-year exams start next week, which means outside of attending those, my days in the classroom are done. I'm unshackled from the restrictions of a schedule, let loose from the expectations of the state.

Nine hours of testing to go, and then I'm officially a school-leaver.

An adult.

I rearrange my bag to act as a makeshift pillow and lean back, sliding my sunglasses over my eyes as Kate rummages in her bag. "Dad said I could go to Scott's party next weekend. Even told me he'd buy me something to drink."

Kate frowns, carefully peeling the wrapper from the

base of her cupcake. "I thought we weren't doing that?"

"Why not?"

"Last week you said you didn't want to go."

"Yeah, well last week I didn't have a personal invite from Scott."

"No way." Her eyes go wide and her jaw hangs slack.

"Way." I lift my hand for a high five.

She slaps it with her own. "When did he do that?"

"Third period, English."

"Tell me everything then." She takes a bite of her baked goods, smiling around the mouthful while she watches me, and then swallows. "What exactly did he say?"

I grin at the memory and stretch out. "He said it would be a shame if we never got a chance to hang before we go our own way."

"Hang out." She scoffs before she takes another bite. "Whatever. We're totally getting shit-faced and *you* are getting it on." She waggles her eyebrows at me before she seemingly stares off into nothing. "Damn. What am I going to wear?"

"You look fine whatever you choose." It frustrates me; she really does. The girl could wear a thrift shop bargain two sizes too large for her and still look hot.

The guys are bound to love her, and as usual, she's bound to make me invisible in the process.

"Dad's picking me up, though." I groan. "Said he'd pick us both up, actually."

"We'll tell him I drank too much and Scott's mum

gave me a bed for the night."

"Yeah, I'll think of something."

"I'll tell my parents that your dad is getting us and I'm staying at yours."

"He works nights now." I don't really know why I choose to share that with her other than the change in hours has niggled at me since he took the offer a month ago.

We need the extra money, and moving to the late shift means penalty rates. The decision was a no-brainer, which is exactly what I told him when he asked if I was okay with the idea. Still, it sucks. Dad and I might not have done much in the evenings, but those cheesy TV shows, the two of us cozied on the sofa together... that was our time. That was what we'd done since Mum left. I guess the realisation that I'm growing up—that those moments won't last forever—took me by surprise.

I've been so focused on proving that I'm a young adult that I forgot to make the most of being a child.

"Must be quiet on your own then." Kate sets her rubbish aside and promptly hitches her tank up her stomach to tuck the hem beneath her bra. She wriggles on the grass, scrunching the legs of her shorts together until the black material almost resembles a belt, and then spreads out to catch the rays.

"It's not too bad." I shrug. "I've got Netflix and a ridiculous amount of data."

She chuckles, brushing her hair aside. "I'd love to be

on my own at night. The things I'd get up to, the guys I'd sneak in...."

"You're a fucking nymphomaniac," I say with a laugh. "It's all you think about."

"Babe." She lifts her eyebrows. "I'd have to *be* fucking to be a nympho."

"True that."

"Speaking of...."

I slip my sunglasses to my forehead and turn my face her way. "Yeah?"

"Would you mind if I invited someone else to join us at Scott's?"

"Who?" I get the distinct feeling I'm not the only one who hasn't been sharing everything of late.

"So, there's this guy that does my brother's mechanical work, right?" She bites her bottom lip, fighting the most ridiculous goofy smile. "He's twenty-one, and babe, he's so fucking fine."

"Have you...?"

Her eyes go wide. "Not yet. No way. Damn, I'd tell you if I had." Her cheeks flush as she smiles at me. "I've been drooling over this guy for weeks, Belle, and Saturday he *finally* decides to talk to me."

"Why the hell didn't you tell me?" I ask. "Hello. Messenger, bitch."

"I wasn't sure if he was keen, you know? Like most of the guys always see me as Trent's baby sister and give me hell. But the signals he was throwing off...." She sighs, her eyes glazed as she loses herself to the memory.

I clear my throat, lifting both eyebrows. "And?"

"He messaged me last night. I swear to God I almost died when the notification came up."

"What did he say?" I cry, damn near hysterical. The suspense is killing me. I live my love life vicariously through her escapades, each story like a new hit.

"He fucking sent me a picture," she groans. "You know the kind."

I make grabby hands for her bag, and she swats me away.

"No way. I'm not ready to share yet. But I promise...." Another sigh. "You'll love him, Belle."

"So ask him to come." I narrow my gaze on her. "You think a guy your brother's age wants to hang out with school leavers though?"

"Only one way to know if he's keen." She smiles woefully. "I reckon if he does come out with us I might be able to, you know...."

"Get him liquored enough to go through with it?" I tease, slipping my glasses back on.

The back of her hand collides with my arm. "Hush, woman. He's not that far out of my league."

"Didn't say he was. I mean he's only three years older, right?" Not as though he's in his thirties....

Something twists in my gut as I recall the crush I developed on Dad's best friend a few years ago: guilt, shame? Whatever it is, the unease that builds and flows into my chest is unwelcome as I think back to how hard it was processing those new feelings, how long I struggled before I managed to remind myself how wrong it would be for anything like that to happen between Zeus and me.

Still, I can't deny that half the reason why I've never had a steady relationship with a guy since is because I subconsciously compare them to Zeus. *Apples and oranges.* How could a boy ever compare to a man such as him?

Simple: they don't.

"You don't mind if I message him, then?" Kate asks. "He could probably give us a lift to Scott's if your dad's okay with that."

"Has he got friends?" I need options. If things with Scott don't pan out, I want someone to help me push those kinds of thoughts of Zeus back into the darkest corners of my mind.

I need a distraction.

"Has he got friends," Kate mutters, mocking my question. "Of course he has friends."

"But not your brother." I point a finger at her. "I'm not going to be stuck hanging out with your brother all night."

"Nah, Trent will have something else on with his motocross crew." She rolls away to retrieve her phone as the rugby boys erupt into frustrated cries of defeat.

I prop myself up on my elbows as they attempt to retrieve the ball from the macrocarpa hedge. *Good luck with that.* Kate taps furiously to my right, wriggling around from butt cheek to butt cheek. It's almost sickening how excited she is; the guy *must* be hot.

Still, I could guarantee he's got nothing on Zeus. *Why am I back there?* I dealt with this obsession ages ago. I was young, it was a tough time, and he had been a shoulder to lean on—that's all.

Whatever makes you sleep at night. Fuck.

I lie back and close my eyes, frustrated as my mind continues to wander while Kate's immersed in her phone. He was the extended family I never had. I loved him, before I *really* loved him. And then he vanished. Just up and—*poof*—gone one night.

Dad won't tell me why. I blame myself. Why else would him leaving coincide with when Dad realised how I *really* felt about his best friend?

"Done," Kate announces, tossing her phone down. "He'll meet us there if your dad doesn't agree."

"Sweet."

She sighs, settling on her back once more. "Do you ever freak out a little at the fact school is almost over?"

Yes. "No," I lie, thankful for the change in topic.

"Really?" She pauses, positioning her backpack above her head to block the sun from her eyes. "I do. I wonder if I'll ever achieve anything great, you know? Like, will I be someone important, or will I just coast through life never really making a difference?"

"You think too much," I mutter, knowing exactly what she's talking about. "What are you going to do anyway?"

"Ugh," Kate complains. "Dad wants me to go to Polytech. But I don't know what I'd study."

"I thought you wanted to be a nurse?"

"I do... sort of. I don't know. The more I think about it the less I can make up my mind." Kate rolls to her side as the rugby boys give up and jog past to head for the change rooms. "What about you? You never talk much about what you want to do after school finishes."

For good reason. People expect some grand dream when they ask you what your plans are: to travel the world as a humanitarian, study to be a doctor, or dive into the start of a great investment property portfolio. If you tell them that your dream involves eight hours a day permanently etching colour into a person's skin... yeah. The comments aren't usually all that supportive.

"I have an idea," I say. "But I want to look into it more before I commit."

"You're not still obsessed with tattoos and shit, are you?" She crinkles her nose.

"Nah. Something else." *Case and point.*

Why would she want to know a thing about the hours I put in studying artists I admire, sharing my designs on my Instagram page, when to her the dream is ridiculous? What the hell is it people find so trashy about being a tattoo artist? If it were that easy, anybody could do it. But it's not, and I respect the hell out of the people I follow.

Takes guts to permanently etch your art into somebody's skin with the hope they'll love it.

Kate huffs, settling back as the bell sounds to signal lunch is over. "Damn it."

We each retrieve our bags, and I brush a few pieces of dry grass off Kate's backside as we start toward the buildings. I love her to pieces, but at times I wonder if deep down we're just too different. She loves school life, the drama and the social aspect of seeing the same people day in, day out. Whereas I can't help but feel dread as I look up at the two-storey complex before us.

I can't wait to get out of this prison. I know what I want from life, and I want to be given the chance to get it. I'm ready to prove myself, and above all else, I'm ready to prove that I'm not a kid anymore.

I'm Belle. Not John's daughter. Belle.

I want to be defined by more than just my age. I don't want to be seen as a child anymore; I want to be recognised as a young woman.

I want to be taken seriously.

TWO

Zeus

"I guess you can take the dining set," Jodie says with a sigh as she links her hands atop her head.

I frown, frustrated how after everything we've been through I still get drawn to the way her tits push out when she stands like that. No matter how bad she burned me, I guess a part of me will never forget the way I loved her—once.

"I don't have anywhere to store it." Let alone any use for it when it's just me. "You put it in your new place until you get your own furniture."

"Are you sure?"

"Positive."

She drops her arms, her lips turned down as she looks across to where I stand leaning against the kitchen counter. "You haven't even told me where you'll go. Where are you planning on staying? You can't crash at a motel forever; you don't earn enough."

"With friends, I guess." I didn't tell her where I'd go because I don't know. Fuck—until last week I thought we could work this shit out between us. But the more she pulled away as I reached for her at night, the more I knew there was nothing left in her heart for me.

I'm all out of chances with her. All out of fucks to give, too.

"As long as you have everything you need." She glances at the meagre pile of boxes near the door. "I guess I better start getting ready to head out." Her gaze snaps into focus as she lifts her head and starts for the bedroom.

"Where are you off to?" I'm a sucker for punishment.

"Oh, just a few drinks with the girls from work," Jodie calls on her way down the hall. "We're celebrating a birthday."

"Sounds like fun."

"Yeah." she says as I track her through the house to what was once our room. "It should be." Her hands still in her hair, the long blonde locks falling over her shoulder as she smiles softly at me. "You should get out more, too."

Maybe when I can afford it. But unlike her, I don't have years of savings from my work to fall back on. "Yeah. I should." I thumb over my shoulder, doing everything I can to ignore the fact she openly undresses before me. "I'll get this stuff in the car and head off. I've got something for you first, though."

"Really? Okay." She pauses before the wardrobe in her lingerie. "I'll come out to grab it from you once I'm dressed."

"Sure thing."

I back away, the feel of her curves burned in my brain despite the fact I haven't touched the woman in months. Jodie is an attractive woman, stunning, which is why it's no surprise she wasn't short of offers when I went inside. I naively assumed that she'd be strong enough to resist, though. Yeah. Stupid.

We fought about it, we made up—angry sex with hollow hearts—and we reached the point of no return. I had to get away. These fake niceties, this pretence of a mutual split... it's killing me. She's toxic, plain and simple.

I hate her. I hate that I still love her even more, even if it's not *as* a lover.

The four boxes fit easily, side by side, on the back seat of the car while I mentally bitch slap myself for being such a walkover. My life has been reduced to a handful of possessions, all of which have no sentimental value whatsoever. I made sure anything that held any connection to Jodie stayed with her. Why would I want reminders of how badly I fucked up while I start again? What kind of masochistic arsehole would willingly do that?

I take the plain envelope off the front seat and head back toward the house, eager to wrap up the visit. My decision rests in the papers contained within, my standing on our relationship clear.

It's over for good. I don't see this getting any better no matter how many times she tells me it's just a matter of time, that we need space. She can say anything she wants and it doesn't change the one thing that cemented my decision: she doesn't say what she should.

She never says "I love you" anymore.

She hasn't for years. I was just too blind to see it.

"Oh, I was on my way out to find you," she says as we meet at the corner of the hall.

I let my gaze fall over the tight blue dress she wears, noting the way it hugs her every curve. "Saved you the trip."

"What's that?" Her eyes drop to the envelope as her brow pinches.

"A little something to say goodbye."

I hold steady as she reaches for the papers, and watch her slide a manicured nail under the lip. She billows the sides to slide the sheets of A4 out, her head tilting slightly to the side. The lawyer's logo stands proud at the top of the page; the severity of my "gift" is undeniable.

Her eyes track the words, her breathing picking up pace as she reads the formal documents.

"You want a divorce," she whispers with barely restrained anger. "Already?"

"You know as well as I do that it's over, Jodie."

"Fuck, Zeus." She takes a step back, slumping against the wall as she reads the page again. "I mean...." She shakes her head, seemingly lost for words before she whispers with discontent, "Couldn't you at least give the separation time? I thought it might have been a decision that was better to ease into, you know?"

"Why drag out the inevitable?" I counter, the timbre of my voice rebounding off the walls. "*You* were the one who made the decision for us when you fucked him, Jodie. You could have walked away. You could have told me at your next visit, but no, you took the offer and jumped on the first hard dick that was swung at you after I was safely behind bars."

"Mince your words, why don't you?" she seethes.

"Fuck what words I use to share how I feel." *This woman....* The audacity of her to make out *I'm* the one who ruined us. "The pain *you* feel right now is *nothing* compared to how I felt when *he* told me what you two had done." I shake my head and laugh. "Jesus. You're my wife and you didn't even have the guts to tell me yourself."

"I didn't want to," she admits, a hell of a lot more subdued.

"You didn't want to, or you didn't think you'd have to?" I ask. "Hoped you'd get away with it, perhaps?"

"Zeus," she levels. "You're not being fair."

"Life isn't fair, Jodie. You of all people should understand that."

"You were in prison," she whispers.

"Exactly. In prison, not dead. I was coming home. I was always coming home to you." I huff a heavy breath out my nose, taking a step back toward the door. "Not that it fucking matters now. I'm tired, Jodie. I'm done. Let's just get this final bit over and done with and move on."

20

Tears wet her cheeks as I pause to really drill this moment into my memories. Every time a woman promises me her love, every time a woman tells me that I'm all there is for her, I want to remember this. I want a reason why I can never commit again.

Fuck going through this a second time. Fuck having to do it once.

"Enjoy your night out." I open the door and make it as far as the front step before her deep sigh makes me hesitate.

I turn, surprised to find her clutching the divorce papers as though they're a shield. From what? Her truth? Our truth? Her shoulders rise and fall, her chin to her chest. I don't need to see her face to know it's bad.

It's always bad with my wife. Has been since I was released four months ago. One shit fucking revelation after another. Nothing surprises me anymore.

"There was never any girls' night out, Zeus."

Except maybe that. *Proves there was never any love, either.*

"I'm going to dinner at the sports club with him, and then he's asked me to spend the night at his place." She lifts her chin, challenge in her eyes as she adds, "He wants me to move in with him, really make a go of this."

"And yet you had the fucking gall to stand there and have a go at me for bringing you the divorce papers?" I holler.

She cowers as I march back into the house, stopping nose to nose with the bitch.

"This has been coming for a long time." Her words waver, her trepidation evident. "I didn't want to turn down an opportunity at happiness if things with us didn't work out." She shakes the papers weakly between us. "And they haven't, have they?"

Some kind of sick pride swells within me knowing she still feels enough to be intimidated by me. Good. She should hurt. It's about time the scales of pain tipped her way.

"*You* might have known for a long time," I say as I take a step back and look her over with disgust. "But for me, I loved you until the day *you* gave me reason not to." More fool me. "I was loyal to you, Jodie. Always."

"I know." She hangs her head as I turn for the door. "But you can't blame me for the fact you were either too ignorant, or too stubborn to see that we weren't meant to be."

"Can't I?" If I remember right, it was *her* who first suggested marriage. "When did it stop?" I ask. "What was it that changed for you? When did you stop loving me, because you did love me once, right?" I turn at the door, one hand on the frame as I look to her, hopeful for just one small fucking olive branch.

She frowns, swallowing hard.

"When, Jodie?"

Her lips part as she sucks in a heavy breath. "When you couldn't give me the one thing I wanted."

Nothing I say right now could be good. Nothing I want to say is anything I will look back on without regret.

So I stay silent. I stay silent as my wife walks back to the bedroom to finish getting ready to go fuck another man, and I stay silent as the divorce papers hit the floor in her wake.

No wonder she didn't want the dining table.

THREE

Belle

"You're bad," Kate teases as we stroll up my drive- way. "I can't believe you're skipping this exam, girl."

"It's Biology," I say with a laugh, pointing my finger at her. "You tell me how many people *actually* need Biology under their belt, and I'll go."

"You have a point." She shrugs.

I smile as I dig my keys out of the bottom of my school bag, and then unlock the front door. "Have you figured out what you're going to wear this weekend, yet?"

"Ugh. No." Kate walks inside and drops her things behind the sofa, flopping dramatically over the arm as I head for the kitchen.

"Is that guy still coming?" He's all she's talked about this week after he apparently stayed the night at theirs on Sunday after one too many.

"Brock. His name is Brock." She sighs. "Even his name is sexy."

"Jesus, girl." I laugh as I open the fridge. "Get a grip."

"Have you talked to Scott this week?" Kate calls from

her position splayed out on the sofa cushions.

"Briefly before we had our English exam together yesterday." I stick my head around the dividing wall. "We exchanged numbers."

"You are so in, Belle."

Kate's excitement is infectious, swirling in my gut as I pull two Cokes from the fridge. "I don't know." My insecurities strike the butterflies down one by one. "As keen as he is, I don't think he sees me like *that*, you know?"

"Long-term?" She props herself up on her elbows as I enter the room.

"Yeah." I pass her drink over, and she twists to tuck her legs beneath her. "Should I feel bad if I'm just another conquest?"

"You want long-term out of him?" she asks.

"I don't think so." The condensation swirls beneath my finger as I trace the logo on the can. "He's cute, but he's not really my type."

"What is your type?" She frowns as she takes a sip.

Tall, part-Polynesian, and about twenty years older. "I'm not sure. Maybe somebody who has his life a bit more together?"

Kate chuckles, setting her drink down on the coffee table to shoot me an admonishing glare. "Babe, we're eighteen. No guy our age has it together. Fuck, *we* don't have it together."

Little does she know she's struck the nail on the head. I want older. I want more mature. I want to thrive off a guy who's left the experimental part of life behind. Someone I can be sure of and know I can depend on.

"Well," I announce, raising my can. "Here's to getting our shit together."

She snatches hers up and clangs it against mine. "And to best friends."

I smile as I swallow the acidic drink. She is my best friend, the one person I can count on. My circle is small, and Kate has never given me reason to hate that.

"What?" she asks as I continue to look at her.

"Just thankful to have such a kick-ass bestie."

Kate knocks my arm. "You can't get rid of me now. We're like fucking Thelma and Louise, man." Her eyes go wide as a playful smile parts her lips. "Hell. Promise me you won't go driving us off a canyon or anything."

I laugh, catching my breath to reply, "I'd need a damn car to drive first."

She erupts into laughter, and yet my blood chills. *Speaking of cars....* "Did you hear that?"

The undeniable thump of a door sends us both scrambling. I sling her bag behind the TV cabinet and kick mine under the dining table as we slip and slide over the kitchen tiles toward the rear of the house. Kate crashes to a stop against my back as I brace in an X against the open hallway door.

Bootsteps echo on the front path, and then still. If we cross over the threshold now, we'll be spotted trying to make a getaway, given the front door is directly opposite the back one.

Shit.

"What do we do now?" Kate whispers, trying and failing to disguise her nervous giggle.

"Panic." I snort in an effort to stop my snicker from breaking free.

The front door swings open, two definite bootsteps resonating throughout the otherwise quiet house as Dad steps inside.

I should feel bad that I've let him down by skipping my exam, feel bad for being so selfish. But the adrenaline still runs fast through my veins, keeping me in the thrill of the moment. He said he had errands to run before work; he shouldn't be home.

Kate tugs on my shirt, and then points to the far side of the room. The dining room has two sash windows that open out onto the backyard, but the damn things always stick on their wooden tracks. There's no way we could open them quietly enough.

I'm in the midst of whispering this to her when her eyes go wide and she slowly stands up straight from our crouched positions. "Hi."

"Belle?"

Shit. Shit, shit, shit. So not Dad. Excitement conflicts with regret at the sound of his best friend's voice.

"Zeus." I straighten also and slowly turn to face him. "Why are you here?" It's been years since he disappeared without a word. For some reason, the thought of disappointing him eats at my gut worse than upsetting Dad.

"I think the more important question is, why are *you*? Your dad said you'd be at your exam." His steely gaze flicks to Kate. "And who's she?"

"I'm Kate. Belle's friend." The hussy pops a hip as she sticks an arm past my shoulder, hand outstretched.

He simply stares at her, eyes hard and his lips set in a firm line. Her smile fades, and she slowly lowers her arm, stuffing her hands in the pockets of her jeans.

"We, um, we left some study notes here," I lie. "Thought we'd pick them up before the next one."

Zeus's cool indifference slides my way, his eyes unusually void of expression. "Bullshit."

I frown a little, my jaw slack as I try to work out what the hell happened to the fun, carefree guy that I last knew.

Kate gasps behind me, retreating toward where I threw her bag. "Um, we'll get our things and head out, okay?"

"What are you really doing, Belle?" Zeus asks, his eyes narrowed as he waits on my answer.

"Skipping my exam," I murmur, head down.

"Skipping your exam," he repeats with a dissatisfied huff through his nose. "Still too cool for school after all these years, huh?"

I simply shrug. What does he want me to say? That yeah, I'm a selfish, spoilt bitch who's yet again chosen to do what's more fun for me, than easier for my dad to handle? Because that's totally what I am.

Selfish.

Wonder which parent I learned that from?

"Don't tell Dad," I plead. "Okay?"

"Don't worry," he grumbles, stepping forward into the kitchen and forcing me back in the process. "I won't tell him. *You* will."

Kate stands wide-eyed, her bag now slung over her shoulder. I'm sure my expression is much the same.

"Zeus—"

"No." He spins around, finger pointed my way as he frowns. "Maybe once I was okay with being the go-between, with trying to get it through your immature head what the fuck you're doing to your dad by being such an ignorant little shit. You think you're big enough now to make your own decisions about what's best for your future? Well, then you're big enough to see the effect those decisions have on the people around you."

Jesus. Wherever he's been the last few years, somebody's been stealing all his porridge. The man is one grumpy bear.

"Fine," I huff. "I'll tell him." *Not.*

Zeus nods as he takes an elastic off his wrist and proceeds to pull back his long thick hair. I stand in rapt silence as he lifts both arms to tug the black locks into a rough ponytail, noticing for the first time he's in his gym gear: long shorts and a *very* revealing tank. He's been busy while he was gone, or maybe I simply don't remember him quite the same as I thought I did—the guy is huge.

I'm not the only one whose teenage hormones take

note of his built physique, given the way Kate stands in rapt silence also, her hand flexing in intervals on the strap of her bag.

"Get back to school for your exams, girls," Zeus instructs as he tucks the pony into a knot. "I'll ring and let them know you've both been held up. Maybe you'll get special consideration or some shit." He glares at me. "Maybe not."

Really? "Come on," I plead. "You don't have to go that far. We'll go back, I promise. Isn't that right, Kate?"

She stares silently at Zeus as he leans both palms on the counter behind him, making his triceps pop.

"Kate?"

"Huh?"

Fuck my life. I bend down on my way across to her and snatch my bag from under the table. "Let's go."

"Yeah, okay." She flashes one last smile at Zeus. "I'm really sorry we put you out."

If looks could kill I'm pretty sure he would have incinerated her into a pile of ash.

She giggles awkwardly as I throw a hand up over my shoulder to wave goodbye, pushing her toward the door with the other. "Bye, Zeus. See you in another couple of years."

"I'll see you when you get home tonight, Belle."

Wait. What? I make a move to turn around and ask what he means, but Kate has me by the wrist as she tugs me viciously out the still open front door. I stumble behind, managing to wrench my arm free when we reach the footpath.

"What the hell was that all about?"

"Are you fucking kidding me?" she whisper-yells in response. "*That* is the Zeus you told me about in Year 11?"

"Yeah." I frown. "So? Don't tell me you think he's hot." I roll my eyes, feigning disgust at the idea when in reality it pisses me off somewhat. He's *my* guilty pleasure, *my* eye candy.

Fuck, I've missed him.

"Of course I think he's hot." She skips backward, tugging me away from the house, presumably so we're out of earshot. "Old, but hot."

Old. I snort at the idea. Not as though he's like seventy or something ridiculous. He's only... I don't even know. Younger than Dad, I think, but not by much because they went to school together. So that would make him at least *thirty-four.* Shit.

"Are you okay?" Kate ducks her head as she falls into step beside me.

"Yeah. I just... how am I going to tell Dad I skipped my exam?" I do my best to deflect the issue onto something more believable.

Kate shrugs. "Buggered if I know. Remind him it's just Biology."

"That's not the point. He'll be pissed if he knows I'm not taking this seriously."

"Well then, sucks to be you."

"Yeah." It does.

More than she really knows. More than I let anyone know.

FOUR

Zeus

"How did you go?" John rises from his seat at the dining table and carries his empty coffee mug to the kitchen.

I toss my gym bag down next to the sofa, and shrug. "As well as you'd expect."

After sending Belle back to school for her exams I moved my shit into the spare room, and then headed to the gym for a session with the weights. The mundane routine of lifting, pushing myself to do better, be better, calms my soul. The heavy metal that blasts through my headphones helps too, but mostly it's that charge of adrenaline that I need to see my problems with a new clarity.

I was still mad at Jodie this morning for stepping out on me, but the truth is she saved me wasted years if I'd stayed with her. I was too blind to see what was happening with us.

Now I have a chance for a fresh start. A fucking hard one thanks to my record, but a new start all the same.

"Want one?" John lifts a cold beer from the fridge.

I nod, walking over to accept as I frown. "Did you tell Belle I was moving in?"

"No," he scoffs as he uncaps his bottle. "Mate, this is still my house. I gave up letting a woman dictate what I do in it years ago."

"Amen to that."

He leans a hip into the counter and narrows his gaze on me. "What makes you ask?"

Fuck. "No reason." Almost sprung the fact I caught her out. "Just wondered what sort of grief I'd be in for," I tease.

"She'll be okay," he muses. "I know it's been a while since you've seen her, but not much has changed." *Everything has changed.* "She still skips school—even though she thinks I don't know it—and she's still stubborn, just like you were at that age." He smirks around the lip of his bottle.

"At eighteen, you and I were a lot more than stubborn."

John shrugs. "Fair point. I don't think you need to worry about her jacking cars anytime soon, though."

He's right, although I don't doubt she'd do it if the idea struck her as a good one. Unlike John, Belle has always been fearless. The girl shows no consideration of the consequences at all, and more than a few times I've wondered if my influence here will have a negative effect on that trait of hers.

"What are you thinking?" my best mate asks as he gestures to the living room with a jerk of his head. "I can see the cogs working."

"You think I might be a bad influence on her if I'm here?"

He frowns as he takes a seat in his armchair. "Do you think I'd let you around here if you were?"

He has a point.

"You're the extended family she missed out on," he continues, kicking the recliner out. "The uncle she never had a chance to know. I don't give a shit about what you've done, as long as you don't glorify it when she asks about why you've been gone for the past two years."

"As if I'd do that."

To make prison out to be something to look up to, I'd have to be proud of the fact I served time. But I'm not. Fuck that shit. Not when it makes me everything I swore I'd never be: my father.

I used to feel sorry for John when we first struck up a friendship as teenagers because he didn't really remember his parents. Orphaned at a young age, he doesn't have the extended family most of us do, and so ended up in the foster system. The fact that he wished he knew his parents, and I wished I didn't, was one of the many things that set us apart. The other major one being the fact he's a lean, tall white boy with golden hair, and I'm the tan-skinned half-caste with jet-black locks.

You couldn't get two men more polar opposites if you tried. And yet I wouldn't trade our friendship for anything.

"What's she planning on doing after she finishes

school?" I ask.

John shrugs, lacing his fingers behind his head as he stretches his arms out wide. "She's still stuck on using her drawing skills for an apprenticeship as a tattoo artist, but if she doesn't lift her test scores, I don't know if she'll get into tertiary courses."

"Does she need to do any more studies?"

"You think she could slip straight into an apprenticeship without it?" He frowns as though the thought hadn't crossed his mind.

"Don't see why not. She's bloody talented." Belle started drawing as a distraction after her mother left. I don't think either John or I expected her to be so damn good at it.

"I thought perhaps she could find some fill-in work to save money to back herself with, but then I don't want her to get comfortable." John sighs. "You know how it is when you get your first paying job: the cash is such a novelty that you don't care what you're doing as long as you get paid for it."

"Yeah, I remember how that was." Awkward silence hangs between us. "The whole rebellion thing is just a phase, J. She'll grow out of it."

"I hope so." His eyes sharpen as he snaps out of his daze. "I better chuck this back." He lifts the bottle in his hand. "Time to head to work."

"Thanks again for the room." I twist the bottle in my hand, choosing to stare at the label. "You've saved my arse. Promise it'll only be temporary; a few weeks at most."

"Where will you go?" The smile slides from his face as he leans forward in the seat and rests both elbows on his knees.

He doesn't have to say it; the insinuation is there between his words. I'm going to need all the time I can get to find a willing landlord, considering my criminal record. People don't readily let ex-cons into their investment properties very often, especially re-offenders.

Some of us don't learn.

"I'm not sure where I'll end up. The new job with Gillies doesn't earn a lot, and I've only just finished paying what was left on the car. I've got nothing saved."

He hums as he nods, hands clasped. "How *is* the new job going? I may have a solution if you don't have any other plans."

"It's going all right, I think. But you know how it is." I pick at a loose thread on my jeans. "I'll get the trial run, they'll tell me that my history doesn't matter as long as I work hard, and then after three months they'll let me go using my criminal record as an excuse so that they get casual work at permanent rates, just like the last crowd did."

"Arseholes."

"Yep." I take a deep breath and shove the negative feelings aside to ask, "What was your idea?"

"I took a position on the night shift a couple of months back. The pay is another two dollars an hour, which adds up. I need it. *We* need it, but I don't like leaving Belle on her own."

"You saying I should stay here?" I frown, turning my head slightly.

"If you're okay with that." He spreads his hands wide and then claps them together again. "Look, I don't expect you to babysit Belle, but it would make me feel better if she wasn't alone."

"I can do that." Shit, he's probably saved me a grand in bond and setup costs on a new rental.

"Sorted then." He rises, bins his empty bottle, and then hesitates with keys in hand. "End of an era, huh?"

"Sure is." I've kicked around with John since we were kids, and Jodie had been there too in one way or another. Back when John was dating his ex-wife the four of us used to head out to the bars at the weekend. Fuck, how times change. "Thanks for this, bro. It's a real help."

"We're friends, Zeus," he says. "This is the exact stuff I'm supposed to help with. You should have said something sooner."

"I guess the right opportunity never came up."

"Probably because I've seen you all of what? Twice since you got out?"

"As shit as it sounds, I was just busy, mate." Busy trying to save a dead marriage.

"Yeah, well, I'll probably be sick of your ugly mug soon, huh?" He chuckles, making me laugh also.

I give him a simple shrug as he heads for the door. "You had your own problems to worry about, anyway." I tip my head toward a picture of John and Belle on the side table. "And we both know that she's way more important than my cheating wife."

He chuckles, ducking his chin to his chest. "I guess you have a point. Still"—he lifts his eyes to mine—"we're here to help, both Belle and I. I sometimes think that kid loves you more than I do, mate."

Yeah. Sometimes so do I.

••••

The incessant tick of the cheap clock mounted in the kitchen matches the beat I tap on my thigh with my phone. Legs kicked out before me, I sit in John's armchair and close my eyes. My body wants to rest, but my mind refuses to take its foot off the gas.

So many things to think about: money, the divorce, and most importantly what the fuck I plan on doing to keep my stupid arse out of the correctional system.

Six months for theft the first time was an easy stretch. Maybe too easy, considering it wasn't enough of a deterrent when I weighed the tyre iron in my hand and made a choice.

Fucker deserved it.

That much hasn't changed in the least; I don't regret a single fucking second of what I did. Only what it meant to the people who mattered: John didn't have a helping hand in raising Belle, and Belle didn't have someone other than her dad to lean on for advice.

Belle. Everything comes back to that kid.

She's got the fiery pig-headedness of her mother, but beneath all that I was lucky enough to be given the occasional glimpse of John—the cool, calm, compassionate side. The better side. She was every part the young woman when I went in, every part the old soul back when she watched her mother tear the family apart for the sake of a fatter bank balance, but now…. Shit. I can't stop thinking about how much she's matured in two years. Maybe not mentally, given she was here when she was supposed to be taking an exam, but damn, that body.

Long, lanky teenage limbs have given way to a fuller, curvier woman's body. She filled out, and the fact I noticed has me torn on what exactly that means. I guess it's okay to look if I don't touch.

Fucked. That's fucked logic, old man.

The staggered beat of my ringtone breaks me from my thoughts, pulling me back to the here and now as I answer the call. "I'm not going to sit around waiting every time if you plan on always calling late."

"I said *around* three," Jodie snaps.

"You said *at* three."

Her frustrated sigh punctures the line. "I didn't call to argue, Zeus."

"I know." I drag a hand over my face, already tired with the prospect of another slinging match. "Have you signed them?"

"Yeah." She hesitates; the fact there's more inferred in her tone. "I don't want this to get ugly; our split. We had some good years, Zeus. Made some good memories. I'd like to leave them like that."

"The wounds are still raw, Jodie."

"I know," she breathes. "And I'm sorry. I really am. There were better ways to tell you I was done, a million ways I could have handled it better. I guess I got caught up in the moment."

"That's not a valid excuse for fucking my old boss."

"No, it's not," she bites. "But punishing me for it repeatedly will only make you suffer too."

Fuck her and her ability to point out the facts. "Give me time." I close my eyes again and drop my head to the seat. "Take the papers back, and give me the space and time you wouldn't fucking shut up about."

"Take as much as you need," she bites, "but Zeus?"

"Yeah."

"I'm serious; I don't want to lose my friend." She sighs. "I sometimes think perhaps that's where we should have stopped all those years ago."

Guilt settles in the pit of my stomach—does she think this is ultimately my fault? She wasn't interested in dating at the start, but after seeing John and Cerise together she gave in to my constant badgering of her and the rest is history.

Maybe I should have taken the hint and left her alone, but when we were repeatedly thrust together by our best friends being in love; *something* was bound to come out of it. I guess happily ever after wasn't it, though.

"I'll be in touch when I'm ready."

I end the call, catching her faint "Take care" before I press the icon.

My eyes lift in time to catch Belle as she turns up the front path, walking with her head down and earphones in. The students in the final year at her high school get the luxury of not having to wear uniform, and I can't decide if that's a good or a bad thing. Pass her in the street without the bulging backpack, and you'd be forgiven for thinking she's several years her senior.

She's a young woman in every way—no longer a gawky teenager—except for her damn attitude. Maybe John isn't hard enough on her, sure, but I can understand why. His no-nonsense attitude was the very thing that finally made his wife give up, made Belle's mother pick another man over what she should have cherished most—her child, her family.

The front door opens, followed by the thud of Belle's bag as it hits the floor.

"Enjoy the rest of your afternoon?" I call.

Her shuffling stops for a beat before she pokes her head around the doorframe. "My maths exam was *swell*." Her dark-rimmed eyes narrow on the relaxed position I've got in her father's chair. "How was yours?"

"Productive."

"Huh." She disappears again, presumably going through her bag by the sound of it. "You going to answer my question now?" she calls from behind the wall.

"What one is that?"

"Why you've suddenly turned up out of the blue

after...." She steps into the room. "How long was it exactly?"

"Two and a half years."

"Hmm." Her lips purse as she glares at me.

Fuck—she's just as stunning as her mother was at that age.

"So where did you go, *Z?*" She sneers the nickname her father uses for me.

"Thought I'd trade my freedom for three meals a day and a complimentary movie channel subscription."

She folds her arms over her chest, drawing my eye to her narrow waist slightly hidden beneath a loose T-shirt. "You went back to prison." Her brow furrows.

I nod.

"Why the hell didn't Dad tell me?"

"Didn't want you to think the wrong thing." I shrug. "I don't know."

"Huh." She crosses to the sofa and drops onto the cushions. "What was it for?"

"Assault." The change is slight, but it's still there; she's nervous. "I'd never hurt you, Belle."

She swallows, hand clutched around her phone, and nods. "Still doesn't tell me why you're sitting in Dad's chair like you live here, though." She snaps out of her daze and turns her focus to the screen in her hand.

"Your dad's offered me a place to stay for a while."

Her thumb stills on the phone as she drags her gaze back to me. "Pardon?"

"I'm staying here for a while, Belle."

She frowns; her eyes go back to the phone as she says, "Why? Don't you have your own place or some shit?"

"Did."

She pauses again, this time setting the phone down beside her. "What happened?"

"Moved out."

"Why?" Her gaze darts around the place. "Where's Jodie?"

"Gone."

"Gone?"

"Divorced, split... gone."

She doesn't offer condolences, or even pass comment—pretty much what I'd expect from someone her age. Instead, she picks up her phone again and resumes scrolling.

It's refreshing.

I cast my eyes over her as she frowns at the device, clearly trying to avoid any further conversation, and can't help but smile. She fights her natural instincts, always putting on this "tough girl" show as though letting people know that she cares would be a sign of weakness.

It's sad, really, that she denies the world such an amazing young woman.

"What time does your dad usually get in from work?"

She pulls her bottom lip between her teeth for a moment, still focused on the phone. "He'll be done before midnight; he has to pick me up from a party.

Why? You want to organise a late-night sit-down when we get in?" She lifts her gaze momentarily to slap me with a scathing glare.

"Do I have to? Or can I trust you to bring up what happened today on your own?"

She sighs, closing her eyes briefly. Her long lashes rest on her high cheekbones before she slays me with what has to be a well-practiced puppy-dog stare. "Do I have to tell him, Zeus? I mean, the school said they wouldn't contact him since you'd already phoned, so...."

"You think one cute stare can sway me?" I chuckle. "Think again."

"Was it cute, though?" She smiles. "Did I pull it off?"

"Adorable," I deadpan.

An awkward beat passes. Does she see the line we just crossed as well as I do? Never once over the years have I commented on the way she looks. Even when she was young, I always kept those kinds of observations to myself. After all, she's not mine. It was just weird to call her cute and pretty when she's not related to me. Even weirder now.

"So," Belle exclaims, returning her hard-edged stare to her phone. "What's the plan for a Friday night then? You heading out to the pub soon, or what?"

"Thought I'd cook dinner tonight."

She snorts, tearing her gaze away from that fucking thing in her hand. "You cook?"

"Why? Does that surprise you?" I smirk.

"I've only ever seen you man a barbecue, or devour

45

takeaway pizza."

"Well, I cook. So how about you tell me what things you *don't* eat?" I push out of the chair as she swings her legs up onto the sofa and stretches out.

Her T-shirt rides up over her stomach as she slides lower on the cushions, revealing smooth pale flesh. I move my gaze to the wall behind her, focusing on the split in the plaster as she answers.

"As long as you don't sneak anything weird like eggplant or brussels sprouts in there, you're okay."

"Deal."

You're okay. If she only knew how far from the truth that is.

FIVE

Belle

"Kate. I've been looking for you for ages." I push past a couple of shit-faced girls to fit in the narrow gap between the garage and fence, tucking the bottle in my hand to my chest to protect it.

I managed to avoid a landmine with Dad and Zeus, delaying my "confession" until tomorrow since Dad is at work. Brock picked Kate and me up as planned, much to what seemed like Zeus's dislike, and brought us out to Scott's for a night of letting loose.

I haven't seen Kate since we got here.

"Hey, Belle." Kate flashes me a smile before she twists in the narrow space to face Brock and kiss him.

Scott's parents aren't here, and the party has spilled across the lifestyle block with drunken teenagers dotted across the property like ants at a picnic. Beer flows freely from kegs lined up along the back deck, and the array of liquor on offer across the kitchen counter would put most bars to shame.

It's fair to say I've had more than my "one drink per hour" quota set down by Dad.

"Jesus. Don't go out of your way to spare me any time," I snap, fuelled by the liquid courage that burns in my empty stomach.

"What the hell?" Kate rolls her eyes at me, missing the vicious look Brock and I exchange.

He's quiet, sullen, and seems not to like me, which in turn makes me like him even less. The guy grunted at me when I got in his car—grunted, for fuck's sake. I'm not convinced he's good for her, but then again when has my taste in guys ever been that great?

He gropes her arse as she pushes off him and heads towards me, shepherding me back out the way I came. "Belle, please don't fuck this up for me," she mumbles under her breath, presumably low enough he can't hear her. "Seriously. I'm so in love."

And I'm so being ditched. "I thought we were supposed to be hanging out together tonight?"

Her eyes dart toward where Brock lights a smoke before she graces me with a weak smile. "We can hang out anytime, babe."

"But not tonight, right?" I fold my arms across my chest, and then promptly put them back at my sides when my ability to stay upright decides to take a break.

Guess the drinks have got to me more than I give them credit for.

"Don't be angry," she says with a pout. "Be happy for me." She grabs my arm with painful urgency. "Legit, he's so sweet, Belle. You should hear the things he's been telling me."

Things that he knows will get her to loosen up and offer what he's looking for, no doubt. Yet I don't voice the thought. I don't say a thing as Kate loosens her grip on my bicep and strokes my arm instead as though to sweeten the next blow.

"Brock said he wants to take me home to his place." She gives the guy lovey eyes even though he's now sharing a joint with his friends, paying her no mind.

"Yeah? And what about me?" I slump against the fence to save my unsteady legs.

"Your dad mentioned he'd pick you up, right?" She frowns. "You'll be okay on your own until then."

What the fuck happened to Thelma and Louise? Seems Thelma found Brad Pitt, is what.

I seriously can't believe my best friend is doing this. Not only did she disappear over two hours ago, but now I find her picking a guy over me. Maybe I'm being petty, selfish even, but this was supposed to be *our* night out. I agreed to let him tag along, knowing it would make her happy, but shit, the guy's hijacked the whole fucking evening.

I lift my drink and drain the remainder of the bourbon premix. "Dad's going to ask where you are," I point out as I ditch the bottle in the long grass. "He'll want to know in case your parents ask him."

"Tell him I'm staying the night here, that Scott's parents offered me one of the spare beds when I got a migraine."

"I can't believe you're using an actual problem of

yours as an excuse to hang out with some guy."

Her eyes go wide. "Belle, he's not just *some* guy." Her freezing cold hands slap against the sides of my face as she twists my head toward him. "Look at him. He's *gorgeous.*"

I squint a fraction in my effort to focus. "So?" Doesn't mean he's going to take care of her. "Have you even met his friends before?" I gesture to the guy with the cloud of smoke trailing out his nose.

"No. So?" All humour slides from her face, as her hands do from mine.

"So, I don't feel right leaving you with people we don't know that well. It's not safe."

"Just because you can't trust people, Belle, doesn't mean I'm not allowed to."

Ouch. "I didn't only mean that," I say. "What about the fact they're all smoking up, getting high. Who's driving?"

Her eyes narrow as she takes a step back. "You need to loosen up. You sound like your old man."

I harden my gaze and give her nothing but silence.

She sighs. "Look. He's cute, I have a condom burning a fucking hole in my bag, and I'm determined I'm not going to university a virgin. This might be my only chance."

"I can't believe you're so shallow," I snap. "You really think the fact you fucked a guy will make people like you more, or something? Initiate you into some elite club for the cool kids?"

She chooses not to reply, instead huffing as she turns

away and storms back to the admittedly hot Brock.

I remember being upset back when I was twelve because a friend of mine at the time took my skirt and then lied to her mum when I asked for it back, saying it was a gift and *I* was the thief. Dad eventually got the skirt back after speaking with her parents, but as he said afterward, "Friends don't often last forever, princess. Not everybody has a permanent place in your life." I'd done everything I could to deny the glaring truth that the girl wasn't my true friend. I finally ceded when I watched Dad interact with Zeus, hoping one day I too would find that person who stood by me through thick and thin.

I thought Kate was it. And the fact she's just proven that she's not... well, that burns.

I'm literally alone, on my own after slowly losing every friend I thought I could count on over the years. And all I have to ask myself is why? Why did they all go? What did I do wrong?

What is it about me that everyone seems so keen to run from?

"Everything okay here?" Scott steps up beside me, sliding a fresh bottle of drink into my hand.

Yet another person who disappeared with no reason close to an hour ago. "You're still alive," I say slightly too bitchy.

"I had a few things to organise." His arm slides around my waist as he guides me away from Kate and her heated stare.

I flip her the bird as we leave, snuggling into Scott's side a bit more. *He smells good.*

"Having fun tonight?" His thumb strokes my waist as we walk.

Correction: *he* walks, *I* stumble.

"Not really."

"Why?" His brow furrows as he helps me up the back steps of the house.

I frown as he casually elbows a couple out of the way to give me clear passage into the house. "Seems my friends aren't exactly who I thought they are."

"Shame." My back slams into the wall as he pins me in the hallway. "Anything I can do to remedy that?"

I turn my head to fit the bottle to my lips without clocking him in the face, yet keep my gaze on his as I take a long pull. "Maybe." Liquor coats my lips, drawing his eye.

My breath hitches as he leans in and licks the residue from my bottom lip. *Do I like this?* I can't decide. It feels… good, but also wrong for some reason. Not that I hold much hope of figuring out why when the wall is the only thing stopping me from wobbling on my feet.

"I've been watching you all night," Scott whispers against my mouth.

"You have?"

He nods as he steps away and holds his hand out for mine. "Ever since you marched that sexy arse through the front door."

I set my palm in his, a strange swirling taking root in

my gut as he leads me toward the opposite end of the house. The party noise dies off as we head to the far rooms, the people thinning until all that remains is a girl passed out, her back against the hallway wall. I step over her, following Scott's lead, and stare down at her sleeping form. Something registers as familiar between her and me, yet I can't work out how that's connected to the anxiety taking root in my head, or why that should even matter.

"Lie down. It'll make you feel better." Scott nods toward a bed in the centre of the room as he shuts the door behind us, blocking my view of comatose girl.

Somehow I don't think a lie down is the only thing he has in mind to make me feel better.

Shit.

SIX

Zeus

The banner for an oncoming call slides down over the top half of my screen. *Fuck's sake.* I tap to answer, pissed off that the call interrupted the Insta-stalking I'm doing. I wasn't allowed a phone in prison, even though I was minimum security, so exploring the rise of the Instagram model has been a pleasant visual treat to say the least.

"Hey, John."

"Hope I didn't interrupt your Friday night, mate."

Nothing I'd share with him, anyway. "No. You're all good."

"I need a favour."

"Sure thing."

He sighs, frustrated. "I've been asked to stick around another hour. The guy who comes in after me is running late—some car trouble thing—and so they want me to fill the gap."

"Yeah?" Don't see what that has to do with me, but okay.

"I need you to pick up Belle for me."

Fuck. Of course. "Sure. Send me the address."

"Done." His voice is distant, telling me he's got me on speaker as the chime of an incoming message sounds in my ear. "Thanks, Z."

"No sweat. I'm not doing much anyway." Just looking at women with fuck-all clothes on. Totally ordinary Friday night.

"I told her I'd be there at midnight. It takes about fifteen to get out to the property."

I pull the phone from my ear and check the time: eleven thirty. "Just her? Or am I taking her friends home, too?"

"Shit, yeah. Kate as well."

"I'll flick you a message when we get back, let you know she's all tucked up safe and sound."

John chuckles while I visualise his daughter in bed. *So, so wrong.* "Yeah, that'd be great. Thanks. Catch you when I get in."

He ends the call while I drag a palm over my face and blow out a heavy breath. Who the fuck am I? Sitting in bed with my cock in a semihard state because of women my age on Instagram, thinking about a girl who's closer to twenty years my junior. *Jesus.* Maybe it's time I took a walk back to prison with my hands held out before me, ready for cuffs.

Fuck me. I've got to get my head screwed on straight.

Disgusted with what I was satisfied doing mere minutes ago, I toss my phone aside and reach for the dirty denim next to the bed. Pretty sure Belle is going to be shocked when I turn up to get her. But maybe then she'll be relieved? Always did suck being picked up by your parents from a get-together with mates.

Especially when it was your dad dragging your sorry ass outside before he beat your nose bloody for lying to him. *Good times.*

I slip my phone in the back pocket, and then tug a clean T-shirt on. My eye catches the door to her bedroom as I step out into the hall to retrieve my boots from the front door. I shouldn't, but the opportunity is there. *So going to hell for this.*

Her space smells like vanilla and some berry thing I can't place. It smells like youth and innocence, only our girl is anything but innocent. At least, that's the feeling I get. Her bed is made, although not neatly, and she has the toy elephant I remember her dragging around as a kid propped against the footboard. I step further in, casting my eye over her furniture. Books are stacked on the left side of her dresser, makeup piled in a messy heap on the right. But what catch my eye are the pictures she has jammed around the frame of the mirror. My heart jackhammers in my chest as I step closer, leaning in to take a better look—this is so wrong, a violation of her trust.

And yet, I. Want. More.

The top row is old photos taken when she was ten or eleven at most: pictures of her and John. There's one I know contains her mother, Cerise, and yet Belle has carefully folded it to exclude her. *Cold.* I run my eye down the left side of the mirror, noting how she gets older in each picture. A birthday party, a day at the lake, and what steals the air from my lungs: *her and me.* I don't remember the photo being taken, but I remember the day—John's birthday. It was a month or so before I went inside. He'd been so down, so miserable, that I did what any mate would: I phoned around and got together a bunch of guys he hadn't seen for a while and brought them around for a barbecue and drinks.

Where are they now? What kind of fair-weather friends are they?

Even worse, am I any doing any better by being here, considering it's his daughter that my gaze fixes to? Belle stands behind me in the shot, her arms looped around my shoulders as she rests her chin on my left. Time was, I would have looked at this picture and seen the whole shot, the day for what it was: friends and family in the sun, sharing stories, making memories. Except time has passed, Belle has grown up, and the way she looks at me now has me eyeing the picture with a fresh perspective.

Her arse is high in the air, her legs straight where she stands behind my seat. The hold is innocent enough, but she rests a hand on my chest, palm flat. Her eyes aren't on the other people in the circle, she doesn't engage in the conversation or watch the guy who clearly speaks— she stares at the ground as a smile pulls at her lush lips. She holds me *possessively* as though nobody around us in that moment matters.

I swallow hard and pluck the picture from the

mirror; my eyes glued to it as the revelation smacks me like a steel bat. Did she *always* look at me like that? Was I blind to something that was right under my nose all those years ago?

Fuck. Fuck, fuck, fuck.

My phone vibrates in my pocket to remind me I have an unopened message, jolting me from my thoughts. *Shit.* I have to get on the road to pick her up.

How the fuck am I supposed to sit in the goddamn car with her after this? Knowing she saw me as something more—whatever that is—all the way back then... it changes everything. If I didn't see how she acted around me years ago, then what the fuck aren't I seeing now?

Only one way to find out, and that's by taking the bull by the horns. Fifteen minutes in the car together at least, and however many it takes us to get back home from Kate's, alone.

What better time to ask the hard questions than when she can't up and leave?

SEVEN

Belle

Scott's bedroom is everything I'd expect for a guy our age. There's dirty laundry heaped in the corner, a desk covered in scraps of paper, litter, and motorcycle parts. His bed is unmade around me; mismatched sheets on an oddly fitting mattress and base.

Scott flicks the lock, and then tugs his T-shirt off over his head while he stalks my way. *He certainly doesn't like to muck around.* "You want to finish your drink?" He nods toward the bottle in my hand.

I lean to set it on the nightstand; the thought of having more turns my stomach to acid. "I think I've had enough, don't you?"

"Your choice." He shrugs, drawing my eye to his naked torso. He's cut, but he's also small. Not big like Zeus.

Zeus. Jesus, not now. The first guy in years to make moves currently stands before me with a hungry look in his eye, and I still think about the unobtainable.

Reality check, Belle. It'll never happen, no matter how attracted you are to a guy who's old enough to be your father. Zeus is smoking hot and kind to me, but that's where it ends.

That's where it has to end.

My gaze drifts to Scott's bedroom door as he crosses to a music dock. The logical decision-making part of myself drifts separate in this moment, as though it stares down at my vessel of a body from a distance.

Scott wants sex. Scott invited me here for what he probably thought was an easy score. I mean nothing to him. But then again, he means nothing to me too.

So who's using who?

"What kind of music do you prefer?" Scott stares down at his phone, oblivious to my internal debate as he scrolls through playlists.

"Rock, house music... I'm not fussy."

Music erupts from a set of speakers behind me—the beat heavy and bass laden, drowning out the tunes that play at the party. *I should do this.* Use the alcohol that swims in my veins to lose myself for a while. Kate's fooled around with guys plenty and she's happy. Scott doesn't promise anything other than a bit of fun, and just like riding a bike, I have to start somewhere, right?

I need to open the final door to my adulthood and explore my sexuality.

And if not with Scott, then who? Sure, he's cocky and selfish. But he's also cute, fit, and eager to break me in. If it all goes south then what does it matter? School's over, exams are finished, and the chances we'll see each other around town are slim. Since when have I given a fuck what anyone thinks of me anyway?

Scott tosses the phone aside, seemingly satisfied with the soundtrack for our escapades, and then regards me with a cool stare.

"What's on your mind, Belle?"

"Trying to work out your game, is all."

"I have a game?" He crosses the room back to the foot of the bed, yet this time he stands towering over me with a cocked eyebrow.

"You asked me to the party yourself, and now here we are in your room with your shirt off, listening to…" I tip my head to the side. "Closer?"

Really. Could he be any crasser?

"I like music. You like music," he coos as he tucks his fingers beneath my chin to tilt my head up. "What's the big deal?"

"I can enjoy music with all my clothes on," I deadpan.

"It's so much better if you don't." He hooks a finger in the neck of my shirt and tugs. "Promise."

"What do you want from me?" I ask, pulling away.

"Same thing you want."

"Which is?" I frown as he takes hold of the hem of my shirt.

"Release." He pulls the material over my head and sucks in a sharp breath. "You're cute, Belle, and I'll be blunt and admit I've wondered for a while what you'd be like in bed." He smiles as his thumb sweeps my bottom lip. "You, however, need to loosen up and live a little. I'm going to show you how."

"Such a Casanova," I taunt, although the thought of losing my innocence to him seems less like a bad idea as we go on, and more like the commonsense thing to do.

He won't care if I'm terrible at it; he probably expects it. And when we walk away afterward, I don't have to worry about it changing how he thinks of me, because who gives two shits what his opinion is if I never have to see him again?

He gives me a cheeky smile. "Is your answer no?"

That small percentage of me fighting this pushes to the forefront of my mind. Isn't the first time supposed to be special? *Maybe.* But when there's only one person I'd rather give this moment to, and the chance of ever going *there* with *him* is about as rare as hen's teeth, then who exactly am I holding out for?

"It's not, is it?" Scott asks, interpreting my silence.

"I still think you're a jerk, though."

"And I still think you're a moody bitch." He winks. "But angry sex is the best kind of sex."

I wish I could say I understood. My chest heaves with my steadying breath. "How do you want to do this, then?"

He steps back and goes to work on his buckle. "What made you change your mind?" He smirks. "I saw the look on your face when you walked in here; you were ready to bolt."

"I haven't changed my mind, as such. I'm just more open to the option." I cast my gaze down over my sensible denim shorts and high-top boots, coasting back up to my plain black bra. *Do I have to take it* all *off?*

Scott's denim drops to the floor with a dull thud as the metal of his belt hits the carpet. *My God.* The bulge in his boxers is nothing short of impressive. No wonder the girls seem so smitten with the guy. His body's not all that bad, either. Definitely a touch on the lean side like I guessed, but he's eighteen; I can't expect too much of the guy.

He's certainly no Zeus, that's for sure. A pang of nauseous guilt fists in my gut at the thought. *Stop it.*

"You need to get at least half naked for this to work, Belle."

I shudder in a deep breath and stand. My hands gingerly undo the snap on my shorts and pull the zipper down. Scott watches keenly as my cut-offs drop down my legs and I step out from both them and my boots in one movement. His boxers tent under the strain of his erection when I shift closer to him.

"You look as good as I thought you would, Belle. You know how gorgeous you are, right?"

Hurl. "Guess not." I glance over at the bed, longing for the modest safety of the sheets.

"You can lie down if it makes you more comfortable." *Ever the gentleman.*

I shrug. "I really don't know." I choose to give it a shot anyway, considering everything about this is uncomfortable and new.

Scott holds fire where he stands while I get onto the bed on all fours and crawl up to the head of it, tugging the linen over my legs as I settle. His hungry eyes devour my every move as I strip my panties off under the covers and drop them out the side of the sheets.

"You have protection, right?" I ask, shifting myself down to lie flat on my back as a roar goes up from somewhere outside.

"Yeah, sure." He takes two long strides and arrives at my side. I flinch as he drops his boxers and his erection springs out inches from my head. Still, it's the first real, living penis I've seen and I can't stop myself from ogling it.

The beast rises as Scott takes note of my observation. "Like?"

"Let you know when we're done." It's normal to want to throw up, right?

He chuckles, getting under the sheet with me. I shift aside, giving him room to lie on his side, mirroring my position. We stare at one another. "How do you want to start out?" he asks. "I'm assuming you haven't fucked a guy yet."

My face flames, and I fight the urge to run right there and then. "No, I haven't." Is it that obvious?

Suddenly the rest of that bottle of bourbon looks a damn sight more appealing.

"We'll start slow, then." He places a warm hand on my collarbone and traces a line down and over my breast, continuing along my side to my hip.

I break out in goosebumps.

"Sensitive, huh?" His eyes light up.

"You're the first person to touch me like this, so yeah, it's a little new."

He continues his lazy trail down as far as his hand will reach on my thigh, and then reverses the path. "You can touch me, too, you know."

Shit. I've got no idea what to do, so I echo his movements. He pauses in his caressing of me to lift my hand and place it over his cock. I freeze. He rocks his hips forward, stroking the length of his shaft over my palm. Instinct kicks in and I wrap my hand around his length and stroke slow and even. He groans, closing his eyes for the briefest of seconds. *Guess I must be doing something right.* My body reacts to the sound, and to my horror, a wet sensation floods the space between my legs.

He can't be turning me on, surely. I don't even fancy him all that much. Still, I remind myself this is the exact reason I'm here—to prove I can get what I need from somebody other than Zeus. *Fuck, Zeus.* Why do my thoughts always come right back to him?

Scott's fingers rub in a slow circle on the flesh of my clit, setting fire to the nerves below. My hips rise to meet his hand, searching for more of their own accord. He pushes his index finger between my legs, and runs it along the lips of my pussy. "Fuck, Belle. You're ready for this, aren't you?"

I nod, biting my bottom lip. I'm ready to be fucked, to have sex, just not ready to make love—because that's not what this is. It's simply two bodies needing release.

Nothing more. Possibly less.

His fingers continue to explore my slick folds, teasing them apart so he can circle my entrance. I moan at the sensation, a tingle spreading through my legs and lower abdomen. I knew it would be better to have somebody else do it, to give that control over to another person, but damn have I missed out. Scott rolls me on to my back, using his shoulder against me to push me over. I oblige, already languid with the incredible reaction my body has to being touched so intimately.

The sheet is strewn aside, along with my inhibitions as Scott slips a finger inside my tight hole. I gasp, unsure if it feels amazing, awkward, or both. "Fuck yeah," he mumbles. "So tight." He slips his finger out, back in, and out, over and over again as he finds rhythm. My muscles relax, inviting more.

I can't pick if the swimming sensation in my head is from the alcohol, or him. Maybe both?

His free hand scoops behind my butt, lifting my hips slightly as he shifts himself down the bed so his face is even with my belly. The change in angle is unbelievable, placing his thrusting finger against an extremely sensitive spot. My breath comes in ragged pants as I focus on solely the sensation of what he's doing and not the why and how of where we are.

Fucking. Drunk. At a goddamn party.

A fragment of me aches thinking of how low I've stooped in the name of ticking losing my virginity off the to-do list. I should be doing something this important with a man I care about, if not love, not with some random guy from school. But I pathetically justify the loss of this moment by reasoning that experience might make me more appealing to Zeus. That maybe, just maybe, if I crest this last blockade to adulthood he might see me as a woman worth pursuing.

God—everything I said to Kate seems so two-faced. Now who's losing their V-card simply to fit in? *Way to go, Belle.*

"How you doing?" Scott asks, his breath tickling my clit.

"Good," I moan, shutting all reason out. "It feels good."

"One more, okay?" He circles my pussy with his fingers, and then presses inside again with two digits. I cry out, and stiffen, causing him to stop. "Okay, Belle?"

"Yeah. Just adjusting." I take a deep breath. "Keep going."

His eyes connect with mine over the length of my torso. "This might help." His fingers push inside again, but at the same time he leans down and licks the tight nerves at my clit.

I damn near throw him off the bed with the violence of my hip thrust. "Holy hell."

"Good, right?" He goes in for a second lave, suckling the hood a little on the tail end of his lick.

I answer with nothing more than an incomprehensible moan.

His fingers push harder, faster, his tongue lapping

quicker the more I buck. I'm seeing stars, swearing my allegiance to the first sex club I come across if this is how good it can feel, when he pulls away.

"What did I do?" I push up on my elbows as he sits back on his haunches, wiping his mouth clean.

"Nothing. We're ready for the next stage."

Fuck. "Yeah?" Already?

"Lie down again."

I flop back on the mattress as he stalks over me, resting his hands either side of my head, elbows on the bed by my shoulders. "I've heard it hurts."

"Sometimes." He talks about it with the kind of casual demeanour you'd expect when you discuss dinner. "But you're wet as hell, and you took finger fucking real good, so...."

"I might be okay," I finish.

"Should we find out?"

I nod, closing my eyes. He scares the living hell out of me by pressing his lips to mine, teasing and coaxing my mouth open. I reciprocate, well aware this is another area of intimacy I'm not very well versed in, and get lost in the sensation of his tongue as it dances with mine.

Pressure at my pussy snaps my eyes open in a heartbeat when he pushes his rigid cock slightly inside. "Condom," I cry out, breaking from the kiss.

"Oh, yeah." He laughs—actually fucking laughs.

I lie still as a dead thing while he casually wanders over to the desk, dick bobbing. With his back to me I catch the slide of a drawer, and watch the way the muscles in his back work as he fiddles with what I assume to be the condom. I throw an arm over my eyes and let out a long breath, psyching myself up for the finale. Before I know it, there's an impatient dick waiting for permission again... and a cock prodding my vagina.

"I'm ready." I nod as though I'm giving a body piercer the go-ahead. *Guess I almost am.*

Scott nods, and closes his eyes as he eases his length inside. The fit is tight, and it burns a bit, but the pain isn't anything I can't handle. I marvel at how silky it feels, even with the latex of a condom between us. They really have nailed making those things feel invisible.

"Tell me when you're ready to go faster." He clenches his jaw, easing out and pushing in slowly.

"Ready," I say on a whisper, the pleasure overtaking the pain. "It feels okay again."

Scott's hips quicken pace, and I lift my legs in response, opening myself further to him and allowing him deeper. He drives into me with short, sharp breaths, eyes shut tight as he bites his bottom lip.

I match him, closing my eyes to focus again on the "what" and not the "who." The giddy tingles spread again, but this time they're relentless in their search, zapping to every inch of my body as I jolt with each hit of Scott's hips. Tension builds in my gut, coiling like a snake ready to strike. My muscles twitch around his cock as he punishes me with hard, even strokes.

"I think... I think...." My thoughts are interrupted by

Scott's cries of pleasure as he stills and then jerks erratically inside of me. *Well, that was a disappointment.* I wait him out as warmth spreads inside of me— *Wait, what?* Why the hell is everything so sticky while he's pulling out?

I jolt upright, staring at his *naked* cock with an accusatory stare. "What the hell, Scott?" I shriek. "Where the fuck is the condom?"

He stares down at his softening dick, and shrugs. "You're on the pill, right? I'm clean. What's the big deal?"

What's the big deal? What's the.... "I never said I was on the pill," I holler. "I'm a fucking virgin—I have no reason to be!"

"You *were* a virgin," he points out with a smug smile. "Go get the morning-after pill. Relax."

I slip off the bed, cum trailing down my legs as I yank my shorts on to go clean up. "I could get pregnant, you moron."

"It's your first time, Belle. What are the chances?"

Yeah, I forget he has no idea how my mother got pregnant; she thought the same thing. "You're a fucking arsehole, Scott. A fucking arsehole." I tug my bra and shirt on with jerky movements. "I can't believe I thought this might make me feel better."

"Made me feel better."

Fucking. Pig. I flick the lock on his bedroom door and fling it wide hard enough that it ricochets off the dresser behind.

I made the biggest mistake of my life and there isn't

a single fucking person I can talk to about it.
What's new?

EIGHT

Zeus

The tyres dig into the gravel as I throw the car down a gear and twist the wheel hard left and then right to gain control of the slide. *What the fuck is she doing?* I just about ran her down.

My heart resides in my throat as I toss the door open and step out into the cloud of dust that drifts past where the car sits idling on the side of the road. "What the fuck, Belle?"

She looks up from where she now stands on the grass verge, her hands clearly shaking as she dusts herself off. We're a kilometre at the very least from where John said she'd be.

"I'm sorry."

"I almost ran you over. There aren't any streetlights out here, for fuck's sake."

She nods furiously, swiping at her eyes with the backs of her hands as I advance. "I know."

"Jesus Christ. You're mostly wearing black." My heart still hammers, but her tears calm me. She's as frightened as I am by what just happened. "I could have killed you."

Her hummed reply hiccups from deep in her chest as her tears strengthen.

I step toward her and take a firm hold of her shoulder to yank her into me. "I'm sorry, dove. You scared the fucking daylights out of me, though."

"I thought I'd start walking," she murmurs against my chest. Her slight hands fist in my shirt, and fuck it all if that right there isn't the most perfect sensation ever. "Where's Dad?"

"He got kept late at work. Had to cover for another guy."

She pulls in a shaky breath, and nods against my chest. "Lewis. Apparently, he's always got an excuse."

"Belle, tell me. Why are you so upset?" I know I lost my shit at her reckless behaviour, but hell, it wasn't that unexpected, was it?

"No reason." Her body quivers against mine.

"Are you cold?"

"No."

I lean back, Belle still in my hold, to try and see her face. She tucks her chin down, staring at the road. "Why did you leave the party? It's not safe out here on your own."

"It's not safe there, either," she retorts bitterly. "I wanted to leave, okay, so can we leave?" She pulls away, brow furrowed as she looks up at me with her hands still on my chest.

I wipe away what remains of her smudged make-up with my thumbs and sigh. "Talk to me. What happened?"

Belle's frown deepens, and she looks at the hand over my heart. "I can feel your heartbeat. It's so strong."

"Because I'm fucking angry."

"At me?"

"At whoever upset you and made you think walking out here on a fucking country road was a smart idea." I settle a hand over hers and trap it to my chest to remind her how serious this is. "A name, Belle. Give it to me."

"No. Let's go home, okay?" She tears her hand away and takes an unsteady step toward the car.

"You're drunk."

"Not as much as I was." She laughs.

I lift my gaze to the horizon, to the glow of lights in the distance. She fumbles with the door of the GTO, giggling as she finally gets it open to climb inside. The gravel crunches beneath my boots as I stride up to my still open door and lean down.

"Name."

"No." She closes her eyes as she rests her head back on the seat.

"Name, or I go and ask somebody else at the party."

That grabs her attention. Stormy eyes snap open onto mine. "Leave it." The quiver of her chin shreds any resolve I had at keeping this civil.

"Stay here." I slam the door and start toward where music ebbs and flows on the night breeze.

"Zeus!" Her panicked cry erupts behind me. "Stop."

I keep walking, even as her frantic footfalls catch up. Eyes wide, Belle steps in my path and sets both hands on my chest. Her boots dig into the loose road as she anchors herself and pushes against me. "Just take me home. Please?"

"Not until you tell me what the fuck happened to make you so goddamn upset." Fuck. I want to kiss it all away, make her forget.

Right after I murder some punk-arse motherfucker.

So wrong. And yet, for some goddamn reason it feels as though I'd be the only one who could make her happy, solve this for her.

"Okay," she whispers.

"Okay?"

"If it stops you marching up there to crack heads together, then sure." She forces a smile.

Red rings her puffy eyes. "Not promising a thing."

"Please?"

"You're hurt."

"I'm always hurt," she bites out, slapping me with the force of her words. "What's new?"

"Dove...."

"Stop calling me that." She yanks her hands from my chest and takes a step back.

"Why?" Why the fuck are women so confusing?

Belle's eyes close, her long hair drifting side to side as she slowly shakes her head. "Because... because I can't deal with how it makes me feel."

"I can't deal with the thought of somebody upsetting you."

"*You* upset me." Her eyes narrow. "So what now,

Zeus? What are you going to do to tell *yourself* off?"

Fuck it. "When did I upset you?" I ask softly, careful not to spook her.

"When you went away." She marches past, feet thumping the ground the whole way to the car.

I take a deep breath and look toward the flickering lights again. *Fuck.* I'm in the mood for a fight now, the adrenaline still fresh in my veins at the thought of putting some little fuck in his place. Because of course it would be a guy. With a girl as stunning as Belle, it'll always be a guy.

"Are you coming?" she calls from behind her open door.

I stride back to the GTO and drop into the driver seat without a word. She closes her door and buckles up seconds before I drop the hammer and tear the grass out as I spin the car around.

"Talk to me." My breaths come even and slow, in and out my nose, while I work on tempering myself just like the prison shrink taught me.

"I got punked."

"Punked?"

"You know? Made a fool of?" She glares from where she's leaning against the door.

"I know what punked means, Belle. I meant how? Tell me more."

"I don't want to." Her words are a mere whisper as she gives me her shoulder and shuts down.

No. *Nope.* She doesn't get to do that. Not tonight.

Her back goes ramrod straight, shooting her up in the seat as I shift down the gears and pull to the side of the road. "What are you doing?"

"Turning around."

"Why?"

"To ask somebody at the party why I picked up a crying, upset Belle who was walking down a dark fucking road on her own when she's supposed to be at a fucking party." *On her own....* "Where's your mate, Kate?"

"Who cares?" She leans forward in her seat, alarm in her eyes. "You're actually turning around."

I pull the wheel straight and nod. "Told you I would. I figure you have less than a minute to start talking."

"Shit," she whispers, eyes glued to the road.

"Down to thirty seconds, baby girl." I catch the reflection of the number on the mailbox—we're close.

"Okay! Just stop."

"Don't believe you." I kill the gas, letting the engine slow the car.

"I slept with a guy, okay?" She cowers in her seat as I punch the pedal and tear past the party. "I slept with a guy because I thought it would be the right thing to do."

She's drunk, and *I* want to vomit. "Why?"

"I just did." The resignation in her voice tells me she doesn't really know.

What the fuck did you do, Belle? I want to yell at her, ask her how she could be so fucking reckless. But what would that achieve? She's confided something pretty serious in me, and one glance at her sullen face as we leave the party behind tells me she's beaten herself up about it enough already. No point making her feel lower.

"Do you think I'm disgusting now?" Her quiet question shakes me to the core.

"What? No."

"*I* feel disgusting."

Jesus, this girl. "Well don't. You're old enough to do what you want with your body, Belle. You have been for two years." As much as it pains me to admit so.

"He doesn't like me."

"My first fuck didn't like me either." God knows why I told her that, but shit, anything to make her feel less stupid about what she did.

We all make mistakes. Don't I know that?

"Really?"

I glance over and find her looking up at me, hopeful. "Really. She was a cousin of a guy I played rugby with. Long story, but clearly you know how it ends."

She snorts a bitter laugh. "Clearly."

Silence hangs in the air between us as I turn onto the next road that leads back to town. It's the long way back—the quicker route is the way I came—but something tells me she needs this time.

I need this time with her.

"Why did you get upset when I left?"

The spill of the dash illuminates her face in a soft glow as she stares out at the dark fields. "I missed you."

"Why?"

"Am I not allowed to?" She chooses not to face me, hiding behind her hair as she tips her chin down.

"I just don't understand why." Fuck—this conversation was so much easier in my head. "You miss all your dad's mates when they leave?"

"You were the only one that mattered."

"Why, Belle? Tell me why."

She huffs, shaking her head gently. "Because you were the only one I saw. The only one who saw me, too."

NINE

Belle

The ride into town takes nineteen minutes. Nine-teen tense, awkward, agonising minutes where all I can do is sit as rigid as rock in the passenger seat of the GTO as

it flies along the straight roads. I stare out my window at the passing scenery as it morphs from dark shadowy shapes into buildings with lights on, and then into the lit suburban streets of Longdale. Zeus sighs beside me, but I don't have the guts to face him. I stare instead at the darkened houses we pass while I sober up, creating profiles for the people inside based on how tidy their garden is and how many vehicles they have parked in the yard—all the small things that can tell you so much about a person. The houses eventually spread out, becoming semi-residential before we hit the agricultural hub of the town. Instead of muted lights through curtains, I'm staring at tractors that sit idle in sales yards, and large signage that announces this week's special on stock feed. All staples of a mostly farming orientated community.

Zeus slows the car to take a left, the revs high as he uses the natural braking of the engine to bring the beast to a crawl around the intersection. I focus on the inside of the McDonalds building situated on the corner as we enter the driveway, casing out how many other partygoers have decided on a feed to soak up the alcohol in their gut. As harmless as his seemingly impromptu idea is, the gossipmongers would have a field day if they spotted me here with him, more than likely sprouting rumours that I'm sleeping with Zeus. *As if that would happen.* My lurid thoughts drift to what sex with him might be like... a man that muscular, the way he'd move.... *Damn it.* I slam my eyes closed and frown at the wash of shame that envelops me. I've just fantasised about a man twenty-odd years my senior. What the fuck is wrong with me? How can I even think like that after what happened with Scott tonight?

Because it's easier than worrying about the fact the insensitive jerk came in you without protection.

"You okay?" Zeus asks as the GTO rolls to a stop in the parking lot. The vehicle gives one last shudder as he kills the engine.

"No, but I will be."

"Did he hurt you?" Zeus's eyes roam my body, but with none of the unwanted lust I got from Scott. He looks over me with care, as though I'm a fragile keepsake that's fallen from the shelf.

"Not physically."

He reaches out and straightens my oversized T-shirt

so it sits on both my shoulders. "Sorry I lost my temper, dove." I flinch at his pet name for me, and he sighs out his nose. "Habit."

A beat passes where neither of us appears to know what to say. The engine ticks as it cools, the gentle rush of his breath as Zeus sits beside me almost calming.

"Belle," Zeus offers, low and quiet. "Are you sure you're okay? We don't have to get a sundae. I just thought it might cheer you up *and* give you something in your stomach other than alcohol."

The first tears fall and run a path over my flaming cheeks. I'm too embarrassed to admit to him the truth of it, that what burns more than what Scott did is the fact that my agreeing to it, the fact that I went along with it, only cements how immature I am.

I've got so much to learn. So far to go before Zeus could ever look at me as an equal. *Why do I keep on with the fantasy?* He's never going to want me, especially now.

"Don't cry," he pleads. "I don't know what to do when you cry."

"Neither do I." A jaded laugh falls from my lips as I wipe the depth of my pain from my cheeks.

I'm a complete idiot for making it through five years of high school without a single legitimate boyfriend. Sure, it's not the be-all and end-all of life, but fuck, I'm a teenage girl and hormones are doing a number on me. *Probably why I went through with it.* I'm only human; I lust after people, too. But when the biggest object of my affection doesn't return the feeling, it's only natural that I seek out the affirmation I miss from somebody else.

I need to know I'm enough. I need to know I can be who somebody wants.

As much as I make out I'm happy hanging out on my own, I'd do anything for a boy who gives enough of a shit about me to hold my hand in front of my peers, a boy who is proud to call me his despite the lies that follow everywhere behind me like a burnt black veil.

A boy who treats me like more than an item on his high school bucket list.

"Belle?"

"I'm okay. Are we doing drive-through, or what?" I wipe my eyes once more and give him my full attention—a decision that turns out to be detrimental to my mental health.

He talks, but my focus is on the sharp line of his jaw as it moves, contrasting with the soft pout of his lips slightly hidden by his goatee. His cheekbones are high, leading to eyes that are dark and framed with the blackest of lashes, adding another touch of softness to an otherwise harsh face. He's so confident in himself, so sure, and I find myself wanting that. I want a bit of him to rub off on me.

I want him, full stop.

"...and you can kick back for a while before we get you home." I come around to his words, realising how much I've missed while in my daze.

"Sorry, I... I drifted for a bit there. What did you say?"

His eyebrows pinch together for a beat. "I said we'd go inside so you can chill out for a bit. If your dad sees you like this you can kiss goodbye to being let out again while you're under his roof."

Just another reason why I love Zeus: he gives a shit about the people in his life. He could take me home, throw me under the bus, and leave me to explain to Dad what happened. But he doesn't. Instead, he brings us here and spends time he doesn't have to waste on me making sure I'm okay before I walk through the door.

"You're too good to me." I avert my gaze.

"Hardly. This kind of shit is what you do for the ones you love," he remarks casually as he stares out the windscreen.

Heat rushes to my cheeks and I fidget with my hands. Zeus has known me since I was born, in the background when Mum and Dad were still together as a familiar face but nothing more than the guy who'd drop Dad off after a "boys' night out." After Mum left, he came around more; he was there for Dad while I was too young to help, too young to understand what it was that my father needed to process his heartache because I was only just coming to terms with my own. This whole situation here, now, sitting in his car while I wonder if he could ever love me in a non-platonic way—it's insane.

"Let's go inside, then," I cede. "Some time to wind down would be the sensible thing to do."

He shakes his head slowly. "Sensible would be taking

you home to your father and having him lock you away so horny fuckers like that can't take advantage of you again."

I chuckle at his amused smirk. "Why aren't you then?"

"Because I was young once too, Belle. I know what it's like to need independence."

I reach for the handle, the air in the car suddenly too thick around us.

He huffs a heavy breath and reaches for his door as well. We rise from the car as one and I make my way towards the brightly lit building before he's had time to lock the vehicle. He still manages to catch up without breaking stride. *Stupid height difference.* Zeus holds the first door open for me, and I pass by, doing the same for him on the second. We line up together behind a sleep-deprived-looking mother with a toddler in pyjamas. Zeus turns his head to look down at me and gives an amused smile.

"What?" I lift a hand to my hair. "Do I need to go freshen up?"

He chuckles. "Depends who you're trying to impress."

"God, is it that bad?" I wipe under my eyes again for added measure.

Gentle fingers turn my face to his. "You look fine." He drops his hand and nods toward the restaurant that hosts no one other than a pair of young farmers still in their dirty work clothes. "Go save us a table."

Not like there's a rush on. I do what I'm told anyway and pick a booth seat beside the wall that backs on to the kitchen area. Sauce is still splattered over the table. *Great.* I mean, honestly, is this how people leave their dining table at home? I rise again, passing the farmers to get a few serviettes, and note that their previous rowdy banter has stopped. They watch me as I return, wipe the table, and bin the dirty paper napkins. I catch the eye of one of them and he smiles before his lips fall sharply south. The heat at my back tells me exactly what the problem is.

"Where are we sitting?" Zeus's deep voice rumbles in his chest, directly behind my head.

"Over here." I break away and scoot onto the bench seat, expecting he'll take the other side.

Zeus slips in beside me, effectively blocking me from the farmers' view. "Caramel," he announces, presenting me with a gooey sundae. "Your favourite."

The table before him sits empty. "What are you having?" I ask.

Amusement flickers in his eyes. "Nothing."

"I thought *we* were having something to eat."

His lips curl up at the corner. "Does it look like my diet has space for a sundae?"

I roam my gaze over the bulk of him squeezed in between the seat and table. "I'm sure *one* wouldn't hurt."

He shakes his head and reaches for the hem of his T-shirt. My hand falters on the plastic spoon as he tugs the shirt up to his breastbone and reveals perfectly sculpted abs. The damn things bulge out at the top—the separation between each one evident, even whilst crunched over. "I start eating shit, and these puppies disappear." He slaps his palm against them twice before dropping his shirt back down.

The man has a point. I can also see why he'd want to keep them. "Fair play."

Zeus's chest rises and falls slowly. He brings his arms onto the table and clasps his hands before him while I eat my sugary sin. I steal a look at him every so often as he stares into the distance, evidently lost in his thoughts. I don't know his exact age; I'm not sure Dad's ever mentioned it. But the rigidity to his structure, devoid of any youth, confirms he's every part the man I appreciate he is.

And I'm eighteen.

Don't do it, Belle. Don't go there. I need to get my thoughts squared away, make myself think of him like an uncle, remove any attraction from the equation. I'm a schoolgirl—although not for much longer—and nothing he'd be remotely interested in. But with every sneaky glance his way, my heart falls a little more hopelessly in lust with this man. He's exactly that—a *man.* He's confident and sure in himself without the teenage hang-ups boys my age bring. *Boys.*

Fuck—why did Dad tell him he could move in?

I swirl the spoon around the remaining caramel sauce at the bottom of the plastic cup, utterly disgusted with how hormonal I am. "Are you sure I can't tempt you?" I hold out a walnut-sized dollop on my spoon, wiggling it a little in Zeus's direction.

He breaks his concentration and looks down at me. "I'm sure." That devastating smile returns.

"Go on...." I arch an eyebrow, wiggling the spoon some more, desperate to return our relationship to the teasing, fun way it used to be before I realised what love truly is.

He chuckles and turns in his seat to face me. "You trying to ruin me, Belle?"

I tip my head to the side. "Ruin you how?" Is he prepping for a bodybuilding contest or something?

"Making me less desirable to other women." Zeus's eyes widen after the words leave his lips, the realisation of what he's alluded to clearly hitting home. "I... I didn't mean it like that."

Swallowing thickly, I choose to be the adult in the situation and ignore his faux pas. "I doubt that would happen after one mouthful." I thrust the spoon his way. "Entertain me, Zeus. Show me you're human."

He smiles and leans forward, those full lips parting to envelop the white spoon. I'm transfixed to the way the plump flesh pulls over the plastic surface, a drop of caramel stuck to his bottom lip. He leans back, gaze holding mine as he slips his tongue out and catches the drop of gooey sauce.

"Good?" My word is a breathless whisper.

"Too tempting. I could have more."

I slam the spoon into the plastic cup, eager to repeat the intensity of the moment, but his hand falls over mine and stills it.

"Time to get you home, Belle."

I can't break my gaze from his flesh on mine, his fingers wrapped around my shaky grip on the spoon. His thumb twitches and strokes mine in a single, slow sweep... and then he's gone. He pulls away and slips out of the booth seat with a stealth that betrays his size. I pass him by, eyes to the floor, and bin my rubbish. He's already at the exit holding the door open when it dawns on me that we're the only ones remaining in the place. I've been so caught up in him, in his proximity, that I never noticed the other customers leave.

We walk in silence to his car and I stand awkwardly by the passenger door while he unlocks his and gets inside, leaning over the centre to unlatch mine. I pull the heavy door open and drop into the seat, closing it securely behind me with a thud as I count out the seconds between my inhale, exhale, doing everything I can to act cool, calm, and collected. Zeus watches me the entire time I straighten out the twisted seat belt and click it into place, jamming my hands between my knees when I'm finished. *Start the damn car already.*

"Things got a bit confusing for you just now, huh?" he asks.

For you. The arsehole. I huff out a sharp breath and cross my arms over my chest. "That would be right— blame whatever is going on between us solely on me, why don't you?"

"I never said that."

"It was implied." I stare petulantly out the window and refuse to acknowledge the fact he hasn't even put the keys in the ignition yet. "Can you please take us home before I tell you something else I shouldn't?"

He slots the key in, twists it, and brings the car to life. We reverse sharply out of the parking spot, and leave a strip of rubber as he rockets us with more force than necessary through the empty lot towards the driveway. His hands flex on the steering wheel in my periphery as we idle at the roadside, waiting for a lone car to pass.

"If it's any consolation," he bites out, "it was confusing for me too." My heart swells, and then deflates with what should be an audible pop on his next words. "Whatever you think you feel about me, whatever you think I feel about you—none of it matters."

"Why?" I bite my lip to save from crying again. Destroyed by two guys in one night—lucky me.

"Because something like *that*," he says, damn near growling the word, "could never happen. Understand?"

Great. Just fucking great. "Loud and clear."

TEN

Zeus

Fuck. *Fuck.* Fuck.

I scrub a hand over my face as Belle heads down the hall to her room. John isn't home yet—thank God. *Shit.* When did my hands start to shake?

What the fuck were you thinking, idiot? Telling a teenage girl that yeah, she wasn't wrong, lines got muddied back there? *So much for being the adult, you dropkick.*

Her door closes hard as she barricades herself in her safe haven. Do I go say something? Would that be even weirder? *Deny, deny, deny.* I need to act normal, as though I didn't just look at my best friend's *eighteen*-year-old daughter and wonder why she thinks of me as more than a family friend.

Because fuck—turns out I think of her as more than a kid.

A kid. I need to remember that. Yes.

Light spills from the fridge as I search for something to dull this ache in my brain. The whole night turned out fucked. I was supposed to kick back, relax, celebrate the fact I still have a job come Monday, and forget that my soon-to-be ex-wife is out fucking the guy who made our relationship that way. But then John got kept late at work, and I thought nothing of agreeing to get Belle.

How hard could it have been, right?

I'm sick. Isn't that what they call men my age who find teenagers attractive? *She's legal age.* Still... God, I'm so fucking confused.

Foam spills from the can of beer after I crack the tab, the bitter taste welcome on my tongue as I suck the aluminium rim clean. I tip my head back and shotgun the whole fucking thing, retrieving another before I toss the first empty in the bin and head toward the living room.

My heart seizes at the sound of Belle's door opening, her soft footsteps padding in the opposite direction before the bathroom door shuts. My thumb tracks a slow path around the rim of the can as I wait with bated breath to see if she'll return to her room when she's done, or come talk it out some more. Although I'm not really expecting her to do anything but hide away like any normal teenager would, avoiding conversation and even eye contact for the next week or however long it takes her to get over it.

Only I don't really want her to get over it. I want to understand what was going through her head when she looked at me like *that.* What exactly was she thinking?

Come on, Belle. Come talk to me.

I down half the second can before the bathroom door

opens and her footsteps track in my direction. She pauses at what I assume to be her bedroom door, and I hold my breath while I wait for the click of her latch.

Yet it doesn't come.

Eyes closed and my hand firm on the can to ground myself, I lean back in the armchair and wait.

"Zeus?" Her voice is barely a whisper, soft and comforting in the darkness.

"Yeah, Belle?"

"Can I ask you something?"

I open my eyes, thankful, so fucking thankful that she chose to thrash it out, talk through whatever the fuck that was, because sure as shit it wasn't just an ice cream. "Fire away."

"Do you still think of me as a child?"

Fuck. Maybe talking with her wasn't such a great idea? "Why are you asking me this?" I pinch the bridge of my nose, eyes closed tight as I wait on her reply.

"Because who else do I ask when your answer is the only one that matters?" The soft scrape of fabric suggests she's seated opposite me now. "I want to know if you still look at me like a kid, or if you see that I'm pretty much an adult now."

I open my eyes to find her watching me with a worried frown, hands jammed between her legs. She's changed, dressed now in her pyjamas: a pair of long black cotton pants and a pale blue tank top. Thank fuck she's kept her bra on.

"You're a young woman, Belle," I say on a sigh. "You

gave up being a kid when you learned how to take care of yourself."

She huffs a bitter laugh. "Awesome job I do of that, huh?"

"You've done it just fine, for years. Since you were barely a teenager. You can cook, clean. Hell, you could even organise to get yourself to school when you wanted to go," I tease. She smiles. "You can take care of yourself."

"Unless I'm in situations like tonight." Her lips fall to a flat line, her eyes distant.

My free hand fists on the arm of the chair as I down the last of my second beer. John mentioned something in passing about trouble he had with Belle while I was inside. Something to do with a bunch of kids at her school bullying her when they found out about why her mother left, spreading lies that—as they always do in school—became gospel.

"What exactly happened tonight, Belle?" I frown. "How did you even get in that situation?"

"It doesn't matter." She stares at the floor.

I point to the bruise on her neck—the *hickey.* "That tells me it does."

She slaps a palm to the darkened flesh, her eyes wide. "Shit."

"Yeah, shit. You know what your old man will say about that. So, I'll ask you again, Belle, what *really* happened?"

She pulls her legs up before her, tucking them inside

her arms. "I'm such an idiot."

"Why?"

"Because I knew he would be trouble. I know he doesn't actually like me, but I let him convince me anyway."

Breathe, Zeus. It'll pass. I spread my hands over the arms of the chair, burying my fingertips into the fabric. "Did he...?"

"Rape me?" she asks, wide-eyed. "God, no."

Thank fuck for that, because I was about ready to head back inside for the rest of my sentence. "It seemed as though you didn't want it to happen, though."

"I did." She turns her head to the side and sighs. "Just for all the wrong reasons." Her face twists in disgust. "Damn it. Why am I telling you all this?"

"Because you have to tell someone," I say carefully.

"He knew I was drunk, and that's what makes me so mad about it all. He should have known I'd feel differently sober."

"Not as brave?"

"Not as rebellious," she drones. "God. I'm such an idiot."

"You're not an idiot." I lean forward, drawing her attention back to me as I reach across the gap between us and prod her in the side of her stomach. "You just need to learn to listen to this. Always. Fuck what anyone tells you, fuck what you think other people reckon; your gut instinct always knows best."

"Is that what you listened to when you beat the hell

out of someone?"

Her question takes me by surprise. Not because she's raised a fair point, but because the hurt in her eyes tells me she's angry that I served my time inside. I never considered the fact she might feel betrayed, upset by it all. Never gave it a single thought in all the years I sat in my fucking cell wondering what everyone I knew was doing on the outside.

"You really are pissed about it." I lean back, resuming my position in the chair with my arms on the sides.

"Dad never told me where you went, so I figured it must have been bad," she states. "Who was the guy you assaulted?"

"We're talking about you tonight, Belle."

"I don't want to talk about me anymore," she snaps.

I could kill that little fucker. "I do."

"Don't." She shakes her head, dropping her legs so that they're folded before her. "Not yet, anyway."

The pain is too raw, I get that, but we haven't reached the critical moment yet: when our relationship deviated from the familiar path back at that damn McDonald's.

"Fine. Later," I yield. "How about you tell me what made you ask if I see you as a kid, then?"

Say it. Say the words for me.

"I just wondered, is all. I've thought about it a bit lately, and what you said in the car sort of brought it back to the forefront of my mind. I mean, is that how everyone sees me? Especially Dad," Belle admits, looking to the floor. "He wants to dictate everything I do, but I should be allowed to make more choices on my own, you know?"

"You still live under his roof."

"I know." Her gaze lifts, and fuck me if it isn't the most maturity I've ever seen displayed in those eyes. "But for how much longer? I've finished school now. Shouldn't I be learning how to be more independent?"

"I guess he's not ready to give up protecting you, yet." *I know I'm not.* The empty can creaks in my hand as I take the frustration coursing through me out on its weak structure. "You said my opinion was the only one that mattered, though. Why?"

"Work that out for yourself, Zeus." She holds my gaze, strong and sure.

There's nothing immature about her at all in that moment. Nothing.

"What are your plans now school is done?" I opt for a change of subject. I get the feeling she could dance around defining this relationship of ours all night.

She shrugs. "Honestly?"

"Isn't that why you came to talk to me? For an honest conversation?"

She hums a funny little "hmph" before answering. "Yeah."

"So, what is it you want to do?"

"Tattoo."

Totally not thinking of her with those hands on my skin. Nope. Not at all. "I figured."

"So why ask?"

She's daring *me* to admit the truth now. *Clever way to turn it around, Belle.*

"I don't know." I rub my forefinger and thumb over closed eyes before rising from the chair to bin the can in my other hand. "Are we done here?"

I catch the slight cock of her head in my periphery. "I guess."

Yeah, I'm an arsehole for cutting her off, but if she won't discuss the real issues at hand—like the fact her baggy pyjamas haven't stopped me from visualising how her naked body looks underneath—then she and I have no business hanging out. I'm no better than that jackass at the party who couldn't keep his goddamn hands to himself.

I'm worse.

Belle rises from the sofa and walks toward her room, only to hesitate at the start of the hallway. "Thank you for tonight; for giving me that time to calm down."

"I'm just glad it wasn't your old man who found you."

"Yeah." She turns her head to match my gaze. "So was I."

I should offer some words of wisdom... or she should walk away. One of us should do something to cut the cord, flick the switch off on whatever dim connection we have going here, yet neither of us do.

She swallows, her jaw lifting slightly as she does. I take a deep breath, mentally walking away to retrieve a bottle of water to take to bed with me, yet all I physically do is stay.

I can't walk away—it doesn't feel right, and I don't know why.

It should feel nothing but natural, second nature to shut her off and wipe Belle from my thoughts. But I can't look away from her, even as she drops her gaze and sucks in a deep breath herself, one hand on the other wrist as she slowly rubs it back and forth.

"What, Belle?" I ask quietly. "What else is on your mind?"

She chuckles, her lips tilting up on one side. "I... it's nothing. I should just go to bed."

"Yeah. Same."

She takes a single step and then turns back to face me, her lips pressed in a thin line as though she's resolved to say whatever comes next no matter the consequence. "You're a great guy, Zeus. At first, I thought Jodie was stupid to let you go, but then I realised something." Her chest heaves with her quick breath. "All she did was free you up for the person who appreciates you and loves you like you deserve. I guess she did you a favour." Belle twitches a smile, her cheeks flushed rose pink as she turns away and heads for her room.

I stay rooted to the spot, watching the gentle sway of her hips as she pads barefoot down the hallway. She didn't say it, didn't voice it, but the panic in my chest confirms what was hidden between the lines of that last statement: she thinks *she's* the one who can love and appreciate me.

Belle honestly believes that she could be what I deserve. And what's even more twisted and fucked up is, I believe she could be right.

ELEVEN

Belle

The chill from the thick shake in my hand has my fingers numb by the time Kate steps through the automatic doors. She glances around, her gaze settling on where I sit on the bench seat in the middle of the mall, and smiles.

Maybe there is hope.

"Sorry I'm late." She motions for me to stand with a jerk of her head as she approaches. "Brock had to help his dad with something before we left. He's waiting in the car, so let's make this quick, yeah?"

Maybe there isn't.

I fall into step with her, frustrated that yet again she's placed that fucking guy on the rung above me. "Thanks for coming."

"I need to pick up some more moisturiser anyway, so no biggie." She glances across as we head toward the chemist. "Talk to me. What happened?"

Looking at her, I feel every part the emotional wreck I am in that moment. She's clearly stayed the night at Brock's given the fact she wears the same clothes as last night, and yet if I hadn't seen her yesterday to know, I wouldn't have picked up on it. Her hair is still perfectly straight, her face stunning despite the lack of make-up, and she has this air about her. She's glowing. Not a word I would have thought I'd use to describe my best friend, but there's no other way to describe how her happiness seems to follow her like a sweet cloud of sugary goodness.

"I need to get the morning-after," I whisper as I catch my reflection in the shop windows.

Dad was still asleep when I left, after having got in at some ungodly hour of the morning. Forty minutes in the shower, and I still can't scrub the feeling of filth from my pores. The more I sobered up last night, the more it sunk in. I seriously considered stealing a bottle from Dad's cupboard to reinstate the blissful numb that accompanies killing half your brain cells.

And yet I didn't. One look at Zeus as he sat at the breakfast table and I wished I had.

"Jesus, Belle," Kate hisses under her breath. "How could you be so careless?"

"It wasn't me," I whisper-yell in return, leaning in close as we walk. "He said he was gloved."

"And you didn't notice when he stuck it in that he wasn't?"

I smile sheepishly at a guy who frowns on his way past us. "Keep it down."

She's hit the nail on the head, found the thing that makes me feel most stupid about the whole deal. How did I not know?

Because you're young and inexperienced, that's why.

And it's that inadequacy that made me want to crawl under a rock when Zeus locked his gaze with mine and simply sighed. He didn't say a damn thing; didn't have to. He's disappointed in me. Probably takes one look at me and can't help but see a stupid young girl getting it on with an even stupider young guy.

I'm tainted. Used.

Undesirable.

No guy wants seconds, and when you're trying to score a guy twenty years your senior then you best be bringing your *A* game.

Clearly, I'm not.

"I can't believe you were so gullible, Belle." Kate makes a clicking sound with her tongue as we near the chemist. "Did you see him put it on?"

"Yes. I mean, not really. I thought he did."

She stops in the entrance to the shop, turning to face me. "Did you see his dick sheathed in rubber? It's pretty simple, you know."

I cock an eyebrow at her, stunned by this attitude. I get it—I was naïve to believe he would have enough respect to glove up and not be selfish. But shit, cut a newbie some slack, huh?

"What is your deal?"

"I can't believe you'd be so stupid is all." She flicks her hair and starts walking again, leading us through the aisles. "If you weren't thorough enough to check, then no wonder you're in this situation."

"You're blaming this on me," I whisper as we pass an old lady selecting a heat rub.

"What was it you preached to me? Do you think this will make you fit in? Make you cool?" Kate slaps me with a scathing glare before sweeping around the end of the racking to pluck her moisturiser from the shelf. "Scott? Of all people? Didn't you want it to mean something?"

It takes me a minute to retrieve my jaw from the floor and then set to work on my cracked heart. This girl is supposed to be on my side, telling me what I need to hear to make me feel better. I guess she's got the whole tell-it-how-it-is trait nailed down, but shit.

What do I say when my answer involves the guy I *really* wanted to give it to being my dad's best friend?

"Well, I guess we can't all be you, right?"

"What's that supposed to mean?" Her gaze narrows as she queues up behind some guy.

"Finding the perfect boy to fall in love with." I glare at her, slamming my arms across my chest. "How was *he*, Kate? Was *he* special?"

Her nostrils flare as she simply stares at me a beat. "We didn't go that far."

"His parents have you in the spare room?" I cock an eyebrow, somewhat disbelieving after the way she went on about him last night.

"No." The line shifts and she slams her purchase on the counter. "He had too much respect for me to go there on the first date."

Ugh. I step back as she starts her transaction and get flagged by the assistant at the next till over. "Can I help?"

All of two people stand behind us, and yet it could be a crowd of a thousand for how nervous I am in this moment. I set my hands on the counter and lean over to murmur, "I need the morning-after."

The assistant nods, not a single muscle in her face shifting. This woman has mastered the art of indifference, but then again, she probably sees stupid young girls such as me all the time.

I sweat bullets as she turns and walks several steps to retrieve a box from the lower shelves behind the counter. "Have you had this before?"

I shake my head, which in turn sets her off explaining how to take it and the side effects. I should be listening, but instead I'm focused on my friend as she takes her purchase and walks out of the store.

What the fuck? She's left without a single word. Nothing.

"Any questions?"

I snap back to the pharmacy assistant and shake my head. I'm sure anything I missed will either be on the box or available care of Dr Google.

She rings the purchase up, and takes the better part of my fifty-dollar note Dad gave me for my birthday. I clutch the paper bag to my chest as I walk out and head to the supermarket to get a bottle of PowerAde and something sweet from the bakery to wash this down. The sooner the damn thing is in me, the sooner my stomach can stop turning at the thought of a tiny Scott running around.

I speed through my shopping in record time, intent on taking the pill at the mall. Yet as I step back out into the walkway, I'm overwhelmed by the hundreds of eyes around me as the weekend shopping hits peak hour. People stroll past, filling the floor space and the bench seats, all lost in their personal crusades, but I can't shake the feeling that they all *know*. That if I take a seat and pull the packet from the chemist bag I may as well be waving a banner flag and flicking on a neon sign.

Privacy. I need privacy. My research on the pill last night said I have up to twenty-four hours to get it down before the effectiveness starts to wane, so I've got plenty of time left to get home.

Home.

Part of me considers the logistics of never having to leave the house again. I have no friends left—Kate made that clear—and no job to keep me busy now school is done. What reason do I have to do anything other than merely exist? A week in hibernation working on my sketches sounds like bliss after this weekend. A week to unwind and find myself again, because fuck knows I didn't find her amongst the masses the last five years.

School's out, motherfuckers—welcome to adulthood.

Where mistakes are made, and dreams are shattered.

Living the dream.

TWELVE

Zeus

Dark clouds gather on the horizon, dulling what was an enjoyable spring day. The loud clink of metal on glass tears my focus away from the approaching storm and back to Jodie.

"Are you listening?" Her perfectly drawn eyebrow arches as she leans back.

I focus on where she smacked the teaspoon against my beer glass and frown. "Sure."

"What did I just say, then?"

Fuck. "That we'll split the agent fees down the middle?"

She huffs, her ample chest heaving as she does. "After that, Zeus."

I stare at the woman I once promised the rest of my life to and wonder how I could ever have been so stupid. Dating her in school had been an accomplishment of sorts, considering she was one of the rich, popular girls, and I was... well, the poor half-caste from the wrong end of town.

But pretty girls love bad boys, and a bad boy was all

I was. No entry-level scores for my exams, no perfect attendance. Just a few thousand in my back pocket from the shit I'd stolen and hocked off at the traders downtown, and an entitled attitude that no level of authority could heel.

"You'll have to remind me." I lean back and spread my legs wide beneath the table.

I don't miss the way Jodie's eyes track the shape of my shoulders before she answers. "I said I'd list it as negotiable over four-twenty."

"Sounds fair enough." Last valuation had our house at three-ninety, so whatever she can get over that is more money in my back pocket once we divide the profit.

"Veronica, the agent, has the papers drafted awaiting the price, so I can get them from her for you to sign tomorrow."

I nod, already disinterested in the conversation again. Yet the more amicable this split is, the less it'll cost me in lawyer's fees—money I don't have right now. I shift my gaze to the clouds again, thinking how they look the same as the rain storm that hit the day I spoke to Belle out the back of John's when Cerise left: black and foreboding.

Belle loves storms. Always has.

Even at age five she'd tug on my arm and beg me to turn all the lights off to sit in the dark and watch the lightning with her. John and Cerise would leave us to it, probably thankful for the break. I loved those afternoons. I'd almost go as far as to say I miss them.

"You're not listening again, are you?"

"I think we've covered everything we have to."

Jodie's eyes narrow as she lifts her purse. "I asked where I could find you, so I know where to bring your copy of the documents."

"I'll come see you."

"I don't think that's a good idea." She pulls lipstick and a compact out, her brow furrowed.

"Let me guess." I can't keep the twitch from my eye as I stare down this harlot. "You're at his house now."

"I told you he asked me to move in." She smacks her lips, the look in her eyes fire.

"Yeah, you did, but I thought you'd have more decency than to jump ship before our bed was even cold."

"Don't fool yourself, Zeus." The scrape of her chair on the pavement is as angry as her words. "Our bed was cold months ago."

"And who's fault would that be?" I show indifference to her tantrum by refusing to move, spread out on my seat still.

Her chest heaves once, twice, before the brutality of her words punches a fist into my chest and rips my heart out. "We're trying for a baby." The victory shines in her eyes. "You know, that thing you could never give me."

Bitch is lucky we're in public. I've never hit a woman, but goddamn she makes me want to start.

"Go play happy families, Jodie. I'm at John's when you've got the paperwork ready for me." Sooner we get this shit tied up and finished, the better.

I push to my feet and make it as far as swiping my keys from the table before she digs her talons in that extra inch.

"John's? How's that working out for you, sharing the same roof as his melodramatic bitch of a daughter?"

"Say something else about Belle," I threaten with a finger pointed her way. "And see what happens."

Her freshly painted lips curl up on one side. "A bit on the defensive side, aren't you?"

"Sick of this shit, is all."

She huffs, slinging the strap of her purse over her shoulder. "Admit it: drama follows that wee madam everywhere. He spoiled her after Cerise walked out and made a rod for his own back."

"He hardly spoiled her." He barely had two coins to rub together at the end of the week. If anything, he sacrificed to make sure she didn't go without. John never lost his physical size because he stopped working out with me, he lost it because he couldn't afford to maintain it anymore. Shit, some weeks he only ate because of the help I gave him.

"You're as delusional as he is." Jodie shakes her head. "Just make sure she doesn't try to manipulate you as well. Last thing you need is that little leech sucking you dry."

I scoff as I march past her. "No, Jodie. Not when

you're doing such a great job of that all on your own."

Her response doesn't reach my ears, the words lost in the distance between us as I stride out to the parking lot and drop into the GTO. My heart thunders in my chest, the words she spoke about Belle fuel for the fire I keep dampened inside.

I have a tendency to become violent when provoked, especially when it comes to the people I care about. Hell, one look at the reason I was sent inside proves that. But I've spent years with the custodial therapist working on keeping my fists to myself and resolving issues with words. Fucked if one jaded ex-wife will be the reason why that changes.

My pulse continues to throb fat and heavy in my neck as I drive back to John's. The more I try to calm myself, the more wound up I become. Yet strangely my frustration doesn't have me craving the usual outlet for my anger. A session with the bag at the gym, a few swings of the hammer onto the tyre, and my mood eases. Not today. The more I run what Jodie said through my mind, the more I wonder if that's how everyone views Belle, and why she gets a hard time. The more I want to hold her and tell her I don't think that way at all.

Inappropriate, Zeus. Totally not what I need to do to ease this pressure coiled tight in my chest.

She came to me in confidence on Friday night, and what did I do? I brushed her aside and discounted how she felt, all to save how *I* felt. I did the same as every other fucking person in her life—everyone except her father. And yet, she won't talk to him. Why?

I park the car in John's driveway and wander toward the house in a daze, my thoughts still so tangled in Belle that I don't notice John at the door until he almost bowls me over in his effort to look behind me.

"She's not with you?"

"Should she be?" The panicked look in his eye sets my racing heart back where it left off.

He turns and storms inside the house, leaving me to follow. "She wasn't here when I got up."

"She went to the shops, man."

His shoulders sag as his face relaxes. "Of course."

I slap a hand on his shoulder and smile. "Beer?"

"I think so." He drags a hand over his face as I head for the fridge. "I guess I'm a little on edge."

"You don't say." I uncap the bottle and hand it over. "Why?"

He slumps into a seat at the dining table and looks up at me with nothing short of apprehension.

"What have you done?"

"It's not what I've done," he says. "It's what I'm about to do."

I lean back against the counter and open a bottle of water. "Which is?"

"I got a phone call a few months ago." He chews the inside of his cheek before continuing. "Cerise."

"Fuck off." My jaw sets to stone. That bitch ruined him. Nothing she could have to say would be worth it.

"She wanted to see me, to hear about Belle."

"She's had ten years to hear about Belle," I point out. "And *now* she gives a fucking shit?"

"She had issues to work through, mate."

"She gave *you* issues to work through last time she was around."

He sighs. It's clear that no matter what I come up with, this deal is done. "We've been meeting up, catching up."

"When?"

"Before work. After." His guilty eyes tell me everything.

"You're meaning to tell me that you were worried about leaving Belle on her own while you're at work, but you were okay with making booty calls with your ex instead?"

"Zeus, have some respect, man."

"I am," I deadpan. "You don't want to hear what I really think of her. What happened to Mr Moneybags?"

"They lasted two years."

"Two years." I scoff. "Her affair is over after two years, and yet it's *ten* before she thinks to come ask about her fucking daughter."

"She admits she fucked up, okay? But tell me," he asks with a narrowed glare. "How easy would you find it to walk back into your kid's life after all this time?"

"If I loved her, pretty fucking easy."

He regards me a moment, silent as he takes several pulls of his beer. "We're thinking of a reconciliation."

"Are you high?"

"Z, man. I haven't had a serious relationship since her. Fuck, I haven't had *one* long-term relationship."

"So, you'll settle for seconds?"

"I thought you'd support me—us."

"If I thought it was a good idea, then yeah, I would."

He huffs heavily out his nose. "I need you to try, mate. I need you to put some real effort into seeing how she's changed."

"Why?" I narrow my gaze on him, not liking the unease in my gut one fucking iota.

"Because I want to ask her to move back in as part of the reconciliation."

My bottle hits the counter with a splash. "No fucking way."

"I'm sorry," he snaps with the most balls I've seen on the man in years. "But this is *my* house, so it's *my* decision."

"And Belle is your daughter. You know, the one *you* raised alone the last ten years? How would she feel? You thought about that?"

"She'll either adapt or she's welcome to start her own life under her own roof."

"You'd boot your eighteen-year-old daughter out unprepared in the name of maybe working things out with the woman who fucked around and left you for the next shiny thing?"

"This conversation is going nowhere." He rises, face impassive as he stares me down.

"Too right, it's not. Just like your future with that fucking woman." I snatch up my drink and turn for the door. "I'll keep my mouth shut for you, J, but fucked if I'm going to play nice with her."

"That's all I ask."

THIRTEEN

Belle

The water runs over me in the shower, washing away the last scraps of my self-respect. I can't get enough of the cleansing effect a hot shower has of late. I took one last night when I got home, a lengthy one this morning, and now an even longer one to try and get the last of the metaphorical dirt from under my skin.

Every inch of my body repulses me. I disgust myself. How could I have been so flippant that I not only chose to sleep with a guy who doesn't care one iota about me, but to trust the asshole to use protection? How could I ever think that I could mend a broken heart by shattering it further? *How could I trust my best friend to understand?* My chest heaves, and snot bubbles out my nose as my tears attempt to erupt into a full-on howl. I force my mouth closed, afraid that either Dad or Zeus might hear me, and moan long lamented chords instead. My cheeks puff out as my body does everything it can to try and expel this ache inside of me. I'm a fool, stupid, naïve, and *young.* I've still got so much to learn.

Thump, thump, thump.

"You okay, Belle?"

Dad. *Shit.* Guess I'm not as quiet as I'd hoped. I wipe the snot from my nose with both hands, washing them off under the water as I stand on shaky legs. "I'm fine." Fuck. Even I can pick how ridiculously weak that sounded.

"What's the matter, honey?"

I tip my chin up under the water, hands to the wall as I let the flow wash over my face one last time before shutting the water off. "Just a bad day, Dad. I'm fine." My stomach roils to remind me that I haven't eaten since I downed the pill before lunch.

"Well, I'm reheating casserole for dinner." *Thank heaven for small miracles.* "I know it's nothing special, but I can serve you some."

"Yes, please." I step out of the shower cubicle and wrap myself in the towel. The fog over the mirror smears into arcs when I wipe my hand across the surface. I stare at the broken reflection looking back at me, and scowl. *Stupid bitch.*

I've never kept anything from Dad before, never had reason to lie. Honesty was one of the things he demanded from me after Mum left. I suppose in a way he was worried that if he didn't instil the habit early, he'd eventually lose me too. He doesn't need to worry. I'd never have reason to walk away from him. But if he found out what I did... would he ever find reason to abandon me?

Best not to think too hard on it.

Dried and dressed, I head out to the dining table to try and settle this unease in my gut. Hopefully a hearty meal followed by an early night is all I need. Dad sits on his side, acknowledging me with a nod as he continues to shovel forkfuls of casserole into his mouth. Zeus is nowhere to be seen. *Thank God for that.*

Dad finishes his bite as I take my seat. "Glad you could join me." A smile tugs at the corner of his eyes.

"Hottest date in town," I tease. "Before-payday special?" I move the cut roast meat and vegetables drenched in gravy around on my plate.

"Sure is."

As strange as it sounds, his spur of the moment "use it or lose it" meals are the best. Somehow Dad manages to take last night's (or sometimes the night before's) meat, a few shrivelling vegetables, and a mixture of whatever spices he can lay his hands on and make the best damn casseroles ever. I devour my meal in silence, sopping up the last of the gravy with a slice of the buttered bread he has on a plate in the centre of the table.

"Exams all done, huh?" He pushes his empty plate forward and takes his bottle of beer in hand. "How do you think you did?"

"Okay." I shrug. "Where's Zeus gone?" The seats in the living room are empty despite the fact the TV is still on. "He missed out on dinner."

"At the gym, I think." Dad sighs out his nose, setting the glass in his hand down. "He said he'd sort himself out. Anything you want to tell me? Anything that's bothering you?"

Anything that's bothering you, Dad? The cool tone he used when he spoke of Zeus didn't escape my notice. I shake my head and stand to collect our plates. "Nothing that won't work itself out." *Speaking of which...* My stomach churns, and my face falls rapidly at the abundance of saliva that rushes into my mouth.

"You okay?" Dad asks.

I nod, paling as I turn for the kitchen. *Casserole is working fast.* Or my morning-after pill has kicked in. *Shit.* I manage to get the stacked plates onto the counter before I'm forced to grip the edge and hang my head between my shoulders to ride out the swell of nausea.

"Time to stop bullshitting me, sweetheart," Dad says as he enters the kitchen. He places a hand between my shoulders to rub in circles. "What's going on?"

"I don't know," I lie. "Must be what I had at the mall for lunch."

"Which was?"

"A burger from that place next to the sushi shop."

"Maybe we should let them know in case other people get sick?"

He knows I lie. He knows that I know it.

Dad disappears from my side, returning with a glass in hand. He leans over me to fill it from the tap. "Here. Go sit down on the couch... or the toilet. Whatever's going to make you feel more comfortable." A playful smirk tugs at his lips.

I manage to chuckle at his humour. "Nice visual, there."

"It is what it is." He smiles and shoos me from the room. "Go, before you make me feel off colour."

"Thanks, Dad." He never has been able to handle seeing other people be sick.

I retreat to the safe confines of my room and set the glass down on the bedside table. My stomach flips as I lower myself onto the bed and attempt to lie on my front. An ache spreads through my chest, the source of the agony my meagre B-cup breasts. *What else?* I roll onto my back, barely managing to hold down the bile that ebbs in my throat. My heart pounds in my ears, my skin flushed and my head aching. *No. I can't deal with this too.* Nausea rises like a relentless wave, crashing all over my manageable state. I launch off the bed and barely make it to the bathroom before the contents of my stomach expel into the basin. The toilet's another door down—I had no hope in hell.

I stare at the mess in the sink, tears streaming from my eyes, water running from my nose. *How am I going to explain this?* Round two. I crank the cold tap on, washing away what I can before my stomach clenches for round three. The foam that expels is sickly yellow; I've got nothing left. *Thank God for that.* Still doesn't stop my stomach from cramping in its efforts to find something to gift me.

"Shit, Belle." Dad steps through the open doorway and reaches out to stroke the damp hair from my temples. "Are you sure it's just food poisoning? Maybe it's something viral. Should we go to after hours?"

"No." I hold up a shaky hand in weak protest. "I'll be okay now that my stomach's empty." I expel another load of yellow foam as my body's way of giving me a silent *fuck you*.

"Bed. I'll grab a bucket and a cold cloth."

"Let me wash my face first."

He nods and leaves the bathroom, presumably to fetch what's fondly known as the "sick bucket" in our house; a green plastic tub that only gets cranked out in times like this. Soaking the facecloth in warm water, I run it over my face, groaning at how refreshed the simple action makes me. My stomach doubles on itself again, but this time that's as far as the action goes. I close my eyes in relief, thankful my burning throat doesn't have to endure more.

I guess I deserve it: the pain, the suffering, the stress of upholding my lies.

Dad finds me in bed, tucked under the blankets, when he returns with the bucket and places it on the floor. He takes a seat on the edge of my mattress, placing a hand to my forehead. His wrinkled eyes smile at me, but his mouth remains dour. "I think the patient might pull through."

"Prognosis, Doctor?" I close my eyes, enjoying the fact he's chosen to play a game we had to ease my aches whenever I was sick as a child.

It's a welcome distraction from the betrayal that rips

at my chest when I meet his eyes.

"It's hard to be sure, but I think we can appoint this case of vomiting to acute off-lunchitis."

"Sounds serious, Doctor."

"Gravely. In most cases the spoiled beef means the illness is terminal, but we may have just saved this one in time."

I smile, nestling into my pillow. "Thanks, Dad." My eyes burn with regret.

He chuckles, pulling my sheet up over me as though I'm still five years old. "Anytime, honey." The mattress lifts as he stands. "Light out?" he asks from the doorway.

"Yeah, please." My head pounds as though the devil himself is working the jackhammer.

I'm plunged into darkness when he pulls my door to. I lie for a while, concentrating on willing my burbling stomach to ease. The mind trick seems to work for a while, long enough to let me nod off. I'm woken though by laughter drifting in from the living room.

Only one person with a low rumble like that. Seems Zeus has decided it's safe to show his face.

My eyes shoot open, and I stare out into the black, straining my ears to catch another note. I'm rewarded for my efforts by a long, deep lilt of amusement that leaves me nothing short of conflicted.

I want to go out there and talk to him, prove that we don't have to let one misunderstanding get in the way of our friendship, but at the same time I can't bear to see his face after what I've done. He might have brushed it all off as concern last night, but I glimpsed what he refused to voice—anger, and disappointment.

I've let him down. But if he doesn't want to think of me as anything more than John's daughter, why would that matter so much? I'm not his concern.

My stomach clenches and I roll to my right, grappling for the bucket. I find it just in time to catch another exorcism of the demons in my gut. The acid burns my oesophagus, and the only thing I can do to ease the ache is groan. My body races with heat—sweat breaking out from every pore as the cramps in my stomach bring tears to my eyes. I rip the sheets off myself, and move to sit on the edge of the bed, fanning myself with both hands. The bucket sits at my feet, taunting my stomach, tricking it into having another go. I'm mid-hurl when the light snaps on.

"Belle?"

Kill me now. "I'm fine, Zeus, really." The last word comes out as more of a moan when my throat closes in preparation for the next round. "It'll pass soon."

"Your dad said you told him you have food poisoning." He steps into the room, coming to a stop at the foot of my bed. "You weren't sick when you got home from the mall, though."

"I guess it hadn't kicked in yet."

"Are you sure?" He moves to sit beside me, bringing a hand up to stroke the hair at my nape.

"That's my story and I'm sticking with it." The tears free-falling let him know the truth is bad enough—he doesn't need the details.

"Belle...."

"Zeus," I mimic, managing to grimace a smile before my stomach cramps again.

"Truth about what's going on. Now." His dark eyes hold me captive.

My chin shakes as I stifle my sobs. "No."

"Why the fuck not?" He frowns, his hand in my hair taking firm hold.

"Because...." I can't even get the words out. Fear takes over at the mere thought of what he'd think of me once he knows the whole story. "Because you'll think lesser of me."

"Tit for tat."

"Huh?" I move the bucket away, the thought enough to make me go again.

"Tit for tat," he repeats. "You give me your bad news—because that's what I'm guessing you have—and I'll share something bad I've done with you."

Still doesn't convince me. I shake my head. "I need to clean up." My efforts to stand are halted by a large hand pressing firmly into the centre of my chest, seating me squarely back on the bed. I turn my head to find him staring at the empty packet of Plan B partially visible from where I hid it in my school bag. *Well, that sucks.* "Don't say it."

"Say what?" His brow furrows.

Anyone who didn't know him might think he was cross. But I know better. I've hurt him—again.

Does it ever end?

"That I'm reckless, immature."

"Careless, I was going to say." He drags a hand over his mouth, still staring at the fucking box.

I stretch my leg out and nudge my bag with the tips of my toes to cover the evidence.

"Who was he?" Pained eyes search mine.

"A guy from school." This won't end well. He needs to stop the questions now if he expects either of us to survive.

"Who?"

Fuck, Zeus. "Andrew." I pick the first name that comes to mind.

"Liar."

"How would you know?" I snap back.

"Your ears always go pink when you lie."

Damn it.

"I'll ask again." His jaw stiffens. "Who was it?"

"Why?" I whisper, tucking my legs to my chest as my gut twists again. "What are you going to do if I tell you?"

"Teach the little fucker a lesson about respecting women."

"And what if it was me who chose to do it unprotected?" I need to steer him away from the who, and discussing the why is all I can think of doing that doesn't seem suspicious.

"Belle." He grimaces, rolling his lips together.

I want to kiss him. As fucked up as it is, I want to kiss away his pain and in turn forget mine. I want to pretend that we could be something real and that I didn't screw up any slim chance I may have had—even if only in my wildest dreams.

"Tell me why it matters, Zeus." I drop my legs and twist to face him.

"Because *you* matter," he murmurs, his brow twitching as he watches my every move, his elbows rested on his knees. "Why would you do that to yourself?"

"I don't know, okay?" I can't look at him, can't see the way he judges me even though he promised he wouldn't. "I don't know."

Zeus stays silent as he stands and steps past me to collect the bucket, then leaves the room. I fall to my knees and tear the empty box out of my school bag, maddened by its clear and obvious packaging. Surely they could make this less conspicuous for those of us who don't want to broadcast to the world that we fucked up?

The low rumble of Zeus and Dad as they talk filters up the hall, their tones even and calm. It doesn't stop my heart from trying to beat a path out of my chest. *Would he tell him?* Would Zeus tell Dad what he saw?

I swipe the tears from my cheeks with an angry hand, frustrated that I could be so stupid, so dense. I know what happens when people drink, how the alcohol clouds your ability to make sound decisions. And yet I did it. I drank past the point of a clear conscience and made a stupid decision based on my pathetic wounded pride.

I wanted to fit in, and all I've done is outcast myself from the person who matters most.

FOURTEEN

Zeus

She didn't come out of her room all of Sunday except to use the bathroom or snatch something from the kitchen when she thought nobody watched. Pair Belle's sulking with John's silence over the subject of Cerise, and it made for one hell of a quiet end to the weekend.

In an odd way, it made me glad to go to work today. I needed the distraction, the mind-numbing state of nothingness that accompanies being on the end of a shovel for a few hours. I needed to put myself to work and replace emotional pain with physical pain—something more tangible to focus on.

I succeeded.

My back hurts, my feet hurt, and I swear to God I've even managed to get wind burnt. *Welcome to your new permanent job, motherfucker.* My boots leave dirt halos where I kick them off at the front step, my clothes still filthy despite the fact I spent what felt like the better part of an hour brushing myself off before I got in the car.

Roadwork is fucking dirty work, especially on days

we finish early because of the rain.

Drawing a deep breath, I hesitate before opening the front door. I did my best to keep up Belle's bullshit story yesterday about her food poisoning, flat-out lying to my best friend when he asked me if she told me anything different to what she told him. "Look after her tomorrow, okay?" he'd remarked as he headed off to catch a few hours rest before his next shift.

Yeah—I'm pretty sure he's got no idea exactly *how* I'd like to look after his daughter.

Quit it, dickhead. No matter how hard I try, I can't shift her from my thoughts. The more I replay the sight of her sitting there on her bed, ashamed at what I noticed, the more the memory shows me a young woman seated across from me. A young woman who may have made a stupid fucking decision, but a woman nonetheless.

She's eighteen, but fuck me, I can't wrap my mind around why that doesn't seem to matter. It should. Her age should be the reason why I back away before things get even more complicated.

But if I've ever been one thing, it's a selfish son of a bitch, and I'm not ready to give up Belle just yet. Not when being around her leaves me feeling better than I have in years... as though I'm worth somebody's love.

It's just your divorce playing games with you. The only logical explanation to the way I feel. Yet as I finally twist the handle and push, I know a fragile heart is the last thing that's got me the way I am.

She sees me, just like she said. She sees me and that makes her happy. Nobody is happy when they find out the truth about who I am. Only her.

"How was your day?" Belle pauses in the hallway, presumably on her way back to her room with a bowl of what looks to be muesli.

Seems the appetite has returned.

"Long." Fuck it, I give in and smile at her, because why not when the sight of her immediately lessens my aches?

She squares her stance, and then runs her gaze the length of me. A small frown pulls at her brow. "You're going to track dirt all through Dad's house."

Dust and mud are caked around the legs of my work pants. "Yeah, but how else do I get to the laundry?" Let alone to a clean change of clothes. If I were at my own place, I would have stripped in the doorway and walked through the house in nothing but my boxers.

But... Belle.

"Hold on." She disappears for a moment, returning without the bowl in her hands. Instead she carries an armful of towels.

"What are you going to do with those?" I chuckle.

"Lay them down like a path for you to walk over so you at least save the carpet." She drops the stack, then picks up the top towel and shakes it out.

"And you're going to greet me at the door to do this every time it rains?" I tease.

The corners of her mouth turn down in thought. "You

have a point."

"What we need is a better plan." I look around as though the house itself will provide me with the answer.

I have nothing. No ideas that don't involve me at least partially undressed anyway. *Fuck. They're just boxers.* How different would it be to her seeing me in swimmers? It'll only be this one time; I'll take a change of clothes from now on, be more prepared.

"Honestly, go do whatever you were doing when I walked in," I tell her. "I'll sort myself out."

"If you're sure."

"Positive." One hundred per cent positive I want her to fuck off so I can shed my clothes without things getting awkward.

I wait until the rustle of her moving around in her bedroom filters to where I stand, and then unbutton the cotton work shirt with quick fingers. Dust falls to the floor as I slide the sleeves down my arms, but at least on the entry tiles I can sweep the mess up. My belt buckle clangs as I whip it open, and then shove my work pants down my legs and over my feet. With the filthy clothing balled in my hands, I head for the laundry, hoping like hell Belle stays in her fucking room.

Safe as houses. I make it to the washer and let out the breath I didn't realise I'd held. After taking the wet clothes in the machine out to hang up later, I throw my things in and set the load to heavy. My skin prickles at her sudden intake of breath.

Shit.

"I... um, I remembered there was stuff in the machine, so I was coming to get it." Belle's gaze stays stuck on my chest.

I clear my throat.

That deep rose blush shows itself as she steps forward, careful not to bump into where I stand in nothing but my boxer briefs, and reaches for the basket of clothes. "I'll just take this," she whispers, backing out of the room in a hurry.

Fuck my life. Night shift. John had to go and take fucking night shift.

How the fuck am I going to survive this another day? More to the point, how the fuck is Belle going to survive *me*?

I take a step forward and then freeze as she reappears at the door. "I forgot that." Her hand lifts and she points to the clothes airer tucked down the side of the machine.

Twisting to my right, I slide it out and lift the metal frame to pass it over. Her gaze flicks off my arms as I face her, meeting mine with nothing short of guilt. *Be the adult, Zeus.*

"It's okay," I tease. "I know for a fact I'm not the first half-naked guy you've seen, so no need to act shy."

Her face falls and those soft lips turn down. I didn't intend the reference to her first fuck on Friday night to be so harsh. *What a jackass thing to say, Z.*

"I'm sorry. That was uncalled for."

She clutches the airer in her grasp, swallowing

before answering. "No, you're right. I shouldn't be so stupid about it. What's a bit of skin, right?" She laughs awkwardly before backing out of the room.

I throw my head back, hands over my face, and groan. *Well played, Zeus. Fucking tool.* I'm supposed to be making her feel better, letting her know that we all fuck up sometimes, mostly at her age when the world is still so new and there's still so much to learn.

But instead, here I am making her feel even worse for what happened. Fuck. She said it was her decision to take the guy bare, but I'm not stupid, and I've fucking known Belle long enough to know she isn't either.

She didn't choose to be so careless. She wouldn't roll the dice on a risk that great. It just doesn't add up. Not to mention the fact she said she was punked when I picked her up.

Still, I have to take her word on it, because thinking of what the alternative implies has the blood in my veins charged and ready to take down whatever ignorant fuck thought he could take advantage of her like that.

And for a man who's out on good behaviour? Yeah, revenge isn't exactly on the cards if I want to stay on the outside of the razor wire-topped fences and in Belle's life.

Not yet, anyway.

FIFTEEN

Belle

My hands shake as I set the airer up in the living room; the rain has set in for the afternoon, stealing any chance of drying my stuff outdoors. My heart still pounds in my chest, my body alive, my nerves shot. *I walked in on Zeus in nothing but his damn underwear.* Holy hell, that man is fine.

He acted embarrassed, but if he's convinced that anything between us would be a giant mistake, why would he care what I thought? Why would it matter? I expected that he'd get frustrated with the need to deal with my stupid girly crush. But he didn't, and my afflicted mind can't shake the minuscule chance that implies as I return the empty basket to where it belongs.

"So, um, dinner."

I jolt at Zeus's words as he stands in the doorway, trapping me in the laundry room. He's pulled on a pair of rugby shorts and a T-shirt that hugs his huge frame across the chest and through the shoulders.

I set the basket down and place my clammy hands on the legs of my denim shorts. "Dinner."

"You want me to cook again?"

Fuck, he's beautiful. I mean, men can be handsome, gorgeous, even stunning at times. But it's not often a guy can truly be *beautiful* in his masculinity. Soft lips, a hard jaw, firm brow, and the most intense eyes I've ever known.

"I don't mind cooking this time," I say. "We should do turn-about." I put my chin down and avoid eye contact as I squeeze past him.

He moves, but not by much, meaning I still brush my arm against his hard midsection as I pass by. *I'm going to die.* This tension will surely kill me if I have to endure this for however much longer he'll stay with us.

Way I see it I've got two options: die a slow torturous death, or bear the pain all in one blunt blow by facing the problem head-on. I've spent years at school trying to avoid my problems the first way, letting them eat me from the inside out while I slowly become a shell of the girl I once was. If anything, I'd like to think I took that lesson away from my years at Longdale High: bravery is recognising what hurts you and doing it anyway, aware that your soul will heal quicker if you don't prolong the inevitable.

Zeus follows me into the kitchen as I pull the freezer open to check what's available to eat. My mind is only half on the task and it takes me a moment to focus on what exactly I look at. I cast a quick glance his way as he settles his butt against the edge of the counter and folds his huge arms over his chest. "Am I imagining it?" I ask, my grip tightening on the freezer door. "Tell me right now, Zeus. Is this as one-sided as I try convincing myself it is?"

His steely gaze gives nothing away while he silently studies me. The points of his jaw bulge as he clenches and unclenches, the thoughts tumbling around inside his head almost visible in the stormy depth of his eyes.

"I'm fucking sick." He shakes his head in disgust.

I can't keep looking at him; keep seeing my own turmoil mirrored back at me. So I study the contents of the freezer, although nothing registers. The alarm sounds to tell me the door has been open too long.

"I don't know what to tell you, Belle." Zeus rubs a hand over his face in my periphery. "You're not stupid. You know there's tension between us when we're alone—now."

I nod, unable to form coherent words as I pull a tray of sausages out and shut the door. It dawns on me as Zeus's gaze flicks to my chest that the cold air has had a predictable effect on my nipples. *Seriously, kill me now.* I slam my free arm over the offending pair and take the sausages to the counter adjacent to Zeus.

"Maybe you're looking to me for guidance," he says, his voice low and so damn filled with guilt that it makes my chest ache. "But I can't give it to you when I can't work things out for myself. What do you want me to say that would make things okay? I mean, do we pretend this shit ain't happening?" He chuckles bitterly, tossing his hands briefly in the air.

"I don't think we can do that, can we?" I murmur. "That's why I asked you what the hell is going on here."

He sighs heavily out his nose, his gaze burning a hole in the side of my head as I focus on the damn tray of frozen meat before me. "I can't speak for you," he says softly, "but I *can* tell you what's going on in here." He taps the side of his head with a thick finger, swallowing hard yet again. "I see you, I see a beautiful young woman. I see somebody who wants to be independent but doesn't know how. I don't see a kid, and I sure as fuck don't see an age, and *that's* what the problem is." He inches closer, trying to get me to look at him. "I should look at you and see John's eighteen-year-old daughter. I should see the kid I watched grow up, the little girl who used to make me mud cupcakes in her plastic tea set."

"But you don't." I turn my head and hold his gaze despite the incessant beat of my heart, despite the fact my feet want to run.

"I don't," he confirms. "I left that little girl behind when I went inside. When I got out, she was all grown up. All I see now is the young woman you are, Belle, and she's fucking beautiful, inside and out."

I don't know what was worse: wishing he'd say those words, tell me he sees me as more than his best friend's daughter? Or hearing them and knowing this is as far as we'll likely ever get.

Which rejection hurts worse? Right now they both burn, both at the same time, equally as much.

"Belle," he murmurs. "Say something, because I feel like a right fucking creep after telling you all that."

I relax my stance, which means I lean closer to Zeus. He shifts the same distance, bringing his chest to my arm, his leg against the back of mine. God, I just want to crawl up in this man and feel at home.

"I wish things were different. I wish I was older. Most of all, I was wish I was more your type."

"You *are* my type." A bitter laugh edges his words. "That's what sucks the most." His frown deepens as his jaw ticks.

"But?" I twist to face him, snug against his front.

"But, what would your father do if he walked in right now and caught us like this?" He nods down at our proximity.

Shoving my inhibitions aside, knowing that this is probably the only chance I'll ever get to live out this fantasy of *us*, I lift both hands and place my palms on his stomach as I lean into him.

Zeus hisses his next breath between his teeth, before repeating his question. "What would he do, Belle?"

"He's not here, though."

"And if he was?" He tips his head back, exposing his thick neck as his chest rises and falls with shaky, deep breaths.

"But," I repeat, firmer, "he's not."

"What if he walked in?" Zeus grinds out through a clenched jaw. "Right this second?"

"Then I wouldn't tell myself fuck it, you only live

once, and do this." I reach up and take his face between my hands, coaxing him to look back down at me. My palms are on fire, the awareness of the connection making my touch ultrasensitive.

Zeus's eyes are dark; the pupils large as I push up on my tiptoes and slowly bring my mouth to his. He closes his eyes and stiffens, his entire body rigid against mine as I gently drag my lips over his and do my best to change his mind. His mouth is warm, his breath hot on my face as he breathes deep and slow out his nose. I pinch his bottom lip between mine and relish the taste of him on my tongue as I let the flesh go.

Zeus stares at me, his brow pinched hard, as I lower myself to the soles of my feet—his face still in my hands—and wait.

Please... I'm such a fool. Why I ever thought his would wor—

"Fuck it," Zeus growls as his upper lip crinkles with a snarl.

My next breath is ripped from my lungs as he places a strong arm around my lower back and scoops me off my feet so that we're face-to-face, my body pressed flushed against his. He holds my head in place with his free hand, his thumb and fingers punishing on either side of my jaw as he tilts my head the opposite way to his and kisses me deep, hard, and like nothing I've ever experienced before.

This is how a real man kisses. *This* is what real passion feels like.

This is what I've wanted for so long.

It's everything.

My feet hit the floor so suddenly that I lose my balance for a split second, so lost in his kiss that I didn't expect him to stop.

"What have you done?" he whispers with such venom that I instantly feel filthy in my skin. "What did you do, Belle?"

"What did I do?" I murmur, so damn quiet that I have my doubts he even heard me.

Zeus sidesteps to get away from where I stand in shock, backing along the counter until he's frozen on the far side of the kitchen. A frown mars his beautiful face as he looks me over, head to toe, and shakes his head. "Your father can't know that happened."

Because I was so going to tell him. I mentally roll my eyes at the guy. "Really?" I lift my top lip in disdain, yet mostly to cling to any emotion other than the one that fights most to surface: shame.

What have I done? He's right. *I* instigated that. He resisted at first, and *I* pushed him to continue. Selfishly, might I add, because who has the most to lose in this scenario?

Not me.

"I—I'm sorry."

He says nothing, instead lunging for where his keys sit on the end of the counter and snatching them in his grasp. My heart pounds painfully hard as his heavy footfalls track down the hallway, and then out the door before Zeus slams it so hard it rattles.

I don't know what to do. I don't know how to rewind and fix what I've done. Mostly, I don't know how things go from here on out. How do I spend evenings at home with this guy without losing my mind?

Maybe that's why he left? He doesn't know either?

I tune my ears for the sound of his car, for the squeal of tyres as he peels away, yet they never come. My stomach turns with nerves when the soft click of the door as it opens again leaves me even more confused about what I should do.

Does he expect me to still be here in the kitchen, perhaps making dinner as though nothing happened? Or does he expect me to be crying in my bedroom like any normal teenager would be after being humiliated like that?

I'm not normal though. There's nothing normal about lusting after a man twice your age.

"Belle?"

Shoot. What do I say? What do I do?

I don't need to turn around to know he re-enters the kitchen behind me. My entire body is alive with anticipation as the keys make a soft clink where he sets them on the counter. *One, one thousand. Two, one thousand....* Breathe, Belle.

I wait for his next words, hanging on by a thread. Will he apologise? Blame me again? What?

Gentle fingers brush against my skin. He slowly sets a hand on my shoulder and coaxes me to turn around. *I can't breathe.* I wasn't this nervous before when I threw myself at him, but at least with that, the reaction was predictable. I knew it was wrong, that he'd worry, that I'd push boundaries and most likely make him angry.

But this? I have no idea what comes next as I slowly turn and face him. Zeus shows almost no emotion as he stares down at me, the point of his jaw softly working as he presses his teeth together. He lets his hand slide from my shoulder, down my arm, until he takes my hand in his.

"I shouldn't have walked out like that, but…. Don't take this on yourself, okay?"

I can't do it—I can't look at him with a straight face. He frowns when I crack up laughing and pull my hand from his.

"Are you for real?" Tears track over my cheeks as I fall apart. "I tell myself that this is nothing but a stupid teenage crush, that I'm fucking delirious, and absolutely torture myself over how I feel for years." He opens his mouth to speak, yet I hold up a hand. "And then you tell me you feel the same," I whisper, eyes narrowed on him as he swallows hard. "So I risk it. I put myself out there, knowing this whole thing is wrong because I'm *eighteen* and you're… you're…."

"Thirty-five," he murmurs.

"Thirty-five," I repeat, nodding. "I'm not stupid, Zeus. Despite what you saw on Saturday. I know how the birds and the bees work," I scathe. "I'm not naïve. Just desperate to be wanted." My voice fails me on the last word as I back up, tears hot and fresh as the rejection lances through me all over again. "Wanted by the one person *I* want the most."

"It wouldn't work." He scrubs a hand over his face, and for some fucked up reason his torment makes me need him more. "We shouldn't even talk about it."

"Why? Because society tells us it's wrong?" I slam my arms over my chest. "Tell me one thing, Zeus. One thing that'll help me work past this crush, this whatever it is. Tell me why—apart from our ages—it's wrong."

He turns away and paces to the sink, resting his hands on the edge as he gives me his back. "Because it would absolutely crush your father if he knew."

Neither of us move despite the fact we both appear to be out of things to say. With one line, one reason, he's got me. Dad *would* be devastated.

Zeus stays at the window, staring out over our backyard as I remain rooted to the spot in the kitchen. Perhaps it's because we both know that if either of us walk away now, it finalises what happened here, officially pushes it into the "we shall never speak of this again" category.

At least, I know that's what stops me from walking away.

Which is why he does first.

SIXTEEN

Zeus

The real estate agent, Veronica, shifts her weight between her feet, making her arse roll as she leans both elbows on the kitchen counter to go over the details of some clause with Jodie. I left the paperwork up to her; I've never been good with legal jargon. Ask my public defender.

"Is a week long enough, you think, Z?" Jodie calls without lifting her gaze from the papers spread out before her.

"A week for what?" I turn away from the living room windows that overlook the front yard.

"To vacate."

I gesture to the empty house. "Pretty sure we can manage that." The Salvation Army arrived and took the last of what we didn't need but was too good to throw away a few days ago.

Veronica chuckles, her heavy-lidded eyes catching mine as she taps her pen against her lips. *Not interested, love.* Not when the warm kiss of a girl who could never be mine haunts me every hour of every day.

Four days have passed since Belle confronted me in the kitchen. Four days since I shut her down and felt the pain of rejection echoed in my own heart. The week has gone by with the kind of tension I expected. John is either oblivious, or chooses not to say anything as Belle and I exchange barely a few words in the morning over breakfast. Thankfully he's not there to see how tense it gets in the evenings. I can't deny that there's something about Belle that draws me in, something familiar and comfortable that I want.

That I need.

I could stay away, find something else to do, *someone* else to do, but as torn as I am about what happened between us, the part of me that wants to make sure she's safe on her own won't sit back and let go.

Neither will the part of me that wishes she were ten years older, somebody else's daughter.

"If you're satisfied with everything then," Jodie says, "it's time for us to sign this and make it official."

"Are you happy with it?" I lean over the breakfast bar, my arms folded before me, and hold Jodie's gaze.

I ignore the hungry eyes Veronica gives me. She's here to finalise the deal, nothing more.

"It's reasonable. We walk away with sixty thousand each."

Benefits of purchasing in a slump and selling fifteen years later in a peak. "Good."

Jodie spins the papers my way and holds a pen out. "Initial every page, and then sign wherever there is a

Post-it flag."

"Too easy." I take the pen and do as she instructs, a strange sentiment taking over the closer I get to the end of this enormous contract.

End of an era. John's words echo through my mind as I sign the final page and push it all back toward Jodie. She takes over, doing the same as I just have, while I wander away and head for the bedrooms.

The carpet still holds lines from where the cleaner came through, the walls whiter than I've ever seen thanks to a professional who came recommended by one of Jodie's workmates.

I almost don't recognise the place.

"You okay?" Jodie asks quietly behind me as I stand in the middle of what used to be our room with my hands in pockets.

"Yeah." I turn to find her standing with a shoulder propped against the doorframe, what I assume to be our copies of the contract in hand.

"She's gone." A smile tugs at Jodie's lips as she steps forward. "I think she liked you a bit too much."

I chuckle. "Yeah, so do I."

"It's a common theme, Z."

"You think?" I glance down at Jodie where she stands beside me, staring at the walls much the same as I just was.

"I don't think; I know." Her eyes take on a distant feel as she slowly shifts her gaze left to the window. "You have no idea how many girls' dreams I ruined when we started dating." A small laugh falls from her lips. "Do you remember that time at the Provincial Hotel? When we saw that cover band? It was Cerise's birthday."

"Yeah, I do." It was shortly before John proposed to her.

"I got that graze on the side of my face, and I told it you it was because I tripped on my way to the ladies'."

"Yeah." I narrow my gaze on her as she smiles.

"I didn't trip. Some bitch shoved my head into the wall when I told her to keep her filthy whore hands off my man."

"That brunette with the stinky old guy who followed her everywhere." God, I remember that. I figured the girl was cuckoo, but thought nothing of it since I only had eyes for one woman back then.

I loop an arm around Jodie's shoulders and pull her in as we stand in silence in the middle of our old room. So many memories made in this house—some of them good, but most of them bad.

"I'm sorry I couldn't give you a kid."

She crosses an arm over her chest and places her free hand to my wrist, holding me tight. "*Us* a kid, Z. We both wanted it."

"Yeah." Those years when we first started trying were some of the happiest we had. We'd achieved our goals in buying a house, I'd got a full-time job after my first stint inside, and we were full of nothing but hope. "They were good years, Jodie."

"They were, Zeus." Her hand falls from my wrist and

she steps away from my side. "I'm thankful we shared them, even if they were hard toward the end. I think we both grew as people, don't you?"

"I guess." I've never really thought of it that way. I've always chosen to see the end of our relationship as a failure on my part. But the truth remains: we each had our roles to play.

Sometimes what we want out of life changes, and that's okay.

"I better get going." Jodie holds my copy of the sale document out between us. "I've got some errands to run before Eric gets off from work."

"Bit late to still be there isn't it?" I take the contract from her, rolling it into a tube in one hand.

"He's working on acquiring another major project. Something to do with a development in the city."

"He'll be knee-deep in red tape then." It takes every ounce of self-control I possess to save from saying something a lot worse about the cunt.

"Yeah." Jodie frowns, her eyes narrowed as she holds my gaze. "Are you okay?"

"You're talking about a guy I'd like to be re-sentenced for, so not entirely."

"There's something else," she says, always the perceptive one. "You got the permanent contract at your new job, eh?"

"Yeah. It officially started this week."

"Problems at John's then?"

"You could say that." I lift the rolled contract between

us. "Thanks for this."

She replies with a soft grunt, dissatisfied with my evasion of the topic.

Not as though I'd tell my ex-wife my love-life problems anyway, even if the woman in question wasn't seventeen years younger than me. I give her a nod and leave the room, neck on fire as I head for the door.

If Jodie can pick up that there's something amiss with me, can John? Not as if he'd care anyway. He's got the whole issue of Cerise to sort out yet. I half expect to get back to his place after work each day and find a new car up the driveway. Given our current standing, I don't think John will give me any notice when the bitch is due to move in. He knows how I feel about her, and that's never going to change.

Not after what she did to her family, most of all, her daughter.

I step outside to have misty rain wet my face on the short walk to the car. *Great.* Spring is well and truly in force, summer near, and that means random rain showers for the next few weeks.

But given the heat we've had during the day of late, it also means storms. And storms mean Belle's favourite time of year.

My gut tells me as I start the GTO and then run a hand over my face to wipe the dew away, that my dove is going to need every little thing she can get to cheer her up soon. Because when Cerise re-enters her life, that's going to be one storm she'll wish she could escape.

••••

Belle takes me by surprise after dinner, emerging from her bedroom to join me in the living room. She doesn't utter a word as she tucks herself on the sofa. The girl has to be hungry; she hasn't joined me for a meal all week.

"Can I please have the remote?"

"She speaks," I tease as Belle glares at me from her position. They're the first words she's uttered to me after 4:00 p.m. since Monday.

"She does, and she'd like to change the channel."

"I'm watching this."

"Yeah, well I don't want to, and if I'm not mistaken *you're* the guest here." Her jaw is hard, her lips pressed in a thin line as she curls on her side into the arm of the sofa.

"The program has only got ten minutes to go."

"It's about cars."

"So?" I snap, frustrated by her continual attitude.

"I hate car shows." She looks away, thumb flying over the screen of her fucking phone.

"Seems you're preoccupied anyway." I jerk my chin toward the device in her hand when she glances up.

Belle kills the screen and makes a point of tossing it behind her legs. "Remote?"

"Eight minutes." I stretch out in the recliner and tuck my hands behind my head.

"You've missed most of what's left anyway," Belle

complains. "Come on, Zeus. Don't be an arsehole."

Game on, little girl. "You think making you wait ten minutes is me being an arsehole?" I chuckle, despite the fact I'm dying inside thinking about how long I would wait for her.

She glares at me and holds her hand out.

I pick the remote up off the arm of the chair as I lean forward, tucking the recliner away. The barest hint of a smirk shows at the corner of her lips as I stand and strut over to where she's now stretched out to watch what I do. Her smirk fades as I pop the back off the remote and remove the batteries, pocket them, and then slip the cover back on before handing the control over.

"Oh, very funny." Belle sets it aside as I back away laughing. "You think you're clever, huh?"

Got her talking, at least.

She climbs off the sofa and heads for where I back my way into the dining room. Using the table as a block, I circle around the back of it, still chuckling at her false anger. She fakes left, then right, before chasing me back into the living room. Belle's smaller size gives her a speed advantage over a heavy arsehole like me, and by the time I reach the sofa she's on me.

Maybe not in the way I'd prefer, but to hear her laugh is reward enough.

"Give them back." Belle attempts to reach around to my pocket for the batteries.

I twist back and forth, arms raised as I evade her desperate lunges. "Give it up, Belle. Admit you lost."

"Never." She takes me by surprise as she steps onto the sofa with her left foot, and uses the furniture as an aide to jump high enough to sling her arms around my shoulders.

With the girl on my back like a damn monkey, I spin to face away from the sofa and then tumble backward to pin her beneath me. "Let go before you hurt yourself, dove."

She falls limp beneath me at the use of her childhood nickname. We used to do this all the time when she was a kid, horse around just to make her laugh. But there's no denying things aren't the same now.

Not in the slightest.

"Okay," she mumbles. "You win." Her feeble hands shove against the back of my shoulders to get me off.

I slowly rise to my feet and stay with my back to her as I take the batteries from my pocket. She silently hands the useless remote over and watches as I pop them back in.

"Things don't have to be this way forever," I tell myself as much as her. "I'm sure we'll get past it."

"Will we?" she asks. "Because I don't feel as though I ever will. Right or wrong, Zeus, you've got to admit we changed things forever by doing that."

She can't say it: kiss. *Fuck.* I can't say it. I can hardly think it without feeling that knot return to my gut, without feeling my heart quicken at the memory.

Sick. You're a sick fuck, Z.

"I started looking for a place to buy yesterday," I tell

her, as though *that'll* solve things. "Jodie and I accepted an offer on our old house today."

"Oh." The disappointment is so fucking clear in the single syllable. "Many options?"

"A couple." I set the remote down on the coffee table and suck in a deep breath before turning to face her.

"Dad know?"

"Yeah."

Her tongue peeks out as she wets her lips, eyelashes fanning her cheeks with her downward stare. "I might just...." Belle thumbs toward her room as she reaches for her phone with the other hand.

"Don't."

Her warm brown eyes lift to find mine. "Don't what?"

My arse hits the chair cushion hard. "Fuck, every-thing." I toss my hands in the air before me. "Shut me out, avoid me, beat yourself up over it all."

"Doing those things is the only way I know how to cope," she snaps, rising anyway with her fucking phone in hand. The damn thing chimes, drawing her focus away from me.

I could crush that little plastic attention-seeker.

Belle lifts her hand and checks the screen, her gaze flicking to me before back to whatever shows.

"Who is it?" I've got no right to know, let alone ask, but fuck, the thought some teenage boy might have her number.... *She's not yours to have, Z.*

"Kate." She turns the phone so the screen faces me. "I asked her what she's doing this weekend."

"Yeah? And what have you decided? No more parties, I hope."

"No." She shakes her head, sadness in her gaze that I can't place. "Kate has a boyfriend now, but we're trying to patch up our friendship."

Fuck. That shit never works out. "You don't see her as much then?"

Belle sits again, hands slung between her knees. "Not really. We had a… I guess you'd call it a falling out at the party you picked me up from." She lifts her gaze to gauge my reaction. "Um, and since then things have been awkward."

"And I didn't help."

"You did," she says with conviction before changing her tone. "Well, you did *that* night. Maybe not so much after." She smiles.

It's a start.

"I'm sure it'll blow over."

She nods, eyes averted. Belle chooses to stay silent, seemingly out of things to say. So am I. Everything I have left for her revolves around the use of my hands. *I need to step away.*

"I might head out to the gym. You'll be okay on your own?"

The look in her eyes as she glances my way tells me she knows; she understands the need for physical space. The girl's smarter than I give her credit for, hiding away in her room all week.

"Sure," she snaps, shitty attitude reinstated. "Go. I'll

be fine."

I nod and head to grab my gear, knowing that despite what she says, Belle is anything but fine.

She hasn't been fine for a long time, and unfortunately the catalyst for that change is due back any day now.

SEVENTEEN

Belle

Nothing tells you that you're bored beyond tears more than lying on the armchair with your feet over the back, and your head hanging off the front of the seat cushion. I hold my phone above me, scrolling through my newsfeed and pulling faces at the happy snaps from people I once considered friends. It's funny how when you remove a person's reason to interact with you—which in my case was school—they drop off the radar like a ghost.

With a sigh, I kill Facebook and open up Messenger instead. My thumb hovers over her smug smiling face before I tap it with finality. Silence between friends is a two-way street, and I can't stay angry at Kate for keeping me in the dark if I don't do a thing to reach out either.

Which is why I messaged earlier, when Zeus was still here.

B: What are you up to this weekend?

Sometimes denial is the best option. No better way to draw out how somebody really feels about you than denying there's anything wrong at all.

Her reply had come through, seconds later.

K: I'm staying at Brock's.

Of course. I'd asked the question, only to be shot down.

B: Spare a few hours for a girls' night?

K: We already made plans. Sorry.

"Fuck this shit." I toss the phone aside, unable to come up with anything else to say that doesn't come off as desperate. I roll my eyes when the device hits the arm of the chair and slides off onto the floor.

I could head into town on my own, sure. But Longdale isn't exactly known for its nightlife. The most interesting thing I'm likely to find down at the local are two of the old boys having a neck-and-neck game of darts.

My feet tingle as I swing myself around and sit upright on the armchair, my palms braced either side of my legs. *What to do?* I can't stand sitting around the house another night, but when the only connection I had to the social scene that was our year at school—Kate— won't fucking hang out with me, I don't exactly have endless options.

The front door closes with a soft click, and I find Zeus eyeing me, clearly not surprised to see me where he left me.

"Busy gathering dust, I see."

"Hilarious." I rise and stride into the kitchen to grab a drink.

He shadows me, ditching his gym bag next to the dining table. "Out with it."

I glare at him as he stands there, arms folded and feet wide in that way that makes him seem twice as large. "Out with what?"

"You can't avoid talking about it forever, so tell me why you're so pissed off."

"I thought that would be obvious." I shut the fridge and crack a can of Coke, watching him over the rim as I take a sip.

"You're mad because I shut you down afterward."

"I'm mad because you made me feel like a fucking jackass for doing it in the first place."

He blows a heavy breath out his nose, moving one hand to cover his face. "Belle."

"You asked," I sass, turning away to pinch a snack from the pantry before I barricade myself for the rest of the night.

"You can't keep acting like this all weekend," he growls, slamming a hand on the counter behind me. "How are you going to explain it to your dad?"

"Your problem, not mine." I tug a box of crackers off the top shelf, stretching to reach them. "It's going to be you left talking to him if I stay in my room, not me."

"I thought we were getting somewhere earlier."

So did I, until it became clear that it was a huge mistake to come out of my room: I still felt the same after talking to him as I had in avoiding him—frustrated.

"You're going to have to get over it sooner rather than later," Zeus states. "You can't hold a grudge forever."

"Can't I?"

"Fuck's sake," he mutters, turning in my periphery as I set the crackers down to retrieve cheese slices. Zeus slams his butt against the edge of the counter, arms still folded as he scowls at the floor. "Are you always this fucking selfish?"

"Are you shitting me?" I cry, slamming the fridge closed hard enough that the condiments in the door rattle. "Selfish? By doing what? Telling you how I feel about you?" I snort a bitter laugh and snatch up my less than healthy dinner. "Get fucked, Zeus. I don't care what you do, but stay the hell out of my way."

"You're punishing me as though it's my fault you feel the way you do," he calls after me.

I storm back into the kitchen, anger pumping hot through my veins as I dump my haul on the counter again. "I'm punishing you," I say, advancing on him as I do, "because you refuse to admit you feel the same way."

The arsehole has the audacity to smirk at me as I stop before him. "Do I?"

"What else are you doing then?" I cry, throwing my

hands in the air.

"You remember how I kissed you, don't you?" he asks, his lips still curled at the corners.

"Of course I do," I mumble. How could I forget? The bite of his teeth against my lips... I still feel it.

"What did that tell you?"

"The kiss?"

He nods, eyes smiling.

Fuck him. He has me, again. I really need to stop arguing with Zeus. "That you felt something?"

"Yes, dove." He nods slowly, one eyebrow cocked. "So tell me again what I'm doing."

"Ugh. You're so frustrating."

"As are you." He snags me by the hip when I make a move to step away, pulling me flush against him.

It's déjà vu in the worst kind of way. "What are you doing?"

"Listen to me." His piercing blue eyes hold me captive. "I don't deny how I feel about you, Belle. I told you how I feel. I laid it out bare." He swallows, his jaw hard. "What I deny is that there's any point to starting something between us."

"Because of Dad."

He sighs, his brow firm as he studies me. "Don't you agree?"

I'm stuffed if I know what I do and don't agree to. The whole concept of Zeus even entertaining the idea of my ridiculous fantasy is ludicrous enough. I can't comprehend the fact the object of my affection wants me back, let alone envisage something past that.

"Let me go, please."

His head tips slightly to one side. "I'm not holding on, Belle."

The truth to his words strike home as I move my focus downward—he took his hand away while we talked; I'm still here, still leaning against him of my own accord. *Awkward.*

"I'm holding back out of respect for you, as much as him." Zeus puts his hand back on my hip, his fingertips brushing against my arse. "I'm not the kind of guy who enjoys playing with people's hearts, Belle, and leading you on like that... playing is all I would be doing."

"Is that so bad?" Because I'll take this man however I get him.

"It is if I want to keep you happy."

"Pushing me away makes me unhappy," I point out. "This past week...." I can't say it, can't give voice to how miserable I've been hiding away from him, because it seems so pathetic out loud.

"Tell me. This past week, what?" He pinches my chin between his forefinger and thumb, tipping my face up to his.

"I felt so bad wasting time I'd never get back. I wanted to come hang out with you in the evenings because I enjoy being around you, but I knew this... this attraction I have would get in the way and I'd end up hating it because I couldn't spend the time with you doing what I *really* wanted to." I sigh, looking away, despite the fact he holds my head high. "That's why I avoided you," I murmur. "Not because I was angry at you, but because I was angry at not having you how I wanted."

He stays silent a while, looking over my face as he shifts his thumb to brush the underside of my bottom lip. "How *would* you spend the time, dove? Entertain me. Paint me one of your pictures."

I smile a little, enjoying the moment despite the struggle our conversation is built around. "We'd share dinner, just like we did last Friday, and then we'd switch all the lights off and get comfortable on the sofa. Together. You'd stretch out...." I steal a look at his eyes and stall. *How did I think I could do this?*

"Go on."

"You'd stretch out and I'd lie beside you. We'd pick a movie, maybe. Or listen to music."

"And then?"

I can't tell him that. Heat floods my face as I try to pull away. Zeus holds me firm, leaning in to place a gentle kiss against my mouth. I set my hands on his chest, relishing the slow care he takes as he teases his lips across mine, settling my nerves and erasing my doubts.

"Tell me," he whispers before he pulls back. "What goes on in that head of yours when you think of me?"

"It's embarrassing."

"Why?" He shifts his hand to cup the side of my neck, thumb stroking slow sweeps underneath my jaw. "I'm curious, Belle. I want to know what you'd like me to do to you."

"It's not as though you ever would." His heart hammers beneath my touch, his eyes lazy as he smiles.

"Wouldn't I?"

"But you said—"

"Fuck what I said. Just for ten minutes. Fuck everything."

My head swims as though I'm high on some drug, lost in a sea of impossibilities. He's telling me that he wants to make part of my fantasy a reality, and yet I can't find it in myself to believe him.

This has to be a trick. Nothing but a sick joke.

Zeus sets his hands on my waist and hoists me up. I wrap my legs around his, arms looped over his shoulders as he starts to walk. "Talk to me, Belle."

I keep my gaze trained on his as he carries me through to the living room; my heartbeats almost blur into one with my quickened pulse. "You'd kiss me again."

"Given." He nods his head to one side as he sets me down on the sofa. "What else?"

I suck in a sharp breath as he pushes me back with a gentle hand to my shoulder. "We'd touch."

"How?"

This isn't right. I should stop him, tell him not to take advantage of my feelings like this, yet I don't want to miss out either. I focus on my hands as I lift them and set them on Zeus's strong shoulders, still unwilling to believe that this is really happening. I've thought about being with Zeus for years, let my young imagination run wild and told myself it was okay to think about him the way I did when alone because there was no way in hell this could ever come true.

And yet here we are, alone, with him barely holding himself together as he runs his hungry gaze the length of me.

"You say the word, Belle, and I'll step away. You're in control of this."

I have no doubt that I am, but for how long? His breaths come hot and heavy, his left arm braced on the back of the sofa to keep himself steady as I trace the lines of his body. Zeus's arm quivers beneath my touch, his hand white-knuckled on the cushion.

I let my hands slide to his shoulders again, retracing my path to make my way down his chest. He closes his eyes, a satisfied sigh slipping free as he relaxes, even if only the tiniest bit.

"Come closer," I whisper.

He lifts the leg nearest to me, taking care as he slides it between the back of the sofa and my thigh. I swallow, my hands braced on his ribs as he shifts to hold himself over me, his right leg out straight as it takes his weight on the floor.

"You don't look comfortable," I muse.

"Any closer, dove, and a big bastard like me will crush you."

"So do it," I urge, wanting so desperately to know what that would feel like.

He frowns, his movements measured and clearly thought out as he tucks a hand beneath me and shifts me around on the cushions. I'm fascinated by the way his brow furrows, the lines around his eyes as he concentrates. He tucks his tongue to his top teeth as he looks between our bodies to make sure I won't be squashed against the sofa, and then slowly lowers himself down.

I hold his gaze, lost in the bright azure flecks in his blue eyes as he settles his hips over mine. I'm trapped, and yet I've never felt more at peace than I do now.

"Okay?" he asks, eyes searching mine.

"Perfect." I push my shoulders back, leaning up to place a kiss to his lips.

He hums against me as I taste him, running my tongue across his full bottom lip. My chest grows tight, the thrill sending a bolt of awareness straight between my legs.

I didn't get this with Scott, any of this. With him I dove straight in, focused on the outcome and determined to reach the finish line. Yet with Zeus, I want to wade in the shallow waters and take my sweet time reaching full submersion.

"Tell me what I did," he rumbles. "Close your eyes and tell me what you see."

"I don't want to."

He gives me a lopsided smile, tipping his head to the side. "Why not?"

I set my hands either side of his face. "Because you're

right here."

He answers by kissing my neck, trailing his hot lips over my flesh to place another where my collarbones meet beneath my throat. "One word, okay?"

He's so concerned, so worried that I might change my mind. But why would I when this is everything I've always wanted?

I thread my fingers through his hair as he moves lower, lifting himself off me so he can crawl down my body. His left leg tucks awkwardly against the arm of the sofa, and yet it doesn't deter him as he lifts my shirt and kisses a line across my stomach. My gaze fixes to my pale fingers as they knit through his black locks, the action something I've wanted to do for so damn long and yet never thought I could.

So many impossibilities becoming a reality—it makes me wonder how many other things we could get away with if we wanted them bad enough.

My eyes connect with Zeus's as he climbs off the sofa and kneels beside me. He reaches for my shorts, gaze still on mine as he undoes the snap. "Okay?"

I nod, reaching out and running my fingertips under his jaw. He turns his head and places a kiss to them as his own pull my zipper down.

I'm painfully aware of my nipples as I shut my eyes and let my head fall back into the cushions. He tugs the denim of my shorts, one side after the other, moving them down my legs until I lift my feet one by one and let him slip them off me.

My core clenches in anticipation and yet he doesn't dive straight in like I expected him to. Instead, he sets his palm flat on my lower stomach and slowly slides it up my body, under my shirt and between my breasts. I could get drunk off his touch alone, satisfy my need to escape with the sheer bliss his hands bring. He curls a finger around my bra where it meets between the cups, and tugs. I gasp as the fabric pulls at my hardened nipples, the friction unbelievably erotic.

"Did I do this?" he rasps as his fingertips tease my nipples, one after the other.

"No." I can barely voice the word, my lungs devoid of air.

"Should I stop then?"

"No." The word comes out a guttural groan, the need behind it so great.

He teases them once more, and then lifts my shirt higher so that my breasts are exposed to him. I open my eyes, studying his face as he watches his thick finger circle the rose-coloured tips yet again. Does he like what he sees? Am I enough?

I take the answer to be yes when he leans forward and wraps his lips around my right nipple, teasing the hard nub with his tongue. I can't hold back my groan of pleasure, my hips rolling of their own accord as he palms my left breast, rising up on his knees to move closer to me.

"What about this?" he murmurs against my skin as he skims his lips down over my stomach.

I suck in a sharp lungful of air as he parts my legs and runs his nose over my panty-clad pussy. Fuck—I've never wanted to shed an article of clothing so badly in my life.

"Or this?" His words are a breathless whisper as he gently pushes the fabric to one side and places a kiss to my exposed flesh.

"Zeus…."

He rears back, hand still on my panties. "Yes?" He frowns, his concern clear.

"Don't stop."

A satisfied hum comes from deep in his chest as he resumes his actions, only this time he drags his tongue along the length of me without a single scrap of cotton between us. I arch my hips back, shoving my arse hard into the cushions as my legs clamp around his head. With strong hands, he pries them apart again, chuckling before he repeats the action.

"You taste like the best kind of sin, dove."

I ache with the pressure as I swell, the slick juices of my arousal wet as they run over the swell of my arse. Tension coils low in my gut, the feeling familiar from the times I've masturbated in my room, but the intensity is something I've never managed on my own.

Fuck—it's something I didn't even manage with Scott, and I haven't even come yet.

Realisation strikes me hard. Is that what Zeus wants? Is that where he thinks this will lead tonight?

"I'm not on the pill, Zeus," I blurt out before I lose my

head to the things he does between my legs.

He stills, thumb situated over my clit as he smiles. "I'm more of a gentleman than you might think, Belle. I'm not taking advantage of you like that." His eyes narrow, his smile turning wicked. "Not tonight anyway."

I gasp as he pushes a finger inside my slick channel. "What happened to the whole we-can't-do-this thing?" I sigh as he pumps his digit a couple of times before answering.

"I'm reconsidering."

I press my head back into the sofa as he sets a steady pace with his hand, his hot mouth soon joining in. The way he handles me, the way he knows just what to do—it shows his experience, and I can't help but let doubt set in as my breaths come quicker. Perhaps I won't measure up for him?

Surely he's used to a certain level of knowledge, and as mature as I believe I can be, nothing can replace experience when it comes to this.

"Oh my... oh... fuck, Zeus...." I cast all doubts aside as he hums against my pussy, the vibration driving me over the edge.

"So sweet," he mumbles against my swollen flesh before flicking his tongue over my clit. "So good."

With both hands flat against the arm of the sofa above my head, I press down against him, seeking that teeny bit extra as my climax threatens. He increases pace with his finger, his tongue working the bundle of nerves as I reach release and cry out.

My moans echo around the otherwise quiet house, taking me by surprise with how loud I am. My chest heaves, the thrill consuming me and pulling all strength from my body as I collapse onto the cushions.

Zeus sits back, his lips wet with my arousal before he licks them clean. "You make one hell of an argument, girl."

"For what?" I say with a laugh.

"For why I should say fuck what your dad thinks and make you mine." Zeus sucks his finger clean and then climbs back on to the sofa with me, settling himself over top of me once more.

Only this time, the evidence of his arousal is undeniable between us.

I close my eyes as he kisses me, hard and slow, and thread my fingers through his hair. He pulls back, a look of sheer adoration on his face as I tighten my hold and press my nose to his.

"Fuck what Dad thinks; I've always been yours, Zeus."

EIGHTEEN

Zeus

John turned in two hours ago, opting to stay up late on a Saturday to keep his body clock on work time. He spent the first forty minutes after I called it a night on the phone, in the dark, talking to Cerise while he sat in the lounge. He was so absorbed in whatever bullshit she fed him that he didn't notice me walk through to the kitchen to get a bottle of water.

He didn't notice that my door was half-open when he went to bed either. Enough for me to know that he doesn't bother checking on his daughter.

Sucks for her. Great for me.

It's been a day since I kissed her, a day since I tasted her. More than twenty-four hours that I've had to run through the pros and cons of taking this further in my mind, and every damn time I come up with the same result: I don't fucking care either way.

I'll do what I want, what she wants, and we can deal with the consequences—John—later.

I thought that the weekdays had been hell, having her shut me out in the mornings and avoid me at night.

But damn—I had no idea what hell really is. It's the purgatory I've been in having John around today, forcing myself to keep a respectful distance and act indifferent. It's the indescribable ache in my chest when she passes by with worry in her eyes, the relentless cramp in my muscles as I hold back from reaching out like I want to, and the unwavering tension in my gut while I wonder with every breath I take and every look I cast her way if John has figured out my true intentions for his daughter.

Does he suspect anything? Does he see a change in her? Those two thoughts alone should be enough to keep me from continuing what I started last night, and yet only one answer stands true when I think about the risk I take: I. Don't. Care.

I'd like to think I could take things slow for Belle's sake and give her time to adjust to the idea that she'll have to lie to her father. But who the fuck am I kidding? I give myself permission to chase this wild fantasy, remove the huge fucking warning sign I mentally placed over that girl, and I guarantee control will be the last thing I possess.

The first will be her.

That thought alone drives me to be where I am now: poised in the hallway with all intentions of cementing my place in hell. The house is dark and quiet, John turned in and out for the count until mid-morning tomorrow. I stand for what feels like forever, waiting, assessing, and listening.

Nothing. Nobody is awake at this hour except for the delinquents and the troublemakers. I slip into Belle's room, greeted by the sound of her turning in bed as I quietly close the door behind me.

"Zeus?"

"Ssh." I lift a finger to my lips and step lightly across her floor to the curtains beside her bed.

I want to see her, read her reaction, when I go past the point of no return.

Pulling the drapes back an inch, I let the soft glow of light into her room to shine a path across her bed. She sits up, leaning back on her palms as the light slices a path across her beautiful face.

I'm going to burn in hell for her. But fuck me, she's so worth it.

"You want me to leave?" I ask as I crawl on her bed to settle beside her.

"No," she says with a confused smile. "I just wondered why you're in here."

"I can't sleep," I admit. "Can't rest when you're right across the hall."

She swallows, a frown twitching on her brow as she works through this next step. "What is this, Zeus?"

"It's me, needing you. And you, wanting me."

She glances up at me before averting her gaze to the door while she speaks. "We could get caught."

"We won't." I loop a hand around her ankle and guide her leg out straight. "So lie the fuck down and let me hold you."

She pushes her other leg out and scoots down the bed to mirror my position, her hand on my chest. "You make it sound like if we follow our gut, like you told me I should, everything will be okay."

"Won't it?" I trap her hand beneath mine, holding it against my heart.

"Twenty years doesn't vanish simply because two people want it to," she says.

"Seventeen," I correct her. "There's seventeen years between us."

"Exactly. You could be my dad."

"But I'm not." I tug her hand and coax her to climb on top of me. "Why do you choose to look at it like that?" She settles her legs either side of mine and straddles me.

"I look at it how everybody else does," she admits, wide-eyed and fuckable above me.

"Screw what everyone thinks. What do *you* think?"

She takes a moment to mull the situation over, perhaps choose her words. The hesitation kills me, the wait too long. I pass the time the only way I can think how and run my hands over the heated flesh of her thighs. Her hands rest on my forearms, the connection sublime.

"I think," she whispers, her voice wavering as I let my fingertips dive beneath the cotton of her sleep shorts, "you're the only person who has ever truly understood me, and I'm the only person who's really ever understood you."

Home run. "Exactly."

"I've always felt comfortable being me around you," she continues. "Until lately, of course." She chuckles as I skim where her thighs meet her pussy. "Do you have any idea how hard it was to admit how I felt to you? How sure I was you'd just laugh the whole thing off and tell me to stop being so silly?"

She's got no idea. "Imagine how it feels to realise that the woman you married was simply a practice run until the woman you really want was old enough to reciprocate those feelings." I cock an eyebrow at her. "*That* is fucked up, when you think about it."

"When did you know?" She reaches forward and places her palms to my chest, resting her weight on me.

One shift of my hips, one tiny movement, and she'll know how badly she affects me. "The minute I found you in that damn kitchen doorway, a cheeky smile on your face once you realised you'd been caught. I might not have known exactly what it was, dove, but I knew right then with one look at how gorgeous you've become that the little girl I knew was long gone."

"Everything changed," Belle whispers, watching her hand as she strokes a path down my chest to my stomach. "I've thought for so long that you're hot." She huffs a laugh, seemingly to herself. "Had a crush on you since I was fourteen, but that day in the kitchen it wasn't just adoration. It became something more." Her eyes find mine. "Something unstoppable."

"He didn't deserve you, you know."

"Who?"

"That jackass who took your virginity."

Her eyes glaze over as she stares off to the side. "I know."

"It doesn't change anything," I assure her. "Doesn't make me want you any less."

"I still can't believe that you want me at all." She turns her face back to mine with a smile.

"Makes me want to show you what it's like to have a man's touch." I slide my hold around to her tight little butt and shunt her forward. "To have somebody tell you with their hands how beautiful you are, convince you with their mouth how precious you are to them."

Her hips roll, and she lets out a heavy breath. "Zeus. You already did that."

"Not in the way *I've* thought about it."

She leans in, pressing her chest against mine as she places a gentle kiss to my lips. "We need to be careful."

"I know." Like hell I'm stepping over this line only to fuck it all up with reckless abandon. "That's why when your father is home, we keep it PG."

She frowns, her lips quirked up on one side.

"I'm here to sleep, dove. As much as I want to do other filthy things to you, make you scream the fucking house down, I'm tired and having you in my arms is the only way I'm going to get any rest."

Her eyes close as she presses her nose to mine in the way I'm growing to love. "Okay."

I shift my hands up to the back of her shoulders and then slide them together, crossing my arms over her body as she settles on top of me. Belle fits perfectly in the confines of my hold, small and delicate amongst my raw mass. She was built to lie with me, and I was built to love her.

In all the ways that I have.

Her blankets slide to the floor as she tangles her legs in mine. I kick the corner of the sheet off my foot, confident that body heat alone will be enough to keep us warm tonight. I don't plan on letting her go until I wake—even then it'll be hard. She's the most Belle I've ever seen in this moment: pure, unchecked, and real. She's everything.

And I'm the most scared I've ever been in my fucking life.

NINETEEN

Belle

My eyes open on the tell-tale yellow hues of morning light. It's serene—for a second at least—before the awareness of who I share the moment with strikes me.

I turn to face Zeus, his arm hot and heavy over my waist, and hesitate. He's so at peace with the world while he sleeps, so unaffected by the things that plague him while he's awake, that I witness what a carefree life would look like on him.

It's breathtaking.

Annoyed at having to ruin the moment, I place my hand on his shoulder and rock his huge body back and forth. He rolls to his back with a groan, and stretches both arms over his head, narrowly missing me with his elbow.

"Oh, hey." His voice is hoarse from sleep.

"You need to get back to your room," I whisper-yell.

He blinks a couple of times, looking at the light that penetrates the thin curtains, before where he is registers. "Shit." He bolts to a seated position, closing his eyes as his head presumably swims. "I overslept. What time is it?"

I roll away and smack the home button on my phone. "A bit after eight. Do you think he's up?"

"Fucking hope not." Amusement taints his words as he smiles over at me.

"Go." I smack his arm with the back of my hand, stifling my own laugh.

Zeus leans over, a hand possessively wrapping around the back of my head as he steals my breath with the intensity of his kiss. "Morning, dove." He presses his forehead to mine briefly before pulling away and slipping out of bed.

I flop back on my mattress and unashamedly watch his sexy back and arse as he creeps across my floor and hesitates at the door. Zeus looks over his shoulder and flashes me a wink before he slips out the door and returns everything back to normal.

Well, as normal as it can be after spending the night in your father's best friend's arms.

"Time to face the music," I murmur as I throw the blanket back and slide out of bed.

Zeus must have pulled it over us some time in the night, because last I remember I drifted off to sleep on top of him with the sheet and blanket on the floor. Like the creeper I am, I pull the pillow he used to my nose and breathe deep, relishing the masculine scent of his body wash.

How are we going to do this? How many times can he

slip in here at night before Dad catches wind, or he *really* oversleeps? We're playing with fire, and in a way, I hope we get burnt.

Only then will I know if he takes heed of the warning, or falls in love with the flames like I already have.

I tug on a pair of jeans, the morning cooler than usual, and a loose T-shirt. A few runs of my fingers through my hair, and the straight locks assume some sort of order as I step from my room.

I enter the kitchen to find Dad in his pyjama shorts, making himself a coffee.

"Hey, sweetheart. I didn't wake you, did I?"

"I don't think so." I busy myself pulling the bread out to make toast. "Any plans for today?"

He dumps his teaspoon in the sink with a shrug. "Not many. You?"

"I thought I might see what Kate's up to," I lie, knowing full well she's busy with Brock.

"That'd be nice." He carries his steaming drink to the table, always one to have a liquid breakfast before filling up on the real thing later. "If you do go out, make sure you're back by dinner. I want to have a talk with you."

My skin rushes with heat, the rapid cool-down afterward leaving me with goosebumps. "What about?"

"A few changes around here. Nothing major."

"Oh, okay." I place the bread in the slot and push the handle down.

"Morning, everyone."

I can't look at him for fear I'll give it all away.

"Morning," I mumble, head down as I retrieve a butter knife.

"Z," Dad greets curtly.

I have no idea what the fuck is up between those two, but the thought Dad could have busted Zeus in my room sets my heart racing. *Unless he already knows?* My appetite vanishes instantly.

"How did things go with Jodie the other day?" Dad asks as Zeus takes a seat at the table.

"Good." He looks my way. "Leave the toaster out when you're done, Belle. I'll use it."

"Sure." My hands shake as I twist the lid off the Vegemite.

"Sale all settled then?"

"Signed and final," Zeus remarks. "Got a second viewing on that place over on Fraser I told you about."

"The change might be good, huh?" Dad sips his coffee without so much as giving Zeus the common courtesy of eye contact.

"The change is needed. Yes." Zeus shuts down before my eyes as I wait on my toast to pop.

His whole mood shifts, so starkly different to the man who crawled into my bed last night.

"Any plans today, Belle?" Zeus's gaze tickles the length of my spine, exactly how his fingers did as he drifted off to sleep last night.

"I thought I'd see what Kate is doing. We haven't really hung out since school finished."

He nods, acting as though he doesn't already know

she's occupied like I do. "You, John?"

"A couple of loose ends to tidy up on a project."

The way my father holds Zeus's gaze turns my stomach as I pull the hot toast from the machine. "How many slices you want, Zeus? I'll put them in."

"Two. But don't turn it on just yet; I'll make eggs."

"Sure." I occupy myself with the mundane task of spreading butter and then Vegemite on my toast with such meticulous care that I'd laugh at the absurdity myself if I wasn't so focused on ignoring Zeus as he moves around behind me.

His scent drifts past me as he moves, stirring memories of last night. I rush my way through putting the condiments away, and then plate my toast with such urgency the pieces damn near slide off the other side.

"You okay?" Zeus asks.

"Hungry," I mutter, joining my father at the table.

Dad eyes me a moment before downing the last of his coffee. "Glad you got over that stomach bug."

Kill me now. "Yeah. Me too."

"Ever find out exactly what it was?"

"I think you were right." I examine my toast. "Something viral. I must have caught it off someone at school."

"Anybody else come down with it?"

I shrug, aware Zeus watches me in my periphery. "Not sure. I haven't really kept up with anyone since school got out." I glance up to meet Dad's stoic stare, thankful I've left my hair out so my pink ears should be covered.

"Well, I'm going to have a shower and then shoot out to get a head start on these things I have to do." Dad stands, tapping his knuckles on the table. "Say hi to Kate for me. It's been an age since she's come around. Tell her she should come over for a barbecue soon."

"Yeah. Sure."

Dad leaves; the daggers Zeus shoots at his back pique my interest. Listen to my gut, he said. Yeah, well right now my gut tells me that Zeus knows more than he's let on.

I continue to eat my toast, watching Zeus as he prepares his eggs. He plates his meal and carries it over, settling in the chair adjacent to mine.

"What's going on?" The distant sound of water running in the bathroom tells me Dad's safely in the shower.

"Nothing." He leans down to shovel a forkful of toast and egg in his mouth.

The points of his jaw roll and bulge as they work. I drink in every detail of him while I can freely stare without fear of being caught by Dad. "You're lying."

"Nope." He takes another bite.

I narrow my gaze and huff, frustrated that he chooses to be so stubborn. "I'm not stupid."

"Good." He gives me a cheeky smile before eating more.

I kick his leg under the table.

Zeus shifts his fork to the left hand, and then reaches beneath the table with his right to rest it on my knee. I lean both elbows on the table, smiling at him like an idiot while I finish my toast.

For a second, I pretend that this is us, that nobody else matters, and that in some far stretch of the world this could actually end well.

I've set myself up for the worst heartbreak of all, but for now at least it's easy to forget when the high is so great.

For now, it's easy to pretend that I'm not eighteen, he's not thirty-five, and that none of it matters.

Easy to pretend that maybe, he truly loves me.

TWENTY

Zeus

We started something that neither of us know how to handle. But as with anything new, you persist and you learn from your mistakes, keeping on until what was once unknown and terrifying is as routine as tying your shoes.

I just hope the mistakes I make with Belle aren't too major.

Belle occupies the bathroom now John has finished, leaving me to clear the breakfast dishes. She insisted on helping, but I shooed her away with a smack on the arse, reminding her this is how I repay the favour John has done me.

"Cerise moves in tomorrow." *Speak of the devil.*

I still my hands in the soapy water. "That soon, huh?" I'd hoped to have a new place sorted and be gone before the bitch showed her face.

He slaps me with a scathing glare. "Didn't mention anything earlier, Z, because I didn't want you trying to talk me out of it."

"You know it's a terrible idea then?"

"Lay off." He picks up a dishcloth and retrieves a plate from the drying rack.

"Does Belle know?"

"She will."

"When?"

"In good time." He sets the dry plate down, turning to face me front-on. "Not that it's any of your concern."

Arsehole. "Just want to know if I'm going to have a moody teenager to deal with at night is all."

John appears to soften as he picks up another plate. "I'm going to tell her over dinner."

"And if she doesn't take it well? Doesn't give her a lot of time to come to terms with it if Cerise turns up tomorrow."

He stares at me a moment. Bastard knows I'm right.

"Tell her now." I take my frustration out on the damn eggs baked onto the pan. "Give her all day to work through it."

"You're a fucking know-it-all, you realise that?"

I smile, aware he's teasing from the tone of his voice. "Try to be. I'll step out and give you both some privacy."

"No," he urges, seemingly humble. "Stay." He lifts his eyes to mine. "She might want somebody to talk to about it if she gets mad with me."

I give John a simple nod. Things have been tense between us the past week since that blow-up about Cerise. We've spoken, but only when we have to. Knowing my best friend since childhood could become so distant over a damn woman? Yeah, that hurt. But what stung more was the doubt it seeded in my mind about what I'm doing with Belle.

If this is how dark he can get about his ex-wife, what the hell will it do to us if he finds out I've started sharing a bed with his daughter?

The air immediately thickens as Belle enters the room, oblivious to what's about to go down. John sets the towel down and looks across with worry in his gaze. I catch his eye and nod. He's doing the right thing, giving her warning. Maybe to him Cerise moving in is a return to how things were, but for Belle, it's a big deal.

The mother who walked out and abandoned her wants back into the family home, and it's not because of Belle.

"Hey, sweetheart." John steps up to where Belle reaches for the juice. "Got a minute?"

She looks around and finds me, worry in her eyes before she returns her focus to John. "Sure."

I finish up with the pan and pull the plug.

"I've got some news I want to share." John gestures for her to sit at the table.

Belle glances my way while I dry my hands off, as though to ask what's going on.

"I'll be out the back if you need me." I hold her gaze as I say it, letting her know I mean her—if *she* need me.

"Thanks, Z." John nods as I set the towel down and head for the back door.

Belle's scent fills my nose as I pass her, my palm buzzing with the need to reach out and pull her to me, to kiss her. It's a kind of suicide, holding your love inside. A pain that knows no equal.

My gut tightens as I step outside, the feeling that I'm abandoning her strong. My dove is about to find out she has to share her cage with a crow. A dark beast of a bird that does nothing but bring bad luck and thrive on death and decay.

I take a seat on the back step, raising my chin to the sky to look at the dark clouds that gather in the west. *Maybe we'll get a storm.* Hopefully—it would help to lift Belle's mood after she's done talking to John.

Curiosity gets the better of me, and I pull my phone out to scroll through to Jodie's number. We might have left off on bad terms, but her attitude when I've seen her to deal with the house sale has been more relaxed than when she lost her shit at the café. Perhaps it's not the best idea, but when you literally grow up in your best friend's pocket with fuck-all other friends around, nobody understands the situation the same as your ex-wife.

Z: Did you know John and Cerise are back together?

I send the message and tune my ears for anything coming from inside. Yet it's as quiet as a fucking library in there, no indication of which way the discussion goes. My phone pings with a reply.

J: What the fuck for?

I chuckle at her blunt response. At least I'm not the only one who sees the bad in this.

Z: She got in touch a few months back, so he says. She moves in tomorrow.

Her reply is immediate; the dots dancing across my screen.

J: You're still there?

Z: Yes.

Nothing. The absence of a reply, or even any indication she's typing, speaks volumes. I set the phone down and take a stroll to the fence line, absently pulling out weeds as I go. Where do I see this relationship with Belle going? I started things, crossed that line selfishly without really thinking it through. I want her—always, but the logistics of that are something that can't be handled without copious amounts of heartache: for John, for her, and for me.

My phone pings from the step. I glance up at the dining room windows as I return, but I can't see anyone; they must be in the living room. The echo of a door sounds as I retake my position, followed by the rumble of John's work truck as it starts.

Thunder beats a drum on the horizon as I open

Jodie's reply.

J: How did Belle take the news?

Such a simple question, but one I know would have taken her a hell of a lot to ask. She's never liked Belle all that much, at least since Cerise left. You'd think a woman's natural instinct to nurture and protect would kick in when she watched a child be abandoned by a parent, but not for Jodie. Strangely it was *my* instinct that drew me to the dejected kid playing on her own in silence, and all that happened for Jodie was she grew increasingly wary of Belle, withdrawing further from her the older she got.

My gut knots as the door behind me opens: it was *Jodie* who took that picture of me and Belle at the barbecue. *Shit.* How could I forget that?

"You can come back in if you want." Belle's voice is flat, scarily unmoved.

I turn as I stand, and pocket my phone. "What did he say?"

"You know she never once sent me a birthday card? Not even a phone call." Her eyes are narrow and critical, but the pain is still clear.

"I know."

"And now she wants to come back in here and take Dad like she's entitled to him."

I reach out and pull Belle to me with a sigh. She crashes into my chest, resistant at first, but her body soon settles against mine. "Sometimes you have to let people make their own mistakes, dove."

"Didn't he do that the first time?" she scoffs. "You'd think he'd remember."

You would. John took Cerise leaving hard, leaning a little too heavily on the bottle as his way to numb the pain of betrayal. You'd especially think he'd remember how cold and tactless it was that the bitch brought her new man around to get her shit when she left.

"I wish I could do something," I admit. "Watching your dad make the same mistake twice feels wrong, but he already shut me out when I let him know how I felt about it."

"He doesn't want to face the truth, does he?"

Her question strikes a bit too close to home. "I guess not. Sometimes it's easier to live in the lie than acknowledge how painful the truth is."

And as with any lie, there's only so long you can keep it up before the web begins to unravel.

"Come inside," Belle says as she pulls away. "I'm in the mood for a movie and comfort food." She graces me with a sad smile as I follow her lead, hand in hers. "May as well make the most of the fact Dad's headed out to organise shit for the bitch."

She turns away, missing the worry that no doubt settles across my features. In a way, having Cerise move back in is needed; it forces us to face what this is that we've started. But in the same vein, I can't help but feel unease at what else it means.

Distance makes the heart grow fonder, but what if distance for Belle and me simply clears the fog of lust and shows this arrangement for what it really is?

Wrong.

Controversial.

And ultimately, condemned?

If that's the future for us, then I'll go to bed tonight wishing for the miracle of a groundhog day. Because as much as Belle's pain at her mother's return makes my chest ache, I don't want to ever let this day go.

I'd gladly live every day on a loop if one more step forward would mean an end.

TWENTY-ONE

Belle

An existential crisis—that's what I've been told this is called. That point where you don't know what to do, which road to take... which one will lead to a better future. Cerise moved in on Monday, and for the entire week I've wished for some miracle that would make her realise the whole thing were a mistake and leave. Because if she doesn't, I just might.

I never wanted her back. Not when she left the first time, not now. Some things never change, and my lack of love for my mother is one of those.

"You realise this is your fault, don't you?"

Zeus messaged to say he's on his way home from work, and Dad has not long left for his night shift. Cerise is almost through her first bottle of wine, her words beginning to slur as she jabs her mostly empty glass at me.

"I drank before you came along, sure," she rambles. "But I had control of it. After you were born, though..." She huffs a bitter laugh. "Christ. You wouldn't shut up for the first few weeks. Cried, and cried, and cried." She waves her arms around as she talks, moaning the words. "You were a handful from the get go."

As the days go by, it seems more and more likely that her return coincides with a need to have someone to look after her. I can't shake the feeling that she's taking Dad for a ride, taking advantage of his good nature. I wouldn't put it past the woman, that's for sure. I might not have known much about my mother since she left when I was so young, but I learnt enough from the things Dad told me to know that Cerise doesn't do anything unless it's to her benefit.

She's a user. In every aspect of the word.

I glance over the top of my phone as she leans her head back to take a sip of the wine. Cerise doesn't look like what I imagine a mother should. Pressure makes her veins stand out against her pallid skin, the words she speaks to me gritted out through a stiff jaw. There's no softness, no comfort. Nothing that I longed for as a kid.

I clearly didn't miss out on anything, not having her around.

"What are you going to do with yourself now school is over?" she asks, her hand shaky as she pours another glass.

"I've contacted a few shops about placement as an apprentice."

Dad thinks I should jump straight into what I want to be doing and not waste time saving cash at a regular job for school leavers, like the supermarket, or a takeaway joint. He has a point, in that I should focus on my chosen career rather than waste time in a job that doesn't help me learn or grow in my preferred field. So I started to contact the artists I've followed for years on social media, asking for placement.

A bold step, yeah, but nobody got anywhere by sitting on their hands. The worst they can do is say no—which most have—but a few have either not responded or asked for a sample design to gauge my skill level.

It's a start.

"Apprentice for what?"

I rise from my seat in the living room and head through to the kitchen to get her something to eat, rather than let her consume so much alcohol on an empty stomach.

"Tattooing."

I'm not dumb—feeding her slows her absorption, which in turn makes my life easier.

She laughs as I pull a bag of bread rolls from the pantry and retrieve the butter and ham. "Do you have any plans to get a *real* job?"

Why the fuck Dad thought it was our responsibility to look after her, get her on the straight and narrow, I have no idea. If he wanted a project, he could have adopted a stray animal. At least an animal would have been grateful to have the free roof over its head while it mooched on what we gave it.

"Being a tattoo artist *is* a real job." I slam the ham in her unbuttered bun, my level of care suddenly diminished.

"Don't kid yourself, Belle." She eyes the roll dismissively as I set it down on the table beside her. "You'll never make good money doing that."

"You shouldn't offer advice on things you don't understand." I swipe my phone off the sofa and drop onto the cushions.

I catch her lift the food in my periphery as I flick through my timeline. She inspects the bread roll, lifting the ham as though I would have hidden poison beneath it, and then takes a bite.

My thumb hovers over the screen while I glance her way. "If I wanted to get rid of you, I'd think of something more practical than giving myself a dead body to dispose of."

Cerise sneers before taking another bite and then setting the food aside while she chews.

"You're giving me that look," she says, wiping the crumbs from her lips. "That one that says you think you're better than me."

Because I am.

She lifts her glass and takes a large gulp. "I'm your mother, Belle." *Exactly*. I wish she'd act like it. "You're supposed to respect me."

"Give me something worth respecting and we'll go from there, huh?"

She sets her glass down with a clang and rises abruptly from her seat. I stiffen, ready to flee the room, when the click of the front door freezes her in her tracks.

"Afternoon, everyone."

Zeus. I've never been more thankful for his untimely interruptions in my life.

This week has been hard on both of us, having to hide the connection we so clearly acknowledged on this very sofa. He avoids eye contact, and more often than not leaves the room when I enter. It's painful, especially since my self-doubt has begun to creep in telling me that perhaps he's realised his mistake.

"How was your day?" Cerise asks sweetly, taking a step back to retrieve her glass. "You look tired."

Tension crackles between the two of them as he stares her down without answering. My skin heats when his intense gaze slides to me, his eyes softening a fraction.

"Everything okay, here?"

"Fine," I mumble. "I'm in my room if anyone wants me." I hold his gaze as I stand, willing him to read between the lines.

Cerise knocks back another gulp of her drink and then picks her smokes off the side table as I leave the room. I cast a glance back at her, my gut tight when I catch the way she blatantly looks Zeus over with appreciation while his back is turned. They hate each other—that much is clear—but she still seems to like having him around.

Makes me want to throw caution to the wind and claim him as mine for all to see.

I retreat to my room and shut the door before I cross

to my music dock and set the mood with some sombre rock. My pencils are still spread over my small desk from earlier in the day, the piece I was working on calling to me.

The tip of my red intensifies the shading in the centre of the flower, the work almost complete by the time I hear him enter.

"Hey."

I turn on my seat and fail to find a smile for him. "Hey."

"She's taken her wine outside to have a smoke." Zeus tips his head toward the door as he closes it softly behind him. "We've got five minutes, more or less."

"This is bullshit."

He frowns. "What is?"

"Having to hide like this."

I track the way his body moves as he crosses my room, the roll of his huge shoulders as he takes a seat on the side of my bed. "I know it's hard."

"But?"

"I'm hoping I'll have a place of my own sorted soon."

I don't say anything; the conversation seems so absurd. I feel as though if I talk it would wake me from the dream.

"Come here." Zeus pats the bed beside him. "I miss you, dove."

"Even though," I say as I move to sit beside him, "we live under the same roof."

He wraps an arm around my waist before I can drop

to the bed, and manoeuvres me so that I straddle his thick thighs. "That's what makes it so hard." He pulls me forward, shunting me hard against his hips. The proximity is unbelievably erotic, despite the fact we're both fully clothed. "I want to sneak over here every night, but Cerise is a light sleeper. I hear her get up sometimes, early in the morning."

"I know." I hear her too.

She drinks during the day, and more often than not, falls asleep too. Which unfortunately for us means she doesn't always sleep that well at night. I'm only new to her habits, but already I hate them. She's a waste of oxygen.

"I thought maybe you'd changed your mind," I admit. "I couldn't tell."

"No," he coos, burying his nose against my throat. "No way."

I lean my head back, the heat of his lips against my flesh making my nipples pebble.

"I did everything I wanted to with you, dove."

"Everything?" I tease, smiling as he pulls back to look in my eyes.

He smirks, the tilt of his lips sending butterflies thrumming through my middle. "Everything I wanted to do *that* night," he clarifies with a raised eyebrow. Zeus hooks his fingers in the neck of my shirt, pulling the fabric away from my body so he can peek below. "Everything else will come in good time."

"I need you." The words escape before I have time to

doubt saying them.

He answers by sealing his lips over mine, stealing my breath away as he sets both hands on my butt and grinds me against his thickening erection. I feel nothing like the teenager I am in that moment. I feel respected and revered. Equal with the man I crave.

"We don't have very long, dove, and I don't want to rush things with you."

I lament the loss of his touch as he pulls away, letting me slide further down his legs.

"Who says we're rushing?"

"I am." My feet are dropped to the floor as he stands to run a hand over the back of his neck. "I'm still wrapping my head around exactly how this works. I don't want to screw up because I'm being careless."

"Screw up with who?" I cross my arms.

His silent shrug says it all: Dad. He's cautious because of the chance of getting caught out, not to spare my feelings. *Fuck.* Am I always going to come second?

"You can leave," I say flatly. "I should go make us all dinner, anyway."

"I can help if you want?" Zeus hesitates by my door like a lost lamb.

"I think you've done enough." The blow is low, but it gets the desired reaction as I push past him and head for the kitchen.

I understand the need to hide me away, but I don't want to be shut out in the cold completely. Sure, take things slow in the public eye for my father's sake, but why the hell can't he act on his urges behind closed doors?

Unless that's the problem. What if the trouble I cause is more than the reward is worth? Maybe I'm just too much of a challenge?

Fuck it.

Cerise enters the house as I walk into the kitchen, waving her hand around as though she can simply bat the smell of nicotine off her. "What's got your face looking like a pinched arse?"

I roll my eyes at her and cross to the fridge to retrieve the meat I thawed earlier.

"Do you have your driver's licence?" She rests her butt against the edge of the counter, eyeing me as I prepare the cutting board.

"Why?"

"I'm on my last bottle."

I lift my brow as I draw the knife from the block. "Well, that's your piss poor preparation then, isn't it?"

"There's ten dollars in it for you."

"You can't buy my obedience." I slice the blade into the meat, wishing it were her.

"Fine." Her shoulder bunts me as she passes, making the knife slip. "I'll ask Zeus."

I hesitate to catch my breath after narrowly missing cutting my fingertip off. "He's not your slave."

Her eyes are hard as she swings around to meet my gaze. "And you've got no say in what I do. If he wants to help me when my own daughter won't, then that's his choice."

My heart thunders in my chest; just the thought of her going down to his room to talk to him makes me murderous. My mother was beautiful once, before the poison ravaged her body and aged her prematurely. I can't shake the idea that Zeus might see that, see past all her vices, as absurd as the concept is.

I need to get a grip on this jealousy. I kissed him, and he fingered me—what of it? We're hardly an item, especially after the way he acted just now.

"I can drive you after dinner."

She leans to one side, eyes narrowed on me. "Why the sudden change of attitude?" Cerise lifts a thin hand to thumb toward the hallway. "It's almost as though you don't want me to ask Zeus."

"I don't want you to put him out, is all."

"Huh." She studies me as I cube the meat.

My face flames, my hand clammy around the hilt of the knife. I've tripped the wire, cut the wrong colour. I have seconds to fix this, if any time at all.

"You might be onto something though." My gut twists at the mere thought of my next words. "If he takes you now, you can get yourself another bottle in time for dinner."

I don't want her in the same car as him, let alone the same house. I don't want her to even look at him—not how she did before, especially.

"For once in your life, Belle, you've said something that actually makes sense." She smirks, knowing she's got me, just not how.

I steady my breathing as she turns and leaves the room. She calls out as she makes her way down the hall, "Zeus? I need a favour."

Fuck. I need a lot more than that.

I need a miracle if I'm going to make it through this evening in one piece.

TWENTY-TWO

Zeus

Cerise clutches her babies to her chest as we head home from the bottle store. I glance over at her as I drive, disgusted that I have her in my fucking safe space. But what else could I do when she asked for a ride? Let her drive drunk? Risk the fallout if she were forced to *really* sober up—not just wait between drinks, but be completely dry?

Bitch might think I'm doing this for her, but there's only one girl that came to mind when she asked—Belle. Cerise has been a right fucking cunt to her this week, making her life hell and making sure to remind her daughter at every goddamn turn how little love there is.

What the fuck was John thinking when she called him? He should have hung up on her, saved himself the trouble.

"How much longer do we have to put up with you around the place?" she asks, face impassive.

I scowl at her and then shift my focus back to the road. "As long as it takes."

"To?"

"To buy my own place."

She huffs with a smirk. "Must make you feel like a right idiot, losing your wife because you can't get her pregnant."

"You want to walk the rest of the way?"

She stays silent, yet smiles.

She's done enough, had her little dig. Maybe it was the catalyst, but I know our inability to conceive wasn't the reason for my split with Jodie. Still—I don't have to justify a goddamn thing to Cerise.

"Why did you come back into their lives? Really?" I cast a look her way, pleased to find her wary. "Can't say either of them are all that much happier with you here."

"Is that so?" She tilts her head. "How about you? Are you making either of them happy?"

"What are you getting at, Cerise?"

She smirks again, hands throttling the neck of her bottles. "Oh, nothing."

Our conversation comes to an abrupt end as I pull up the driveway, yet I don't stop thinking about what she said throughout the entire meal. Belle watches me, flashing me looks when she thinks Cerise isn't paying attention.

I can't deal with the pressure: one wants to ruin me, one wants me to ruin her.

So I deal with the tension the way any male would: I busy myself with menial tasks and bury my head in the sand, blocking out everyone around me. By the time I've cleaned up after dinner and tidied the kitchen, Belle is hidden in her room and Cerise has passed out on the armchair. I switch all the lights off and leave the bitch for John to sort out when he gets home. If he wants to take her on as a charity case, then he can fucking well do all the work.

I didn't volunteer for this shit.

If it wasn't for Belle, I would have found myself lodging at a backpackers or the like until I sorted out the new place. But as long as Cerise is here at night alone with Belle, then I'll stick around until I'm satisfied the bitch hasn't got any ill intentions toward her daughter.

I don't trust the woman. Wouldn't put it past her to be scheming something.

Light spills under Belle's door, my eye drawn to it as I hesitate outside mine. *Should I?* I shut her down earlier, telling myself it was for her sake. But she had me all figured out when she pointed out my hesitation is based around John's feelings, not hers.

I push her door open a fraction. "You awake?"

"It's not that late," she retorts. "If you want to know if you can come in, the answer is yes."

I step into Belle's room, pushing the door closed behind me. "I'm sorry, dove, about earlier."

She shrugs, propped up against the headboard of her bed with her phone in hand. "You have a point, I guess. I just think your reasoning is skewed."

"I guess I worry." Fuck—I seem to be guessing everything when it comes to her. "I don't know how to handle somebody…"

"My age?" she finishes with a jerk of her head.

"Yeah." *Fuck it.* "Don't take it the wrong way."

"I really don't know how else to take it."

Stick the other foot in, Zeus. "Tell me, then. How do we do this taking into account you've got no experience with sexual relationships whatsoever?"

The look she gives could strip paint. "Like any other, I guess: one step at a time."

"Dove." I crumple my face trying to work out how to voice the thoughts in my mind. This has always been my problem: I can't formulate what goes on in my head into the right words. I sucked at school because what I wrote out was never a true reflection of what I had figured out in my mind. "Don't make this harder than it already is."

Her face softens at those words, her shoulders sagging as she sets the phone aside. "I'm sorry. I'm just... I worry that you'll get annoyed with how inexperienced I am and change your mind."

"You think experience is what matters most to me?"

"Isn't it? I don't know much about—" She swallows. "—sex and stuff. How do I know what to do to make you feel good? What if I can't do it?"

Is that all she's worried about? I cross the room and sit on the side of the bed beside her feet. "That stuff? It comes naturally. You do whatever feels right."

"Can I tell you a secret?"

"I think we're a bit past worrying about who can keep a secret or not, don't you?"

She giggles. "Yeah. I suppose."

"What have you got to share, then?"

Her ears burn bright red as she turns her phone to face me. "I was doing research."

Fuck me. Her browser is open on RedTube, the video paused on one hell of a scene. All my previous self-control melts into a puddle. "Well then…"

She snatches the screen away, sending it to black before tossing the phone. "It's silly, I know."

I swallow hard and shake my head. "It's fucking hot, is what it is." She had a damn threesome on the screen, for fuck's sake.

"Really?" Her gaze flicks to the door. "Where's Cerise?"

"Out for the count." I lean over and pick up her phone.

She sits still as a statute while I wake the device and re-open the browser. I should walk away, but shit, as soon as I saw that image I knew this was the only logical course of action. "Hold this, and don't take your eyes off it." I hit play and pass her the phone.

She frowns a little, eyes on me.

I tap my finger on the edge of the hard case. "Watch."

Belle draws a deep breath and drops her gaze to the video. *Risky business.* Still…

I move further onto the bed and position myself at her feet. She glances up, looking away when I tut at her. Satisfied she's focused on the video, I hook my fingers in the waistband of her sleep shorts and jerk them from under her arse before I shimmy them down her legs.

"That one finishes, you start another. Understood?"

She nods, eyes still on the screen. *Good girl.* I drop the clothing off the side of her bed, and then as much as I'd love to keep it on, head across to turn the light off. If we're interrupted, I want a chance at hiding—I'm not that reckless.

"Still watching?" I reposition myself between her legs, using my touch to guide me.

She hums her assent, nodding in the amber glow of the screen.

"Take it off silent."

"Are you sure?" She finally breaks her gaze.

"Positive. Doesn't have to be loud, but I want to hear what you're watching." Fuck—just thinking about it gets me hard.

She does as I ask, letting the sound of a woman's moans and slick skin slapping against skin filter between us. I settle on my stomach and nudge her knees wide. My dove is wet and ready, my fingers grazing easily over her slick folds. *Fuck, yes.*

"Remember, you're in control."

She answers with heavy breaths, her gaze glued to the phone as I slowly push a digit inside her willing cunt. I'm fucking sick in the head, perverted to even think of doing this with an eager eighteen year-old. But damn— it feels so fucking good to be so bad.

"You like what you're seeing, dove? Your wet pussy tells me you do."

Her muscles clench around my finger. "Uh-huh." She

can't even form words—nice.

"Tell me what you see."

I slide another finger in to join the first, and then lean in to suck her hood. *Delicious.*

"I… One of the guys has her on his lap."

"Mmm?" I run my tongue around where my fingers join her.

"She faces him, rides him." She hesitates. "Fuck, Zeus."

I lap up what she gives me, loving this idea even more. "I can taste how turned on you are."

"I can't … Can I just watch?"

"No." With a twist of my wrist, I change the angle of my fingers. Her legs quiver beside my head, her knees seemingly weak as I feather her G-spot.

"Okay." She pants, struggling to catch her breath as I intensify my assault. "The second guy… Oh my God."

"The second guy, what?" I slide my fingers out and use them to spread her wide.

She jolts when my tongue pushes inside. "He's… They're… Fuck."

"Tell me," I demand. "I want to know what makes you so wet, Belle."

"They're both fucking her. In both holes."

The visual, along with the building moans from her phone *and* her, have me hard as a rock. I can guarantee it'll take me mere seconds to stroke this one out when I'm done here.

"Got to keep quiet, dove. Don't want your mother

knowing what you're up to."

"Don't mention her," she grumbles. "Shit…" Her legs seize my shoulders as her climax builds. "I'm so close."

I know. "Watch your phone, Belle. Tell me if you like what you see."

"It's so hot. Oh my God. I'm going to come, Zeus."

I stop licking her, and spread her with my fingers once more. "Not until you tell me the truth." I slide one finger in, pull it out, and then add the second.

She squirms on the bed, hips thrusting to find more.

"Tell me: you wish that woman was you? That something that you think you might like?"

Belle rips a pillow from beside her, muffling her moan as I build pace again.

"You want that, dove?"

"Yes," she cries into the pillow as her climax hits. "I want that."

"Tell me what you want."

"I want you," she groans as her orgasm rips through her. "I want you to fuck me like that."

Fuck. Guess I won't need to stroke it out after all.

TWENTY-THREE

Belle

"We need to say something," I whisper as I trace the line of Zeus's jaw with my fingertips.

He jerks his head away from my hold, a frown deep on his brow as he lies beside me on the bed. "Now isn't the time, Belle."

I thought we'd turned a corner with what he did to me last night. But now I'm not so sure.

The void between us has slowly inched deeper and deeper this past week with Cerise here. We've all been caught up in her toxicity, drawn into caring for her as much as we don't want to. One week with the alcoholic bitch, and she's already ruined the best thing to have happened to me ever.

I know it. I feel it.

I can see it in Zeus's eyes when he looks at her, when he looks at Dad. He doesn't want to add to the stress by getting caught out with me.

"This is the first night we've had the house to ourselves since she moved in," I remind Zeus. "I miss you. I miss this, and I hate the fact I have to sneak in time with you where I can."

"That's the price we pay," he says flatly.

His cool indifference pisses me off. Where's the passion, the lust he had mere minutes ago when he brought me to orgasm? I know tension has run high, not only between him and Dad, but between him and Cerise. Still....

"Are you bored with me?" I push up and sit, leaning on one hand. "Because I'm feeling a little used right now."

He frowns, rolling his head to look at me. "No, dove." The guy looks irresistible, laid out in nothing but his jeans. His bare torso flexes and bulges as he rolls toward me. I pinch myself daily that this man chose to risk things with me.

For how much longer, though? I'd love to pass off this fear as irrational, but the change in him is real—very real.

"What makes you say that anyway?" Zeus reaches out and takes my chin in his firm hold. "I could never be bored with you."

"It feels like you are." I mimic his earlier action and jerk my chin free. "You might be here in body, but your mind is elsewhere. You do things with me and then get distant. I'm not exactly high maintenance, Zeus, but a bit of conversation wouldn't go amiss."

We've got a short window of time while Dad and Cerise are at a movie, and the fact he's wasting it like this brings out the sulky child in me. If I could get away with stamping my foot and yelling, "It's not fair," I probably would.

"I've got a lot on my mind." He flops back on the bed with a frown.

I crawl over top of him, straddling his thick thighs, and set my hands on his chest. "So talk to me about it." I want to know everything that goes on that head of his, no matter how tough it seems to be.

Zeus settles his hands on my hips and sighs. He can swear black and blue that he's not tired of me, but in that moment, in the downward curl of his lips, I read it all: whatever bothers him is entirely to do with me.

Me and my fucking age, no doubt.

"I put an offer in on that place over on Fraser."

"That's awesome."

"It's too far for you to walk though."

Oh. "So I bus until I've saved enough for a car."

"Belle...."

"You're making excuses." My nostrils flare as I work to supress my tears. *I won't cry.* I won't show him how desperately attached to this I am.

"I'm pointing out facts." His fingers tense on my hips, biting into my flesh. "I'm facing the truth."

"That is?"

"This... us... it won't last." He hesitates, the battle clear before he adds, "I should have never started it."

I try to move away, yet he holds me firmly in place. "Nice to know how little I really mean."

"You mean everything, dove."

"Stop calling me that." The bite to my words causes him to let go, allowing me to move away.

I sit on the edge of the bed, but it may as well be the edge of nothing. I could topple, fall off that ledge and gladly slip into the dark where nobody can reach me and nothing can touch me.

Where I wouldn't get my heart smashed by the one who brought it to life.

"You tell me," he demands, shifting behind me. "Tell me how you see this working, because I'm all ears for suggestions. I can't keep away from you, and yet I don't understand how I can keep you."

"We tell Dad," I say, twisting to look at him. "Fuck the consequences." Doubt clouds his eyes. "Why are you so afraid of what he thinks?"

"I'm not afraid." His gaze drops to the bed, where he smooths the bedding with his palm. "I respect him."

"Not enough to keep your hands off his daughter, though?"

"That's not fair." Steely eyes flick to mine.

"This whole thing isn't fair," I snap. "We're supposed to be enjoying ourselves while my fucking parents are out and instead we're fighting."

God, I hate that. I hate the fact I have to mention my parents in the same sentence as what I want to be doing with Zeus. I want out. I want independence. I want to remove everything that makes me seem like a child, and that includes this goddamn room.

My gaze drifts across the walls, across the things I've

cherished and harboured since I was barely into double digits. How can I expect to move on and change when I subconsciously hold myself in the past?

Zeus jackknifes to a seated position when I launch off the bed and rip a music poster off my wall. "What are you doing?" He gets to his feet as I tear past, pieces in hand, and head for the kitchen in search of a trash bag.

I don't need any of the shit that I coveted as a child. I don't need to fan girl over rock gods and keep trinkets from the regional fair. I need to grow up. I need to be taken seriously by everyone, most of all Dad if he's ever going to accept that I want to be with Zeus.

"Belle," Zeus snaps as I tear a plastic bag off the roll.

He's every part as desirable as always, standing in the doorway with his arms braced on the frame. But that angry scowl? Jesus—even when I'm mad with him the guy makes me wet.

"Leave me to it," I bite out as I push past him. "You want a woman, somebody you're not embarrassed to show off, then let me be one."

I make it as far as my bedroom doorway before he spins me with a hand to my shoulder and pushes me up against the wall. The bag is torn from my hand, my heart torn in two directions as he looks down on me with a mix of frustration and hunger.

"You think I don't want to show you off?" he asks, nuzzling my neck.

I sigh, my goddamn body sparking alight as he nips my ear.

"I want to show you off. I want to put your sexy little arse in those black cut-offs of yours, wrap you up in one of your fucking tank tops that you love so much, and put your shit-kickers on your feet so every other man out there can see what I do." He pauses to drag his bottom lip over the ridge of my jaw. "You're different, and that"—he nips at my lips, melting me to the spot—"is what makes you irresistible."

"So do it," I breathe. "Take me out."

"I can't."

"Why not?" I murmur against his mouth.

He presses his forehead to mine, his breaths heavy. "What do you think they'd do to a thirty-five-year-old guy who parades an eighteen-year-old girl around? What do you think they'd do to that guy when he puts his hands on her, touches her the way I touch you, kisses her?"

"Gossip."

"Worse." He huffs out his nose, a smile on his lips. "They'd take you from me, Dove."

My heart picks up the pace as he pulls his head back, his hips still holding me against the wall, and watches for my reaction.

Would they? Would people be that bitter against something they don't understand?

"What if I explain that I want to be with you? How can they take me then?"

"Baby," he says on a sigh. "There are always ways for people with malicious intent to fuck over those who just want to live in peace. The world is a jaded and angry place. Most people can't resist the opportunity to make themselves feel better, vindicated, by bringing down others."

"So you'll hide me?"

"To keep you," he presses. "I hide you to keep you, because that's the only way I know how to do it."

I slide my hands onto his waist, tracing the swell of his obliques as I slip my palms to his arse. His eyes narrow, a playful smile on his lips as I reach into his back pocket and pull his phone out. Holding the device between us I hit the home button and light up the screen to show the time.

"We have forty minutes, maybe fifty if we're lucky."

"That we do."

"How are you going to make them worthwhile, Zeus?"

His phone hits the floor as he grabs hold of my hips and shunts me up the wall. I'm so small in his presence, so vulnerable, but it's a surrender I'll willingly make day after day. Anything to lose myself in this man.

"How about," he murmurs in my ear, cheek to cheek, "we take a drive?"

Excitement pulses through me in a wave as I drag my bottom lip over the shell of his ear. "Where to?"

"It's a surprise."

I lose any protest I might have had as he takes my mouth with his, devouring me with a hunger that I understand after a week around each other with only a single stolen moment for ourselves. I wish I could show others how happy he makes me, stick my middle finger up to the world while shouting his virtues from the rooftops.

But I can't. Instead I have to relish these moments, these dirty lies as they leave me high on a deceptive wave of euphoria.

I run my hands up the sides of Zeus's head as he pulls away, the short locks tickling my palm. "Remind me again why you had to cut your hair?"

"Health hazard."

Fuck his work, and fuck machinery with moving parts. He's had gorgeous shoulder-length black hair for as long as I remember, one of those men who can pull the length off. I loved it, and I'm not ashamed to admit how shallow I am in feeling a teeny bit of disappointment at losing it.

"Get your jacket," he grumbles, eyes closed as I run my fingers around to the back of his head. "I'll meet you in the car."

"Okay." I drop my hands to his shoulders, yet he doesn't move.

His eyes stay trained on mine, the slight furrow to his brow adding to the intensity as he whispers almost as if in disbelief, "Life isn't the same when you're not in it."

I cock my head to the side, frowning as I give him an unsure smile. "What makes you say that?"

"No reason." Shutters flick down behind his eyes, his staunch indifference returning as he steps back and gently sets me on my feet. "Get your stuff and don't muck around."

I smirk as he rearranges the obvious erection pressing against his jeans. "Impatient?"

"Like you wouldn't know, dove."

TWENTY-FOUR

Zeus

Summer may be on the way, but the nights can still be colder than a nun's cunt. The engine of the GTO warms while I wait on Belle to come out and join me. I rub my hands together and huff on them as a set of headlights flash in my rearview.

Fuck.

I wind the window down as they pull up beside me, gaze flicking back to the house—no Belle still.

"Hey, mate." I nod at John as he gets out of the car. "Cerise."

"Hi, Zeus." She closes the door and narrows her gaze on me.

I can't stand her, but like a cat and a dog fated to live under the same master's roof, we tolerate each other enough not to draw blood for his sake.

"Where are you headed?" John leans an elbow on the roof of the car, looking down at me.

"Late night eats." I tip my chin up at him. "Why you two home so early?"

"Movie was shit," he muses as Cerise tucks herself in

behind him.

I find myself staring at her a fraction too long, wondering if that's how Belle will look in twenty years. Cerise isn't unattractive by any stretch of the imagination, but what does outer beauty matter when the inside is an ugly rotten pit?

"That's a shame." Awkward silence hangs between us all; John and Cerise don't move an inch, choosing to stare me down. "What?"

"Nothing." John takes a step away, the Cheshire cat at his back smiling.

"Oh, hey." Belle steps out the front door, hesitant as though not sure if she should shut the house up after herself or leave the door open for these two.

"Hey, sweetheart." John moves toward his daughter.

Cerise takes a step back, her body blocking my view as she leans on the car. "Just going to get something to eat, huh?" She tilts her head to the side, talking low enough for just us to hear despite the fact she watches John and Belle.

"Never done a midnight dash?" I ask.

"It's not midnight, Zeus."

"It's also none of your fucking business what I do with my time."

"It is when it involves my daughter," she seethes.

I reach up and grab a fistful of her jacket while Belle and John still talk, tugging the bitch down so she's face-to-face with me. "How does it feel calling her that after ten years, Cerise? Awkward? Uncomfortable?"

"Natural," she sneers.

"You wouldn't know a goddamn thing about how to be a fucking mother if it slapped you in the face."

She jerks from my hold as Belle skips past the hood. "Well, I sure as fuck won't be asking you for advice on how to look after her," she whispers. Her gaze narrows. "I believe if I followed your lead they'd call that incest."

My breath catches in my throat, choking me as she walks away with far too much fucking pep in her step. John raises a hand to see us off before they head inside the house. The car rocks ever so gently as Belle gets in, the slam of her door enough to snap me the fuck out of it.

"You okay?" she asks, buckling herself in.

Guilt washes through me in a hot wave. Belle is such an incredible young woman. She deserves better than this, yet I also know I'm too fucking selfish to give her up. I'll ruin her before she sees the destruction coming.

"What did your old man say?"

"Gave me a rundown of how shit the movie was." She chuckles. "Told me we're off to get a late night snack." She raises one eyebrow as I back the car down the driveway.

"Seemed like a legitimate excuse."

"You ever going to run out of them?"

I smile as I pull away. "Nope."

"So where are we *really* going?"

I tense as her hand rests on my thigh. "Exploring."

She doesn't utter another word, simply rubbing her

thumb in small circles on my leg as I drive us toward her surprise. I told Belle I'd made an offer on a house—I lied a little.

I closed the offer on it.

As soon as the agent walked me in to view the place on a stormy afternoon, I knew I had to have it. The picture windows that face the backyard gave an uninhibited view of the shifting grey hues as the clouds rolled overhead—a perfect picture for a perfect girl.

I'll never think of anything other than Belle when I look out those windows.

Her eyes widen when I pull up the curved driveway, her hand slipping off my leg as she sits forward in her seat. It's a treat in itself to see Belle work through the motions as I park the car.

"We're at a house?" She can't contain her smile. "And it looks like nobody's home."

"The owner just pulled up."

Belle twists in the seat to look out the rear window, and then slowly turns back toward me. "Zeus…."

"Yes, dove?"

"Is this yours?"

I nod. She squeals. And for a fleeting second, everything is right in my world.

"It's amazing." Her words drift off into the night as she launches herself from the car. "Did you really buy it?"

I slap her arse on the way past, and unlock the house while she stands in the driveway taking in the single-storey building. "Yep."

Grey flagstones line the columns that frame the porch area. The weatherboard exterior is painted a similar colour, an established garden providing a green contrast against the wood. Belle trails her fingertips across the hedge plants that line the front, a goofy grin making her whole face light up.

"I love it already, and I haven't even gone inside."

"Get ready to blow your mind, then." I swing the door wide and then step aside to let her go first.

I want to witness every little hint she gives off as she sees the place for the first time. *Actually.* I pull my phone from my pocket and flick across to the camera, setting it to video as Belle exits the entranceway and steps through to the open-plan living room.

"Those windows are huge!" She beelines straight for them, looking tiny in the empty space.

I set the camera recording and follow her in. "What do you think?"

"This place is so you." She runs her hand over the ash wood mantle above the fireplace. "The colours, the size." Her chin lifts and she realises what I'm doing. "Zeus."

"What, dove?"

"Stop it."

"Not until you check out the fourth door on the left." I point down the hallway with my free hand.

She frowns, tipping her head to the side before she follows my directions. I keep the camera trained on her as she makes her way down to the hall, looking back over her shoulder with a suspicious smile every so often.

Her smile turns to a frown as she opens the door and looks around at the empty double garage. "Okay?"

"Open the door on the other side."

"And go outside?" She crosses the concrete floor with me in tow.

I can't help but laugh at the look on her face when she opens the door. It doesn't go outside.

"Holy shit, there's a studio attached?"

"Previous owner worked from home."

She turns, smiling, although I can tell she's not sure why this should be exciting for her.

"I thought you could too."

Her hand lifts and she gently removes the phone from my hold, tapping the red icon to stop the recording. "Getting my hopes up is a horrible thing to do, Zeus."

I lift her chin with the tips of my fingers, hating that she feels she has to hide her true emotions from me. "I'm not getting anyone's hopes up." My hand slides down to her shoulder. "A year, five. Fuck, even ten. However long it takes, I'll have you here working out of your own tattoo studio."

She huffs a little laugh, still refusing to look me in the eye. "You've got this all planned out, huh?"

"Nope."

That grabs her attention.

"I just know what I want, and I figure if I act like it'll

come true, then it just might."

She loops her arms around my neck, leaning in to my body as she places a chaste kiss to my lips. "You're too good to me."

"Because you deserve it."

"Do I?" She frowns a little. "What have I actually done that deserves all this?"

"Be you," I murmur against her mouth before stealing another kiss—a better one.

She tilts her head and parts her lips on a moan, tangling her tongue with mine as I pick her up and walk her into the room. A blush colours her cheeks when I set her down, tucking her to my side to point out how I envision the setup could go.

For those ten minutes while we stand in the middle of an empty studio discussing benches, tables, and facilities, everything else melts away. I forget my concerns about the logistics of our relationship, and I forget about the hurdles we'll face along the way.

The world becomes Belle, me, and a house that checks the most important box on my to-do list for a fresh start. I was an arsehole as a kid, a troublemaker, and I ended up exactly where I put myself. I can blame circumstance all I want, but the truth of it is I resigned myself to what I got. I paved the way, and life took me on a long walk down that road.

I'm don't want to be that guy. I never wanted to be a criminal, a man skimming his way through life, getting by on the bare minimum. I have dreams and hopes—

most of which include the woman beside me.

All I have to do now is convince the other people in our lives that this is it, this is how our futures are supposed to go: together.

Sounds simple in theory, but I'd be a stupid man if I believed it was.

TWENTY-FIVE

Belle

Are you still watching?

I hit "continue" on Netflix and shift position on the sofa as my phone signals an incoming message. The next episode starts as I reach for it. Dad and Cerise have gone out car shopping for her before he starts work, and Zeus hasn't got in from his day working on the road yet. I bring the device to my lap, eyes on the screen, and hit the home button.

Hopefully Zeus is on a break and he's seen the message I sent him earlier. Ever since he took me to his house last week, I've been inundating him with interior design pictures; black furniture, masculine-toned accessories—everything I think of when I imagine him knocking around a house that's just his.

His. Hopefully one day it'll be ours.

I punch in my passcode and then stiffen at the name displayed at the top of the thread: Kate.

Weeks have passed since I met her at the chemist. Weeks without a single word. Weeks where I've avoided social media for the better part, after Scott thought it would be amusing to start taking the piss out of me with stupid memes.

As far as I'm concerned, I left his immature arse behind the day school finished. Until now I thought I'd done the same with Kate.

K: Hey. I spotted your mum in town.

Simple, and to the point. Yet the fact she chose to contact me about it has me suspicious. Either she's worried about how I feel, or she's fishing for gossip. I choose the safe option and keep my reply minimal.

B: Yeah. She's back with Dad.

The dots dance across the screen as I hit pause on my show.

K: Wow. Are you okay?

B: For now. We keep our distance.

There have been no mother/daughter days, no girly gossips on the sofa while she catches up on everything she's missed. Nope. Not with Cerise. Her claws are firmly in Dad, her focus on recreating this perfect ideal she must have of what life with him should have been.

Turns out the split from her sugar daddy was ugly, and he paid a pretty penny to keep her mouth shut about the things she'd seen in her two years at his side.

The woman came back with money, and she's not shy on spending that on things that satisfy *her* wants and needs.

Namely alcohol.

K: What have you been up to? You've been quiet.

No kidding. I roll my eyes and slide to lie down on the sofa as a reply comes through from Zeus also.

Z: Might have to take you shopping with me. Almost done for the day ;)

That's what I've been doing. Spending time with somebody who actually gives a shit about me. I send him a kissy face and then reopen Kate's thread.

B: Not a lot. Trying to find a job. You?

K: Hanging with Brock, but I'm pretty sure we're done.

I smile as I type my reply.

B: Oh no. Why?

K: He doesn't want to travel. I do. We argue more than anything else now.

B: That sucks. Maybe he'll come around.

K: I don't think so. Do you still want to travel?

Do I? Given the opportunity I wouldn't pass it up, but now that Zeus has his place with the studio space I'm torn over what to save my money for when I get a job. Maybe I could do both? Guess it's something to talk to him about....

B: I'd love to see Canada.

There. Doesn't say yes, but doesn't say no either.

K: We should go.

I sigh as the front door opens, Dad and Cerise chatting as they walk in. The idea of a trip with Kate sounds great, but I can't shake the fair-weather friend feeling. If Brock wanted to travel I have no doubt she would have gone without giving me a second thought.

"Hey, sweetheart." Dad jerks his chin toward my phone. "Who you chatting with?"

"Kate."

"She going to come over for dinner one night?"

"Don't know. Maybe," I call after him as he takes some shopping through to the kitchen.

Cerise hangs in my periphery, awkwardly still. I glance over, a creepy feeling spreading over my skin when I find her watching me. "What?"

"Do you have any plans for your future, other than mooching on your father's couch?"

Hi to you too, Mum. I twist around to sit up straight.

Her gaze tracks Dad as he cuts through the living room on his way to the bedroom. "I better get myself ready for work."

"Okay, love," she calls cheerily, her eyes warm as she watches him go. The ice returns as her gaze slips back to me. "Your dad can't afford to carry you forever, you know."

Is this bitch for real? "I imagine it must be hard for him, given you never sent a single cent to help pay for my upbringing."

Her lips twitch as she stares me down. "I moved out of my parents' house at eighteen."

"You had Dad."

"You have someone also, don't you?" She smiles.

I burn alive. "No."

"Huh." My stomach knots as she walks to the bay window and sighs. "I may have been gone for a while, Belle, but I still know when you're lying."

Fucking ears. "What's it to you anyway?"

"I'm your mother. I care."

"I can still tell when you're lying too," I deadpan.

She smiles, almost as though she's proud of my comeback. "His world has revolved around you for the last ten years. You don't know the half of the sacrifices he's made for you."

"And what sacrifices did *you* make?"

She remains silent. I've got the bitch. She did nothing for me. She can't even spin some bullshit story about how she left for the good of the family. My parents didn't hate each other, from what I remember of life before the split. Staying together wouldn't have meant we struggled to get by. She left for her own benefit, fuck what it meant to anyone else.

She hurt the ones who loved her, all for her own selfish need.

"Don't be a burden, Belle."

I open my mouth to give her what for, yet Dad walks back in, dressed in his work clothes. "Everything okay?" He glances between the two of us.

"Fine. Right, *Mother*?"

"Yes. Lovely."

Dad looks at the two of us, his brow pinched, and then turns for the kitchen with a huff. "Women," he muses. "I'll never understand you lot."

TWENTY-SIX

Zeus

"Kate visited today." Belle lifts a box from the back of the car and heads toward the house with it.

Official possession was earlier in the week, but work ran overtime trying to make up for rainy days, and left hardly any time to do any shifting.

"Yeah? How did that go?" She told me a few days ago that the girl had got in touch with her out of the blue.

Maybe I'm too protective, or maybe I'm being selfish with my time with Belle, but I'm not convinced this is a good thing.

"Okay." She shrugs as she sets the box down on my new dining table, free of any connection to Jodie. "It was awkward at first, but I don't know. She seems genuine."

"Yeah, well, tread carefully. She ditched you when you needed her most."

"I know." Belle stares down at the pile of flat pack furniture stacked against the wall and sighs. "You know Dad calls these divorce kits."

"I can understand why." There's always an extra bolt or two, half the instructions you need, and a fucking

Allen key that's too stubby to get a proper grip on. "Which one do you want to do first?"

"I think we should start with your bedroom furniture."

"Agreed."

Belle smiles as she skips past me. "Come on. Sooner we start, sooner we can chill out afterward."

By the time I've shut the car and closed the front door, she's already standing in the middle of the bedroom with her hands on her hips. I take a moment to watch her from the doorway, amazed by the headstrong young woman she is. Belle might feel insecure at times, tell me that the loss of her friends and the way the jerks at school treated her in the past has left its effects on her. But she can't see what I do.

Bravery.

Her dark hair hangs straight, brushing her lower back as she picks an instruction sheet off the end of the unmade bed and reads the diagrams. My gaze traces a path down her slender arms as she reaches for the first board that'll become my nightstand, and then skims over her hips to the line her black shorts cuts across her upper thigh.

Her soul is what I fell in love with first, but her body is what sings to me when I'm alone at night. If there was ever something that would be a blatant reminder of what's wrong with this relationship, it's the fact she can't stay and sleep beside me. What would John think if he found us? What would he say seeing his daughter tucked in my arms?

"Are you going to help me, or stand there all day?" She doesn't turn around, addressing the square of board in her hand.

"Can't blame me if the view is one I want to enjoy a bit longer."

She reaches for me with her free hand as I step into the room, tucking her small hand behind my neck once I'm close enough. "Maybe. But if you stand behind me, then *I* miss out on my favourite view."

I lean in and brush my nose against hers. "Why are you here?" I murmur against her lips.

"Because I want to be."

It's as simple as that—we both want this. *That* is why I keep on going, despite the fear that I'll fuck things up forever if John catches wind.

"I love you, dove."

"I love you, too." Belle drops the board, and then turns her body toward mine. "Don't forget that. Okay?"

I settle my hands on her waist and lift her off the ground. Her legs tuck around my middle. "How could I?"

"Just promise me." Her eyes hold the truth that neither of us wants to acknowledge.

The risk is too great, the chances too high. A fire that burns as bright as ours will barely last the night.

"I promise."

She hums, tucking her face into my neck as her hold on me tightens. "Let's make the furniture later."

"If you're sure." I walk across to the bed and lay her

down.

Belle spreads out before me on the unmade mattress, her arms stretched over her head. She smiles at me, the afternoon sun casting shadows across her face, and fuck it all if that isn't reason to throw caution to the wind right there.

"I wish I didn't have to take you home tonight," I admit as I reach down and pop her shorts open.

"I wish you didn't either." Belle lifts her hips, helping me to slide the black fabric off her legs.

She's chosen dark grey panties today, a beautiful contrast against her pale skin. Cupping my palm to her pussy, I slide my hold up and across her stomach, making her lift her hips for more. *So greedy.* She looks good enough to eat. In fact, I will.

"You'll have to tell me what the sunrise is like in here." Her head turns away as she looks across to the tall windows that showcase the tree-lined backyard.

"You'll have to see it for yourself," I counter.

A sigh falls from her lips as I repeat the action in reverse, applying pressure to her mound as I slip my hand past, and then run the tips of my fingers over her panty-clad pussy. Belle's eyes hold mine as I push the fabric aside and tease her opening.

"Always wet and willing, aren't you?"

"Always have reason to be." She cocks an eyebrow, tucking her lush bottom lip between her teeth.

Doesn't she know it. I hook my thumbs in the waist of her panties and guide them down her legs. Belle pulls one foot free, and then the other, her long legs coming to rest either side of mine as I lean into the end of the bed. I slide to my knees, yet don't make it all the way to the floor before she stops my descent with a carefully hooked foot under my arm.

"Not this time."

I've been respectful, keeping our interactions to foreplay; a kiss down here, a hooked finger in there. My thin tether to control frays every time she bares herself to me, and it's only a matter of time before I lose any and all grasp I have on consideration.

"What do you want, dove?" I ask, rising to lean over her. "Tell me what's on your mind."

She pushes up on her elbows to place a soft kiss on my cheek before whispering in my ear, "I want to suck your cock."

Jesus. Somebody save this girl.

"I think that's the sweetest thing you've ever said to me," I tease as she pushes against my chest to make me stand tall.

My dick strains in my jeans, my beautiful girl rising to her knees as she reaches for the hem of my T-shirt. I lift both arms, aiding her as she peels the cotton from my body. Belle pauses, her lips parted as she runs her eye over my torso. I spend a ridiculous amount of time in the gym to stay in this shape, and this girl, she makes it all worth it with one satisfied "Hmm."

Hands linked behind my head, I tuck my chin to my chest to watch her as she carefully unbuckles my belt, seated on the side of the bed. The leather falls to the sides, her fingers making quick work of the zipper as she reveals her prize.

However she might have imagined this would happen, I'm resolved to make sure it's ten times better. I want this girl going to bed tonight with the feel of my cock still in her mouth and the taste of my cum still on her tongue.

I want her hungry enough to come back for more.

"Lie down." Belle jerks her head to the mattress, switching positions to stand as I do what I'm told.

My gaze catches the small damp patch she left on the side of the bed. *Fuck, yes.* She's barely holding on too.

"Boxers off," she instructs.

Her T-shirt hits the floor, followed by my boxers, and then her bra. The sight of Belle standing at the foot of my bed, dark hair resting on her pert breasts, has me reaching for my cock. Maybe she's going to bed with the memory of my dick in her mouth, but fuck, I'm going to have my cock permanently in my hand if the memory of her standing here like this serves me well.

"Fuck, baby," I grit out as I slide my fist over my length. "You're so fucking beautiful."

She smiles, but what pisses me off is she also drops her chin. My girl has nothing to be ashamed of, nothing to be embarrassed about. She's gorgeous, with a heart of gold. She should be proud.

"Look at me," I demand.

Her gaze fixes to my hand pumping slowly over my

thick erection. Lust fires behind her eyes before she drags them to mine.

"Don't you ever act shy around me, you hear? You never have reason to be."

Belle nods, taking a bold step forward to reach the edge of the bed. She sets a knee down between my legs, and then the other beside my thigh. One delicate hand rests atop the bed while she lets the other drift over my hip, across my stomach, and to a stop on my chest.

I flex my pec with a smirk, earning a giggle in response.

"I'm trying to be serious here," she complains.

"So am I." Taking her hand, I guide it back down to rest over top of mine.

She follows my movement, continuing to jerk me off after I slide my hand out from beneath hers. Eyes shut, I groan behind closed lips. She's touched me before, run her hands over me, but until now I've never been fully naked with her and at her whim. Until now I've focused on her and what makes her happy, not pausing to think that maybe making *me* happy is what she wants too.

Her fist tightens on a slow stroke and she gives a satisfied hum as pre-cum beads at the tip of my cock. Her pink tongue wets her lips before she ducks and sucks the drop from the head. I fist my hands against the bed in an effort not to thrust back and bury myself in her hot mouth.

"That tastes really good," she muses, stroking for more.

Another bead forms, another swipe of her tongue. I'm ready to beg for mercy. *Just wrap your lips around it already.* I'm rewarded on the third taste, Belle keeping her mouth securely around my shaft as she lowers her head to take me as far as she dares. The head of my cock touches the back of her throat; goosebumps erupt across my flesh.

Fuck, this girl has no idea what she can do to me. One glimpse of her naked, one feel of her over me, and I'd give up everything just to go that little bit further.

"Fuck, Belle…."

"Mmm?" she hums in question around my dick.

"Jesus. Do that again and you might get dinner early."

She rears back, hand still on my cock as she laughs. "Really, Zeus?"

I shrug with a smile, loving the fact that even in the heat of the moment we haven't lost the ability to joke around with one another.

"Carry on what you were doing," I say before tapping my lips. "But get your pussy over here while you do."

Belle positions herself top to tail, both legs to one side. Not quite what I had in mind, but as she sinks that heavenly mouth back on my cock there isn't much that I wouldn't forgive her for. I run my fingertips through her slick pussy, teasing, coaxing, and massaging until she rocks her hips in time with my movements.

Her mouth widens on a moan, my dick still buried inside, as I push two fingers into her cunt. It's one thing to finger-fuck a woman, feel her muscles as they pull you in for more, but to watch it as you do... magic.

"Oh, fuck, Zeus." Belle comes up for air, her fist crushing the base of my dick. "Fuck that's good."

"I know, dove. I know." My fingers slide in and out of her channel, her juices slick on my knuckles as I bury them to the hilt.

She quivers when I pick up the pace, her bobbing head growing frantic as I thrust harder, no doubt bruising her swollen pussy while I pull her thighs apart with my free hand. Nothing else matters in these moments with Belle: no doubts, no worries, not even time. The sun coats the room in a dull orange glow as I twist and duck my head between her legs. Belle's knees slide farther apart of their own volition; the sound of her slick lips sucking on my cock as she chases her mouth with her fist is enough to drive me crazy.

I might not have been hungry before, but one taste of her sweet juices on my tongue and I'm a starved animal. She mewls around my dick, pulling off as I bring my fingers out of her cunt and spear her with my tongue instead. Belle tosses her head back, which in turn arches her back and tips her pussy so that she's perfectly positioned over my mouth. Her hand slows, groans spilling from her lips as she's lost in her pleasure.

"Keep stroking me, baby," I coax. "I want to come when you do."

She hesitates, the slightest tension in her hand. It's barely noticeable, but enough for me to rub the heel of my hand over her pussy while I twist and peer out at her.

"You okay?"

"I love doing this," she purrs, eyes on mine. "But I don't know if I want to swallow yet."

God, she's so cute when she worries about shit that doesn't matter. I slide out from beneath her, Belle pulling back to kneel as I do.

"So we swap," I tell her as I lift her hand and coax her to the middle of the bed.

She lies flat, legs slowly inching apart, and damn well licks her lips. My cock jumps at the fresh memory of that mouth of hers. Her hand finds her breasts as I slide my fingers inside her again, palming the soft flesh while I coax her back to where we left off. It doesn't take long before her hips buck and she's licking those fucking lips while her gaze fixes on my dick.

Always, baby. The frustration at holding back, at not taking things too far, too fast, burns at times. But when she looks at me with heavy-lidded eyes, her cheeks flushed rose pink... no need to rush a good thing.

I shuffle my knees along the bed, still plying her pussy with my fingers as I position myself so I'm in reach. Her fingers grip the base of my shaft as I kneel beside her head and she gives me one hard tug before twisting herself to the side so that her mouth can reach my cock. Her hair spills around her shoulders as she rolls to take me deep, my dick grazing the back of her throat. Belle gives a slight gag, the reaction seeming to surprise her before she takes a breath and attempts to deep throat me again.

Got to love a trier.

"Relax, baby," I instruct. "Stop thinking about not gagging, and open your throat." I slide my hand from her cunt as she slows her pace, and lick my fingers while she bobs and ducks in my lap.

Beautiful.

Belle soon finds her rhythm, pushing deeper and deeper on each take. The head of my cock presses against her throat, the muscles tight around the tip before she slides me out again. It's too much, too perfect.

"Jesus, dove," I groan. "Keep doing that, baby. Keep doing exactly that."

I bury my fingers in her tight channel again and build to a punishing pace. She groans around my cock, squirming when I add my thumb to her clit. Her muscles spasm, and then clamp down on my hand as she lets out a strangled moan around my dick. I pull free, respecting her choice, and twist my hips to pump out my release over her chest. Belle cries out with her own, her face and neck flushed, her hips digging down into the mattress as she clamps her thighs around my wrist.

I give my cock a final pump, the sight of my cum on her stirring something primal within me. I want to smear it over her skin and show her to the world like some fucking caveman; tell them all that she belongs to me.

That'd I'd kill the man who tries to take her from me.

"Stay there." I run my fingers across her jaw. "I'll get

something to clean you up."

She smiles up at me, her cheeks still pink, and her eyes shiny with happiness. God, I love this girl.

Love her so much that I'd risk losing my best friend for a chance at forever with her.

If only I could have it all.

TWENTY-SEVEN

Belle

Yet another rejection. I toss my phone to the side after disconnecting from my voicemail. What the hell is it about me that makes people so wary to hire me? What irks more is when the damn people have the audacity to tell me I "don't have enough experience."

What the hell? How on earth is an eighteen-year-old supposed to get experience if nobody will hire them? I want a job to get my freedom. I need money to pay for a car, or to save for a trip overseas. I need money if I hope to ever start my own tattoo business and live with Zeus.

My chest tightens at the thought of him; two days have passed since he dropped me home. Two days with him busy working and setting up his house, and me stuck here without an excuse to get away to see him.

Fuck him living too far away to walk. Fuck Cerise for being unemployed as well and never giving me a break.

She's there when I get up, watching me from the back porch while she smokes her cigarette and has her coffee. There during the day no matter what I do—she's always two steps behind me, lurking in the shadows. I mean, damn, I took the trash out yesterday and turned back for the house to find her standing in the middle of the backyard pretending to be admiring the flowers.

She hates flowers.

I might not remember a lot from when I was young, but I'll never forget her taking the bouquet Dad bought her when I was little and throwing it in the kitchen sink for him to "sort out later."

"Problem?" She nods to where I tossed my phone, a wine in her hand.

It's half nine in the morning.

"Dad still in bed?" He sleeps in later and later these days; the night shift wreaks havoc on his body clock.

"Yeah." Cerise drifts into the room, stopping to rest a hip against the armchair. "I'm having friends over tonight."

"That so?" I collect my phone, ready to leave when she stalls me with her calculated response.

"I haven't seen Jodie in years, so I figured I might as well ask Zeus too, you know, for old times' sake." She smirks when I meet her eye. "Get the old gang back together."

"That ship has sailed, Cerise."

"Oh I don't know." She pauses to take a drink. "Everybody hits a rough patch sometimes. Look at your father and me. True love never dies."

The words sit on the tip of my tongue: *he doesn't love you*. Dad's lonely, that's all. Lonely and desperate.

Zeus... well, what could I say about that? *Does he still*

love Jodie at all? He was hurt when he found out what she did. And really, they only split up a few months ago, right before he... *fuck.* Am I a rebound?

"What do you plan to make for dinner?" I bury the thought and focus on acting indifferent.

"A barbecue is easy." She takes another swig. "You can organize that if I give you the money can't you?"

"Sure. Can I borrow your car?" Kill two birds with one stone.

Her eyes narrow, but she nods. "Of course. Make a list and I'll get you some cash."

I crush my phone in my fist, eyes trained on my mother as she leaves the room via the kitchen, her empty glass clinking as she sets it on the counter. My fingers fly over the screen as soon as she's out of sight.

B: What time are you coming over?

Zeus's reply is instant.

Z: What for? Still trying to figure out how to get you here ;)

B: Cerise mentioned you and Jodie are coming over for a barbecue. I type out the words *she thinks you two should get back together,* and then delete them. No need to put the idea in his head.

Z: First I heard of it. Still... like I'd turn down the chance to see you.

B: I miss you.

Z: Miss you more, dove. He signs off with his usual: a heart followed by the dove emoticon.

Cerise re-enters as I stand before the open fridge with my phone now switched to the notes app. She peers over my shoulder at the list and lifts her eyebrows.

"Add gherkins. Zeus loves them in a potato salad." She nods at the list. "You could make that, right? I haven't given Jodie enough notice to make one for him like she used to."

This bitch…. "Sure. I imagine it's not hard."

"It's not." She holds out a stack of twenties in her hand. "One hundred. Should be enough, right?"

How much money does she keep on her? *Hell.* "Yeah. Perfect." I take what's offered and then accept the keys she lifts with her other hand.

"No speeding, and only to the supermarket. Okay?"

"Sure." I flick my loose hair over my ears, hoping my telltale blush isn't showing.

She steps to the counter and pours herself a new wine as I slip my boots on. "Tell Dad to message me if he thinks of anything else."

"Of course."

I make it as far as the door.

"Belle?"

"Yeah?" The air in the house seems charged, the tension too high for my liking.

"Send Kate a message while you're out, huh? Maybe you could make yourself scarce for the evening."

My heart beats wildly in my chest as I swallow the anger rising to my lips and utter a simple, "Sure."

My mother knows more than she lets on, and given the fact she's back drinking again it's only a matter of time before the alcohol frays the threads of her tripwire and sets the bomb off.

If Zeus wants this to continue between us, then he better figure out a way to break it to Dad. Because right now, I'm ready to pack a bag and drive to his house on a one-way suicide mission—fuck the consequences.

If Dad can choose a life of misery with the bitch that gave birth to me, then why the hell can't I choose a life of love with the man who risks it all for me?

TWENTY-EIGHT

Zeus

Logic would blame the change in the air on the shift-ing seasons, but as I step out into my best friend's backyard, my gut tells me the unease can be attributed to something a lot more ominous.

I force myself to look toward John first, giving him a nod before I send a smile toward Jodie and Cerise, acknowledging Belle last. Her gaze is apprehensive as she reclines on a lawn chair around the fire pit John has lit.

Have to admit I feel much the same seeing my ex-wife here. Curious that she hasn't bought Eric with her.

"Glad you made it," Cerise calls out before turning to Belle. "Get your uncle a beer, would you."

My spine aches at her blatant decision to label our relationship in such a way. Belle seems to stiffen also as she rises to head for the cooler.

What started as a gathering of old friends will be war before the night is out; that much I'm sure of.

"How was the week?" John asks, seemingly oblivious as he rises and turns toward the barbecue.

"Long." I chuckle, choosing to do the usual and join him at the business end of things while the women talk.

What they talk about though, wouldn't I like to know that?

John throws a cursory glance at the women and then leans in close. "You okay with her being here?"

"Jodie?"

He nods.

I shrug one shoulder. "Sure. Where's the arsehole she's living with?"

John smirks, lifting the lid on the barbecue to prepare the plates. "Apparently *he* wasn't comfortable coming along. Not when he heard Cerise had invited you, too."

I chuckle, crossing my arms as I note the bored look on Jodie's face while Cerise talks. "Can't blame the guy, really."

I keep civil for John's sake as it is. He wants to make this work with Cerise, so as much as I can't stand the bitch, I'll play along—especially if it means a chance to see Belle.

Ah, who the fuck am I kidding? Belle is the only reason I'm here.

"Best we get this bad boy started," John says with a smile as he reaches for the tap on the gas bottle. "Belle's made some good-looking salads, and I'm famished."

The girl in question appears at my side, a freshly opened bottle in a coolie. "Here."

"Thanks." Our fingers touch as she passes it to me, and an ache like I've never known settles in my arm as I force myself to pull back.

I want to wrap an arm around her waist and pull to my side, where she belongs. I want to kiss those pink lips until they're swollen and blushed. I want to fucking bite her shoulder at the base of her neck and mark her so that no other fucker looks twice at her.

Jesus. Get a grip.

"It's been quiet without you here," John admits as he fires the elements to life.

I pull my gaze from Belle's retreating arse and smile. "Didn't realise I was that much of a noisy housemate."

"Not particularly." He nods toward his daughter. "But she doesn't talk nearly as much either, so it's as though I've lost the two of you."

"Her and Cerise still not getting along?" I lift the bottle to my lips, aiming for indifference.

He frowns and takes a moment to answer. "No."

Silence hangs thick between us as John reaches for the packages of meat set on the side of the grill. He tears them open, arranging the sausages across the plate first. Jodie avoids eye contact, twisting to give me her back as I shift my focus to the women. Cerise, however... that bitch watches me like a hawk as I lean against the side of house and take another pull of my beer.

Belle is nowhere to be seen.

The whole thing is fucked. I'm surrounded by so-called friends, and yet it feels as though I'm stranded in the middle of a minefield.

"Shoot," John exclaims from beside me. "Could you

nip indoors and grab the tray to put this on when it's done?"

"Yeah, sure." I set my beer down on the side of the barbecue and head for the house.

Cerise eyes me the whole way while my ex-wife continues to chat, seemingly oblivious to the daggers being thrown my way.

I find Belle in the kitchen, chopping fresh tomatoes. She stills as I walk in, her shoulders visibly relaxing. "We have to be careful."

"Hello to you, too."

Her knife lifts and she gestures outside with a flick of her wrist. "I think she's onto us."

"I think so too." Makes me worry if Belle can sense it too. What's the woman said to her?

Belle sucks in a sharp breath as I grab her jeans by the pocket and yank her toward me. Where I stand, we're out of line of the windows that overlook the backyard, out of sight of the buzzard waiting for its kill.

"Can't sleep right without you under the same roof," I murmur against her neck.

She leans into me, her hand held out to the side with the knife still in her grasp. "I hate being so far away from you."

"It had to happen." I couldn't stay at John's forever—especially with Cerise back. "It was only ever temporary, dove."

"I want permanent with you, though." She frowns, her eyes searching mine. "I want to live with you."

I can't hear any more, not when my own heart echoes the same sentiments. She sighs against my mouth as I claim her with the kiss that's been on my mind since I dropped her home midweek. I want to come home to this every day, to walk in the door and kiss my woman so that she knows how much I've missed her.

I want this. I want it now.

I want *her* now.

"I can't do this," I whisper, my forehead pressed to hers as I hold Belle's face in my hands. "I can't keep pretending you mean nothing, that I don't look at you and want to touch you, that I don't want to make every moment we get together count."

"So, let's tell them."

If only it were that simple. "Not tonight, dove. We will, but not tonight." My thumbs grow wet, and I pull away to find tears cutting a path down her cheeks. "Baby, what's wrong?"

"She wants to get you back together with Jodie." Belle frowns. "That's why Cerise organised this."

She has nothing to worry about. "She's delusional," I say with a smile. "Jodie's happy with that arsehole, now. She's moved on."

Yet the words don't seem to convince Belle, her frown growing deeper. "Do you though?"

"Do I what?"

"Still love her?"

Jesus. That's what she thinks? "No." I stroke my thumb across her cheek, wiping away the fresh tears.

"Why would you even think that?"

"Because you only just split." Belle pulls from my hold, resuming chopping the tomatoes as she talks. "You were upset about it, when you found out about her cheating on you. I just figured…."

"What?" Because whatever her mind came up with, she's got it arse about face.

"That I was a rebound."

"Jesus, dove. Fuck no." I step beside her, not giving a single fuck if anyone—Cerise especially—can see us as I reach for her chin and turn her face toward me. "Jodie and I were done a long time ago. It's just neither of us wanted to face the truth. I love you. *You*, Belle. I've loved you for a long time."

"You can love more than one person." Her eyes search mine.

"In more than one way," I stress. "I love your father, I loved my sister, and yeah, I love Jodie because she was a part of my life for so long, but you?" I smile, releasing her chin from my grip. "Baby, you're something that I've never felt so deep before, something nobody can match."

Belle steps away, returning to her task. "It hurts living without you," she tells the tomatoes that die under her assault. "It hurts waking up every day wondering if this is the one where I lose you."

"Why the fuck would you?" I cross my arms; frustrated that she needs to be reminded constantly how deep this runs between us.

"Because you said it yourself." She pauses to look me in the eye, and the ache in her words damn near cripples me. "What we have can't last. There are ways for people to tear us apart if they really wanted to. What we're doing here, it's not normal. It might not be wrong, but it isn't exactly right either. It's dangerous." She sighs, setting the knife down to place her hand on my arm, out of view of the others. "One of us is going to get hurt, and I don't know if I could handle being the one that is, especially if you were the one to do it."

"So stop worrying about it." I hook my fingers in the waist of her jeans to pull her hips to mine. "Because I've got no intentions of hurting you. Ever."

TWENTY-NINE

Belle

"Can I give you a hand?" Jodie steps into the kitchen where I clean up after dinner.

Dad sits outside with Cerise and Zeus, the three of them talking around the fire pit. Zeus kept his distance throughout the meal, barely including me in conversation. If he hadn't stolen those earlier minutes with me in the kitchen, I'd almost think it's over in his mind.

But it's not. He seems determined not to let me go, even if his common sense is screaming at him to do so. And that's what's so hard to process when he says he's not ready to tell Dad yet.

"Help would be appreciated. Thanks." I smile at Jodie as I continue to scrub.

She lifts the dishtowel from the handle of the oven and picks up one of the pots I've just washed. "How have you been?"

I catch her eye as I start on the barbecue tools, wary. She's never liked me all that much; I don't think Jodie is the maternal kind, to be honest. Still, her concern seems genuine as she swirls the checked towel around the base of the pot.

"Okay."

"Your dad said you're trying to find work."

"Yeah." I focus on a stubborn grease stain. "I'm not having much luck though."

"Don't give up." She offers a smile as she sets the dry pot aside. "It'll come." Jodie appears to be thinking over her next question as she lifts the next pot. "Are you saving for anything in particular?"

"Yeah. Either an overseas trip, or equipment to set myself up as a self-employed tattoo artist once I've done an apprenticeship."

"That sounds interesting." She lifts both brows. "And how does that fit in with Zeus?"

Ice washes through my veins, head to toe, as my heart catapults into overdrive. "Excuse me?"

"I asked how your plans fit in with Zeus's," she repeats carefully. "I'm not blind, Belle. There's something going on between you two, isn't there?"

Have we been that obvious? "I don't know what you're talking about."

She sighs, setting the pot aside to wring the towel around her hand. Jodie's gaze drifts to the darkened yard, only the flicker of the fire visible. "Cerise has figured it out too. Been asking me all sorts of questions to try and trip me up. I think she figures if I'm on side, if I disapprove too then she can stir up some shit with your father." Jodie chuckles as my stomach ties itself in irreversible knots. "She forgets we've been friends for over twenty years; I know how she operates."

"She doesn't like me," I admit for fuck knows what reason. "Which is so weird because she's my mother, you know?"

Jodie nods. "She had a rough time when you were young, and to be honest, I don't think she ever made that bond with you."

"I feel as though it's all my fault." I set the tools on the counter to be dried. "I've always wondered what I did wrong for her to leave me."

"You didn't do anything," Jodie says on a sigh. "And Zeus saw that too." She turns face-on to the window, staring off into the black as she absently dries the barbecue tool. "It made me mad, how much time he'd spend with you. I resented you for a long time."

Her admission shocks me. What the hell do I say to that?

"I was jealous," she continues. "Jealous that he found the love with you that I never had."

My hands tingle, my legs growing weaker with every reference she makes to the current relationship Zeus and I have. "I never knew."

"He had with you what he missed out on," she muses, focus on the tool in her hand. "And what I missed out on." She looks up, hurt in her eyes as she locks gazes with me. "You know we tried for ten years to have kids, right?"

I shake my head. "I never knew you tried for so long."

"We couldn't do it. Gave up. And I got angry with you,

because he had a surrogate and I couldn't look at you without resenting what I didn't have." Jodie sets the towel and tool down, turning to face me.

I freeze as she takes my wet hands in hers.

"I'm sorry, Belle." She shakes my hands once, as though to drive her conviction home. "I'm sorry I took that out on you."

"Why are you telling me this now?" I whisper.

Don't get me wrong, it's amazing to hear and I respect the hell out of her for having the guts to admit she was wrong. But why now? What inspired her to confess after eighteen years?

"I'm telling you," she says, squeezing my hands. "Because I've seen the look in Zeus's eye when he glances your way. You guys might think you're sneaking time when nobody else is around, but it's a little suspicious that he seeks out time to talk with you alone so often." She smiles. "I've seen the change in him since he's been here. And although I don't necessarily agree with it, I can't deny you've done good things for him."

"I have?" It always feels as though he's doing everything for me, as though I lean on him far too heavily. To hear I give back without knowing it....

"He loves you, and he's fiercely protective of you." She chuckles. "I learnt that when I said a few harsh things about you that were out of line."

Her hold on my hands slowly morphs from awkward to something a lot more comfortable. I respect Jodie, for telling me this, and for seeing the truth of what Zeus and

I are, for setting her preconceptions aside to recognise two people who are good for each other.

Who truly love each other.

"You," she says firmly, shaking my hands once more, "need to watch out for your mother. She will tear you to shreds the first chance she can get to drive a wedge between you and your father." Her lips tilt in a sad smile. "I'll keep your secret, but you need to talk to Zeus and figure out where you're going from here. John needs to know."

"I've said that to him already."

She smiles again, and then wraps her arms around my shoulders to pull me in for a hug. It's unexpected, yet warm all at the same time.

"You've got a good head on your shoulders, Belle. Ride this out, and you and Zeus will do just fine."

THIRTY

Zeus

"Must feel strange being on your own now," Cerise says. "Big old empty house, all to yourself."

I glance at John, who watches the two of us with interest as he takes a sip of his beer.

"I kind of got used to being alone, what with having a prison cell to myself for so long and all."

She smirks. "Of course. I forgot you were inside Her Majesty's establishment." Her gaze flicks to the back of the house as Belle and Jodie step outside. "What was it for this time?"

Tension coils in my gut as the two women walk toward the fire. Who'd know what the fuck Jodie said to her while they were alone? *Jesus*. I can't protect Belle from everything, but lately it seems as though I haven't protected her from anything.

"Assault," I absently answer Cerise as she shifts on her seat.

Bitch thinks she's digging a nice grave for me, I can tell. She wastes her time though; John's voiced enough times that he understands what I did. She won't turn him against me for this.

I catch Belle's eye.

Maybe she'll turn him against me for her, though?

"Another bar brawl, I'm guessing," Cerise continues, unaware she's not the centre of attention anymore. "Remember those days, Jodie?"

My ex-wife looks across the flames at me as the two women get settled, and smiles. "I do."

I know that look; that tilt of her lips. It's the same one she'd give me in the old days when some arsehole started an argument he couldn't finish down at the local; the one that says, "I have your back."

"You were such a brute," Cerise remarks with a forced laugh. "Poor John would try to keep up, but he was no match for an Islander such as yourself."

Back the fuck up. "What did you say?" I narrow my eyes on her.

She tilts her head, eyes as dead as the night as she simply states, "Everybody knows you island folk are a bunch of savages when it comes down to it."

"Cerise...," John warns.

"What?" She acts surprised. "Everyone knows I'm right."

Belle picks up a stick and pokes it in the flames, her jaw hard. Jodie sighs beside her. *Classic Cerise.* She's always been like this, with a mouth bigger than her common decency.

"It wasn't a bar fight," I state flatly.

"Oh, really?"

265

"He beat the hell out of his sister's husband," John fills in as he stares into the fire.

We're all over the conversation; it's nothing new for any of us. Only for Cerise, but I guess that's what she gets for deciding to spend the last ten years elsewhere. Walk away, and you miss a few things.

"Huh. I'm guessing that made things awkward between you and your sister."

"I wouldn't know," I bite.

"Is she not talking to you anymore?" Cerise uncorks her third bottle of wine for the night.

"She's can't. She's dead."

Her hands still, neck of the bottle to the lip of her glass. "That's a shame."

Damn right it is. The only thing I regret about the whole incident is that Sefina never knew what I did for her. What tears me up the most though, is that it was too little, too late. I should have done it to the arsehole the first time he laid a hand on her, not when he struck her for the final time.

"Oh well. Let's not ruin the night, huh?" Cerise sets her bottle down, immediately guzzling half the glass she's just poured.

"I thought you were managing that just fine on your own," Belle pipes up from the far side of the fire.

She continues to prod her stick into the flames, letting it set alight and then smothering it out on the lawn before repeating the action.

"Belle," John warns. "Let it be."

"No." Her brow furrows despite the fact she refuses to look at anyone. "Ever since Cerise got here, all she's done is stir shit."

Jodie reaches across and rests a hand on Belle's knee. "When do you get your exam results, Belle?"

"January." She finally looks up, choosing to stare at her father.

John matches her gaze, a silent conversation going down between the two while Jodie does her best to defuse the situation further.

"What subjects did you have?"

Belle rattles off the list, slowly succumbing to the question and dropping her frustration. I relax also, teetering on a knife's edge when it comes to how defensive I can get before we look too obvious.

"What's the attraction then?" Cerise leans in close, her wine precariously close to ending up on the ground as it skims the rim of her glass. "Have you always favoured them young, or is this some new fetish you picked up from your friends in prison?"

"Get out of my face, Cerise."

John's gaze flickers across from where he'd been involved in conversation with Jodie and Belle.

"Can't just be the tight pussy," she says with a slight giggle. "Then again, I suppose Jodie's is ruined after whoring herself around while you were incarcerated."

She's drunk. That's all it is. Drunk, and unable to filter her goddamn mouth.

"You should tell John," she instructs, stabbing her

glass toward him. "While we're all here."

"Are you finished?" I turn to face her, and she reels back.

"Only looking out for my daughter's best interests." One perfectly sculpted eyebrow lifts.

"Did it take you ten years to figure out how to do it?" I snap. "Because you haven't quite got the knack yet, love."

"You couldn't let him go, could you?" Cerise's top lip curls, her disgust for me clear as the conversation across the fire stalls. "Always fucking there. Always wanting his time." She jabs her glass toward me again, before thinking better of spilling all her wine and downing it in one go.

"Is the truth finally coming out?" I bait.

She smirks. "At least one of us has the balls to be honest."

I could leave. I could get up right now and walk away. But where would that leave Belle? What would happen then? Who could say what this bitch would do, what she'd say, if I wasn't around to defend myself?

Not that I have a lot to defend against when it's most likely all the truth. I find Belle seated with her arms across herself, eyes wide as Cerise continues.

"What do you think John would say when he finds out what was going down under his roof? Or should I say *who* was going down?" The bitch laughs at her joke, while John shifts closer to the two of us.

"What are you two talking about?"

"Nothing," I say at the same time as Cerise chirps, "Zeus has a confession."

"Z?"

I shrink under the intensity of John's watchful eye. He appears apprehensive, wary, and what hurts most is he has every right to be.

"I think perhaps, Cerise, you've had enough for one night." Jodie rises from her seat beside Belle and circumvents the fire. "Let's head indoors, huh?"

"No." Cerise yanks her arm away from Jodie's outstretched hand. "We're getting to the best part of a bonfire: truth or dare."

"Jesus, Cerise. What are we? Ten?" I make a move to stand, but John's question stills me.

"Is there something I should know?" He glances between the three of us. "How about we skip the school-yard games and just cut to the heart of it like adults?"

Fuck. I chance a look at Belle. She's frozen, her face pale even in the light of the fire, as she watches the shit hit the fan.

"Maybe there'd be a better time," Jodie suggests.

I shift my gaze to her and frown. Why is my ex-wife trying to protect me? Exactly how much does she know?

"When would that be?" John asks. "When people have had time to fabricate excuses and lies?" He shakes his head. "Out with it. Let's get this shit on the table so we can move on."

Only I don't think there is any moving on.

Cerise twists her head from side to side as she looks

between Jodie and me. An exasperated sigh leaves her lips. "Hell. If you two won't, then I'll up and say it." Jodie and I scramble to distract and disarm, yet our feeble protests are drowned out by one simple statement from John's bitch of an ex. "Zeus is fucking Belle."

Jesus. "Are you crazy?" I snap.

"Pardon?" John's grip on his bottle tightens.

"She's drunk," Jodie excuses with a nervous giggle. "Come on, Cerise. Up we go."

Cerise shakes off Jodie's touch and dives straight for the jugular. "Did it not seem strange to you that a grown man wasn't the slightest bit put out by having to babysit while you were at work, John?"

"We're not fucking," I state as John looks my way. The words sound disgusting to my own ears, so God only knows how this sounds to him.

"Belle?" His gaze stays locked on me as he summons his daughter into the fray. "What do you have to say about this?"

Shit. Hopefully it's too dark for those damn ears of her to be noticeable. Then again, she's not exactly lying if she says no; we haven't had sex yet. *Yet.* Fuck me. There's the problem right there—I can't stop wanting her, even as it all blows up right before our faces.

"Are you seriously asking me if her bullshit is true?" Belle snaps.

"Neither of you reacted as though it was some joke," John points out. "If the idea was that far-fetched I would have expected us all to laugh it off. But both of you sat there like stunned mullets, waiting to see what would happen next."

Shit, shit, fuck. "Maybe we were simply all as shocked as you that Cerise would come up with such a vile thing to accuse me of."

"Hardly an accusation if it's true, is it?" She tips her glass back, sucking the dregs dry.

John turns to her, hand flexing on his bottle. "What evidence do you have?"

"I can't believe you're entertaining—"

"Let her speak, will you?" John holds a hand up toward me.

I catch Jodie's eye as she chews on her bottom lip. She and I are having words after this.

Cerise grins, locking gazes with Belle before she wobbles to her feet and stumbles toward the house. "Everybody sit tight," she booms with a giggle. "This night is about to get *real* interesting."

What the fuck could she have that proves Belle and I have been intimate? We were always so careful... weren't we?

"Belle. Get over here." John jerks his head to Cerise's vacated seat. "Come sit where I can see you both."

"John—"

"Let it lie, Jodie." He narrows his gaze on her as she flexes her grip on the back of the seat. "This has nothing to do with you."

Belle drops into the chair, and my curiosity piques when Jodie rests her hands on Belle's shoulders in a comforting gesture.

"We went through this years ago," John says to his daughter. "We discussed this, and I thought we buried the ridiculous idea then and there."

What the hell?

"We did," Belle murmurs, chancing a look my way.

My chest tightens at the regret in her eyes; she hid something from me, something that's proving to be pretty fucking important.

Her fucking dad already knew how she feels about me.

"So?" John asks, setting his beer down. "What do you have to say? What's your mother going to bring out here?"

"She's not my mother."

"Unfortunately, the fact she gave birth to you means that she is, no matter how much you two don't get along." John sighs, dragging a hand over his face. "If you want the upper hand on her, now's the time to tell me what the fuck is going on."

Belle looks down in contemplation, which gives John ample time to glare in my direction. I could shrug, but that would seem as though I'm trying too hard to play it cool. I could also open my mouth to protest again, but if there's one thing I learnt in the slammer, it's that guilty birds sing the loudest.

So I do nothing, instead staring into my best friend's eyes and hoping that he remembers I've always had his back, ever since we were kids. I'd never do something to knowingly hurt him, and if I did, he'd better bet it was because I thought it was worth the pain.

"Nothing to say?" John asks Belle when she remains silent.

"I get the feeling you wouldn't listen to me, anyway."

"The floor is yours," John says with a sweep of his hand. "I'm listening."

"But are you hearing me?" Belle asks as her mother drops off the back porch a little too sharply and reaches for the rail to steady herself.

"Everybody comfortable?" she asks as she returns to the circle.

Mother and daughter spare no love as they stare each other down, the hate almost palpable.

"I thought I'd tidy up after Zeus moved his things out," Cerise says. "Naturally, since I had the vacuum out I did the whole house... including Belle's room."

Belle's eyes narrow, her lips pressed tight as she watches her mother's performance. Jodie tightens her hold, sensing the knife's edge we're on same as I do. If looks could kill, Belle would have her mother dead and buried by now. But I get the feeling in this moment she wants to do a hell of a lot more damage than just a scathing glare.

My girl looks ready to kill.

"I picked up your school bag to move it aside, Belle, and this fell out." Even in her inebriated state, Cerise manages to toss the pieces of the empty morning-after pill packet into Belle's lap with true dramatic flair. "Care to explain?"

"What is it?" John asks.

Belle leans forward to toss the pieces in the fire. "Nothing."

Yet her father halts her with a hand to her wrist. John peels the largest pieces out of her grasp and examines them while the rest of us wait with bated breath.

"Is this...?"

"Emergency contraceptive," Cerise announces smugly.

I groan and bury my face in my hands. This woman.... She has no idea how close she was to pulling her "great reveal" off, and instead she's unearthed a painful experience her daughter would rather forget.

"Belle?" John asks, lifting the scraps between them. "Explain."

She looks my way, her brow pinched. I give a small nod, letting her know it's time to tell the truth. Even if that does still get me in the shit for keeping secrets.

"You remember when I had food poisoning?" Belle asks, returning her gaze to John.

"Yeah."

"It wasn't an upset stomach from food. It was a side effect of that." She points to the remnant of the box. "I made a mistake at Scott's party."

John's nostrils flare, his jaw hard as he looks off into the darkened backyard. Cerise frowns, her master plan unravelling before her eyes.

"Zeus picked you up that night, didn't he?" John asks.

Great. He's resorted to acting as though I'm not here. I frown at Cerise as she smirks, clearly thinking she's still on a winning streak. All fool her.

"Yes. He did."

"You fucking dog," John spits as he launches out of his seat.

"It wasn't him," Belle yells, halting her father before I'm forced to fight back. "It wasn't Zeus, for fuck's sake."

I lift my hands and tip my head to the side. "Easy now, brother."

"It was Scott." Belle's voice cracks.

Jodie massages Belle's shoulders, hands where I wish mine were. "It's okay, honey. You don't have to justify this witch hunt." My ex-wife reminds me what it was that drew me to her all those years ago as she turns her attention to Cerise. "Satisfied?" Her face is a storm as she lets go of Belle and rounds the seat to advance on her former friend. "Is this what you came back for? To accuse people of wild lies and tear your flesh and blood apart? Do you feel vindicated, you callous cow? Do you? Are your daughter's tears worth it?"

"Oh, lay off, you cunt," Cerise bites back. "You know as well as I do that there's something going on between these two." She points wildly between Belle and me while John stands in the midst looking like a lost sheep. "It's disgusting, and it needs to stop."

"What the fuck is going on here?" John bellows. "Will one of you fucking tell me the truth?"

"Yeah, Belle," Cerise sneers, leaning around Jodie.

"Where's the rest of the story?"

"What part?" my girl asks. "The part where the jerk told me he had a condom on, but lied? The part where I was too drunk to know the difference? Where I thought for once somebody actually wanted me, because you know, after my *mother* walked out on me I kind of figured there must have been something about me that pushed people away." Belle rises, moving to stand behind Jodie, my ex-wife the only thing stopping these two from ripping each other apart. "Or do you want to hear about how Zeus wanted to turn the car around and deal to the arsehole once he figured out something wasn't right? Or where I told him to leave it? Or the best part of all: the next day when my best friend told me I was asking for it if I was too stupid to believe that a guy would have the decency to use protection?" The raw depth of her emotion shines its truth on her face, the firelight catching the moisture as Belle's tears track a path down her cheeks.

Yet she cries out of anger, her fists curled in frustration. And I can't do a fucking thing to make her feel better. I have to sit here like a grade-A arsehole while she hurts, because I'm too afraid of the consequences.

Talk about a moral dilemma.

"Why didn't you say anything?" John asks, pulling Belle toward him.

She wraps her arms around her father, and sobs. "I didn't want you to hate me."

"Ssh, baby. I could never hate you."

The look on Cerise's face would be satisfying if the woman wasn't an unpredictable livewire. She may have lost the battle, but this woman never gives up on the war. Jodie lets out a sigh as Cerise turns for the house and leaves the fireside while John consoles his distraught daughter.

I rise to follow her, yet Jodie's hand against my chest grounds my irrational thoughts. There's nothing to be gained by poking the bear. Not when I've so narrowly missed being flayed alive.

"Not now, Z."

I sigh, grateful for what she did to try and help. "Thank you."

Her eyes crinkle at the corners as she searches mine, a small shake to her head. "No. Don't thank me." Her lips press together as she huffs out her nose. "Just you promise that you'll set things right and let John know the truth. Soon."

"How did you...?"

"I was married to you for sixteen years, Zeus. I know a thing or two about what you do, how you look when you're in love."

I can't look her in the eye. We wasted so many years pretending what we had could be salvaged. Years she could have spent finding the right man for her. Maybe she went about it the wrong way, but I guess my prison term gave her the permission she needed to move on. How else could she have made me face the truth when I was so used to living a lie that I thought what we had was what a partnership is supposed to be?

It wasn't until Belle that I've learnt what it's like to *really* love somebody. I loved Jodie, but I never needed her. And that right there is the difference.

When I thought of life without Jodie, I got angry. When I imagine life without Belle, I can't see there being any point to mine.

"I don't know how to do it," I admit as I look across to where John and Belle talk.

"Like a Band-Aid," Jodie muses. "Quick, so it hurts less." She sighs, knocking her elbow into me to grab my attention. "The longer you leave it, the harder it's going to be for him to take."

"I know." That thought runs through my mind every damn day. And yet....

"Do it tonight, while the topic is fresh." Jodie glances toward the house. "I'll get Cerise into bed; she'll pass out soon if past performance is anything to go by, and then you and John have a quiet word alone while I keep Belle busy."

"No. Not tonight." I need time to think about how to tell him. Time to figure out what the best words to use are.

Time to warn Belle.

"Don't delay the inevitable, Zeus. If you mean well by this girl, then you'll do the right thing."

If my heart constricts any tighter, I don't know if it'll still be able to beat. "I'm going to ruin everything."

"Not as much as you will if he finds out about it from someone other than you two."

THIRTY-ONE

Belle

I can't believe the bitch's audacity to fucking stand there in front of everyone and throw my dirty secrets around for the group to see. Show me another mother who'd be so damn heartless, because I swear to God mine is the only one who could pull off that kind of stunt and still think she's in the right.

"I suppose you're feeling smug with yourself this morning?"

I catch Cerise's eye as she shakes a cigarette out of her packet. "Had hoped you'd still be passed out in bed and I might be rewarded with a quiet breakfast alone, but"—I nod toward the coffee in her hand—"I guess I'm not that lucky."

She rests a hand against the doorframe and huffs a small laugh. "He's no good for you. You understand that, right?"

I match her critical eye. "Somehow I don't think that's what you're concerned about, is it?" In fact, none of this makes sense. "What *do* you want to get out of it all, *Mother*?"

I'm met with silence as she regards me head to toe. "You've grown into quite the perfect little princess, haven't you?"

"You almost sound jealous."

"Since the minute you came home with me from the hospital, you were all your father could talk about. 'My beautiful Belle' this, and 'my little girl' that." She makes a choking noise. "Ugh. It's sickening."

"It might come as a shock, Cerise, but that's what a parent is supposed to do; love their child through rose-tinted glasses."

I turn my back to her and pull a mug from the cupboard. The sooner she heads outside to have her lung dart, the sooner I get my coveted peace and quiet.

"You were a twin," she drops so damn suddenly that I almost don't catch it. "I never told you that, and I'm guessing your dad kept the secret all these years too." My heart thunders as she makes a small "hmph" and then continues. "We didn't tell you about her because your father thought you might get survivor's guilt. I guess he didn't say anything after I left because, well, how do you break the fact you've lied to your kid their entire life to them?"

Apparently without an ounce of care.

I turn, spoon in hand, and cock my head. "I was a twin?"

"She was stillborn."

The stainless handle digs into my palm. I guess that explains some of why I've never felt complete, as though

281

a part of me is missing. For the first time, I find what looks like genuine regret on my mother's face, and I have no idea what to do about it. You can't erase years of neglect with one heartfelt moment, especially when with my mother it has to be delivered with an ulterior motive.

"Why are you telling me this now?" I whisper.

"Because you need to know."

"Why?" What does it have to do with me and Zeus? With Dad? Anyone?

"You asked me why I'm doing this," she says coolly as she reaches for the door handle. "So I thought I'd tell you."

I count my breaths, pacing the air reaching my lungs as I wait on her to continue. *I had a twin.*

Yet she doesn't say another word, instead slipping quietly through the door to enjoy destroying the rest of the morning with her toxins.

My phone vibrates in my pocket as the kettle sings. I set the teaspoon down on the counter and retrieve the device, my jaw slack and my eyes still glazed.

Z: Morning, dove.

The message is laid over a selfie Zeus has taken lying in bed, shirtless. *My favourite.*

B: Hey, you. :*

He left last night while I was still talking with Dad,

asking Jodie to let me know he'd be in touch. I guess he didn't want it to look too suspicious if he hung about to talk with me alone. I get that. It still burned though.

Z: How's the battlefield this morning?

I glance out the kitchen window as a wisp of smoke floats away on the breeze above Cerise's head.

B: Full of surprises.

Z: How so?

B: Do you know I had a twin at birth?

The absence of a reply is duly noted as I finish making my Milo and lean a hip against the counter. I stare at my phone, mug cradled in my hands. The screen remains black for what seems like an age before it lights up with Zeus's name.

"Hey."

"Can you talk?"

"Sure."

He sighs, making me long to reach down the line and touch him. "I knew."

"Did everyone?"

"Yeah." He hesitates, waiting for me to say more, but continues when I don't. "Your dad made the call never to tell you. In hindsight, it might have helped you to understand why your mum is the way she is."

Cerise stamps out her smoke. "She resents me, doesn't she?"

"It seems that way. Yes."

Knowing this explains so much, and yet, it justifies nothing. "I still hate her."

"You don't mean that."

She enters the kitchen and sets her empty mug in the sink, eyeing me as she does. "I do."

"We need to talk, dove."

"What about?" His worried tone sets me on edge.

"Us. The future."

Cerise leaves the kitchen, heading toward the bedroom. I wait a minute to ensure she's far enough away before whispering, "Are you home today?"

"Plan to be."

"I'll see you soon, then."

I don't give Zeus the opportunity to talk me out of it before I hang up. Cerise's car keys sit on the end of the counter, helping me form a plan in my head of how this could go. Snatching them up, I head down to my room and grab a sweater, toe my boots on, and visit the bathroom. No sound comes from Dad's room; the bitch has probably crawled back into bed and fallen asleep again with him.

My heart drums in my ears as I step outside, hammering with my pulse as I start her car and let it idle out of the driveway. The fuel gauge shows half a tank, which is lucky, because I didn't bring any money for petrol.

I drive the short trip across town with my heart in my throat, and regret deep in my veins. This is it: I'm choosing Zeus over my family, and I couldn't care less about it. They fucking lied my entire life to me. And to top it all off, Dad took Cerise back after every goddamn thing she's done. He made her a priority over me.

With Zeus is where I'm supposed to be. With Zeus is where my future lies. I'm ready to shake the covers off and let this love see the light of day.

I pull in his driveway and find him seated on the front step, waiting. Yet no smile greets me as I step out of the car. He doesn't so much as stand to meet me when I approach.

"They rang."

"What?"

"They rang," he repeats. "Your dad, and Cerise. They heard you leave."

Shit. "So?"

"So they know where you went."

"I could have gone to Kate's—"

"They rang there first."

Double shit. "Or the shops."

"Belle...."

No *dove,* no sweetness and care. Just Belle. Just the stupid little girl always making mistakes.

"I said you weren't here," Zeus explains, finally rising. "Which wasn't a lie, because you weren't then. But they'll figure it out."

"So then today is the day," I say with raw determination.

His face tells me otherwise.

"It's not?"

Zeus reaches out, pulling me to him with a hand on my shoulder. "That's what I wanted to talk to you about."

"Right." My energy wanes as he leads me inside.

I step into his arms and inhale his familiar scent as he sighs. "I want to wait until you've moved out of your dad's place before we tell them."

"What?" He doesn't try to stop me as I spin out of his hold. "That could be a year away." There's the bond on a rental to save, not to mention money for furniture....

And I don't even have a job yet.

"It would be less of a blow if he thinks you made the decision while you weren't under his roof, don't you think?" He tucks his hands in the back pockets of his jeans.

I've never seen the man look so much like a nervous boy.

"He's not stupid," I say. "He'll put two and two together and realise this has been going on since before last night's near miss."

"Still, it'll be easier to deal with then. You'll be almost, if not, twenty."

I roll my eyes. "Because that's so much better than eighteen."

"Belle. Don't be a smartarse."

"I can't help it." I march into the living room and flop

on the couch in true dramatic teenager style. "You've just told me you want to hide me away like a filthy little secret for *years*. It feels as though you're looking for reasons to push me away." He doesn't say a thing, prompting me to spin on the seat and look back at him. "Zeus?"

"You haven't had a chance to date other guys yet," he says with a frown. "What if you think this is enough for you, but it's not? You might be young and able to move on, but I'm not. This *is* it for me, and if that's going to be thrown back in my face, then I want to know it now."

I scowl at the big idiot, repositioning myself on my knees with my hands braced on the back of the sofa. "Don't project your insecurities onto me, Zeus."

"I'm not."

"You are. You're telling me your greatest fear is being rejected, and you're laying out options for me on how to do it."

He lifts his chin and pierces me with his intense stare. "And what are your insecurities?"

"That I'm not enough for the trouble I cause. That the next best thing will come along, and she'll be a lot easier, a lot less drama, and you'll jump ship."

His shoulders heave with the deep breath he draws through his nose. "You think I'd step out on you?"

"Have you?"

A smile tilts one side of his lips. "Who's projecting insecurities now?"

"I would have said I'm being possessive, jealous

even. But okay." I shrug.

He stalks toward me, stopping to cup my face in his hands. "Fuck, I missed you."

"It's been less than a day," I tease.

"Since I saw you, maybe. But it's been a hell of a lot longer than that since I could touch you without having to overthink everything first."

"I love you," I remind him. "Don't push me away because you're scared."

Those three words feel so much more important in that moment. A deep unease takes root in my gut; something is off, and I can't put my finger on what. Instinct tells me he brought up this crazy idea of waiting out of sheer panic, thanks to last night's drama. But there's more, a reason why one near miss would spook him so bad, and I can't figure out what.

"What else is on your mind?" I ask as Zeus runs the pads of his thumbs adoringly over my cheekbones. "You're withholding."

"Did you ever wonder why Jodie and I never had kids?"

This big fool. That's what he's been worried about? "She told me," I whisper.

His hands still, those crisp blue eyes focused on mine. "She did?" A frown pulls his brow together.

"Last night. Before my mother decided to sour the mood."

"When she went inside," he says quietly, as though piecing the timeline for himself. "I wondered what she

288

was up to."

His hands fall away, but not for long. Instead, he reaches over the back of the sofa and picks me up by my waist, lifting me high into the air to clear the furniture and hold me to him. I'm weightless in his embrace; he reminds me so often how much larger than me he is, how strong.

How safe.

I wrap my legs around his waist, linking my hands behind his head. "She's accepting of us, you know. So maybe Dad would be too?"

Zeus shakes his head as I run my fingers through his lengthening hair. He says he's growing it out a little bit longer, and I can't help but wonder if that's for me.

"It's not the same, dove. Jodie isn't your parent. She has that… disassociation from it all."

"I can't hide how I feel about you forever. Especially when Dad asks why I've chosen to hang around Longdale."

"What do you mean?" He frowns, his uncertainty almost cute in that moment.

"How can I travel if it means leaving you behind?"

His arms relax as he makes a move to set me down. I tighten my legs around him, refusing to budge.

"Baby…."

"What? If you're here, then so am I."

"You can't give up your dreams for me."

"They weren't set in stone, Zeus. I thought about travel back when there was nothing here for me. Now, there is." I punctuate my words by leaning in and running my nose up the length of his.

He sighs, eyes closed, and kisses the point of my chin. "I feel as though I'm holding you back, dove. But no matter how many times I open the door to let you go, you keep getting back in that damn cage."

"Because I like being yours," I murmur against his lips.

He responds slow, and sweet at first, nipping my bottom lip between his. It doesn't take long for desire to set in and his kiss to grow hungry.

"Zeus," I say breathlessly as I kiss my way up his jaw to whisper in his ear, "take me to bed."

He growls, his hands tightening on my butt. I hold on tight as he walks us down the hallway, nestling my head into my favourite space: the point where his huge shoulder meets his neck.

We cross the threshold of the room, and I take his earlobe between my teeth to give it a quick nip before he sets me down. His eyes rove hungrily over my body as I lie on the bed before him; his strong arms braced either side of me so he can lower himself to steal another kiss.

I lose myself to the moment, savouring his taste and letting the sting of his lips bruising mine make me forget what pushed me to come here. I don't need anyone else: not a mother, a father who doesn't know himself let alone his daughter, or a so-called best friend.

I only need the man who loves me, for me to be

complete.

"Is it wrong that I want to lock you in here?" Zeus asks as he trails kisses down my neck to my chest. "Wrong that I want to come home to you every day?"

"Is it wrong that I want you to?" I stretch both arms over my head, lifting my hips as he slides his hands underneath and kisses my stomach.

"Let me taste you."

I slide my hand between us and block his path to my pussy. "Not today."

Zeus lifts his head, peering up at me across the length of my body. He cocks an eyebrow, unsure of what this means—I've never shut him down before.

I don't plan to now.

"Fuck me like you want to, Zeus." His eyes light up, the smile on his lips positively animal. "Strip me bare and make me completely yours."

"Are you sure?" His hesitation is clear.

"Certain." I coax him up me, pulling his face to mine. "I want this."

He tangles his tongue with mine, hands roaming across my flesh as I press myself into him. I want to feel so connected, so close to him that I forget where I end and he begins. I want time to pass without consequence, for nothing to matter other than who we are and who we're with.

"I'll do my best to be gentle," he whispers, kissing my shoulder. "Tell me if I'm not."

"I don't want you to be." I hold his gaze as I lift my

hips so he can strip my shorts and panties off. "I don't want you to hold back."

The smile I love so much graces his lips as he ducks his head. "Dove. If I did what I wanted to with you, you'd be feeling it for days."

"So do it," I urge. "Give me something to hold on to until I see you again."

He hesitates, kneeling between my legs. "I don't want to hurt you."

I nudge the hem of his T-shirt with my toes. "Stop worrying so much. Off."

He strips off his shirt, tossing it aside to reward me with the best view. I push up with my elbows into a seated position, my legs either side of his. Zeus watches in silence as I trace the lines of his body with my palms, tracking the detail of his tattoo with my fingertips.

"You always seem so amazed," he whispers, watching my hands. "As though you're seeing me for the first time."

"Because I can never believe it," I admit. "I never thought we'd have this, that you'd let me touch you like this."

He responds by cupping my cheek in his hand, tipping my chin with his thumb so he can place a gentle kiss to my lips. "I love it." Another kiss. "I love you."

He braces my weight with an arm behind my back and lays me down, holding himself over me with the other. I close my eyes and draw my focus in, blocking out everything but the heat of his kiss, the tickle of his touch, as he makes his way down my body.

My shirt tugs at my waist, and I open my eyes to find him smiling as he tries to pull it off. I help, shedding the fabric, and my bra straight after, tossing them aside.

I cock an eyebrow at his jeans.

He chuckles, backing off the bed to shed them and his boxers in one fell swoop. "In there." Zeus jerks his chin at the nightstand.

I roll to my side and pull the small drawer at the top open to find a brand new pack of condoms. Did he know I'd want this soon? Or was he simply hopeful? Either way, my hand shakes as I reach for it, the reality setting in.

"You okay?" His heat covers me as he prowls up the length of my body, his strong arms either side of me as I remain on my side.

I nod as he places a kiss to my shoulder. "Nervous."

"Why?"

I roll beneath him, dropping the pack on the side of the bed. "I want to be perfect for you."

"Nobody's perfect, dove." He captures my bottom lip between his. "Just do what feels right."

Do what feels right. So I do.

I surrender.

I give in as Zeus masters my body, worshipping every inch of me until I can't take another second without him as close to me as two people can be. He brings me to the brink with his fingers, the gentleness of his kiss in contrast to the strength of his hand as he leaves me writing on the bed, searching for more.

But more what? That's what frustrates me—I don't know.

"You're in control," he murmurs as he pulls his fingers from my slick channel. "You're my guide, dove."

I lie breathless as he turns away to sheath himself, so much more considerate in that moment than Scott ever was. The swell of emotions overtake me, and to my horror I start to cry. *Not now.* Oh God, what the hell will he think if I'm a teary-eyed mess?

I swipe the traitorous escapees away before Zeus notices, so in love with him in that moment that I want to suspend time and trap the warmth in my soul forever. I reach out, brushing my fingers across his back as he finishes up and looks over his shoulder at me.

"Ready?"

Those eyes. They drew me in from the start, always so piercing, so intense. But in that moment they show something new.

They show insecurity.

He's as worried as I am that he'll screw this up. Does he really think he could put me off? That anything he does could turn me away?

"I'm ready." I reach out for him, looping my arms over his shoulders as he lowers himself over me.

He hesitates, the tip of his cock brushing against my sensitive sex as he strokes the hair from my face. "I feel as though this is new for me too," he whispers. "It's never meant as much as this does right now."

"Do what feels right," I tell him with a soft smile.

He regards me with heavy-lidded eyes before leaning down and taking my mouth with his, the kiss hungry yet reverent all at once.

I moan, breaking away as he eases himself inside, careful and gentle. Zeus kisses my throat as I push my head back, lost to the giddy sensation of his length filling me, stretching me, owning me. Part of me revels in the moment, in the knowledge that we've passed this final milestone in our relationship, but a part of me also laments the loss of the anticipation, the climb to reach what we have.

All I hope is that once the appeal of the new wears off, he still loves what he has.

"Okay?" His whispered word tickles my ear as he nuzzles in to the side of my head, slowly pulling himself back out.

"Again."

Zeus starts out slow, easing my body into the rhythm before he picks up pace. I tuck my feet behind his thighs, holding him to me as he moves. My hands roam the muscles in his back, the feel of them as they work a story in itself.

I imagined a lot of things when it came to what this moment would be like, but what I took for granted is how significant each and every little detail is. I absorb them all, stowing the memories away for later so I can replay this over and over as I lie awake at night.

The way his back tightens as he lifts up on the

outward stroke.

The way his hips thrust as he pushes back in.

The feel of his breath as it washes a hot wave across my neck.

The contrast of his wet kiss as he devours the sweat on my skin.

The truth in his whispered words as he murmurs, "I love you, dove."

I cry out as my climax takes me, ripping through my languid body with enough ferocity to make every muscle clench painfully tight. And yet I still want more. I want to scream out as the intensity of the moment tears me in two, and cry as the man above pieces me back together.

So I do.

Fuck the world around us, fuck the doubts hanging on the outskirts of my mind, the worries waiting for an opportunity to sneak back in.

I live in that moment and I own it as Zeus comes apart over me, the sound of his own release music to my ears.

I love this man, and nothing or no one can ever take that away from me.

THIRTY-TWO

Zeus

If I ever had a reason to go to hell that would be worth the suffering, sex with Belle was totally it. *Not sex.* No. Making love. I've always been hesitant to use that term, thinking it was too flowery for a guy to say. But that... that was love without words. It was our bodies saying everything a dumb fuck like me can't voice despite his best efforts.

I roll my head and look at Belle as she lies beside me, arms spread as her chest heaves with her quickened breaths. She's everything I want, and yet I still don't feel as though I deserve her.

"Thirsty?"

She turns to look at me, and smiles. "Parched."

Her grin widens as I lift my hand and gently stroke the backs of my fingers along her jaw.

"What?" A nervous giggle mixes with the word.

"I want to enjoy this a bit longer." Maybe she thinks we've got away with it, but spend enough time with a person and you begin to read them like a book.

John may have chosen to leave the lie where it rested

last night; that the morning-after was from a mistake with this Scott kid, and that the only role I had to play was that of the sympathetic uncle figure.

But once he sleeps on it. Once he replays the night in his mind as he drinks his morning coffee, he'll work it out. Memories are strange like that—the more you replay them, the more you see. Like an artwork that you've walked past a thousand times, it's not until you actually stop and shut out the noise of everything around you that you see what the artist intended.

And intentional or not, Belle and I gave off plenty that proved John has reason to be suspicious of his best friend's intentions.

I push up on one elbow and lean across to place a kiss to Belle's lips. She sighs against my mouth, her eyes slipping closed as I gently cup the side of her neck. I love this girl. Love her enough to do some pretty fucking stupid things to protect her, but what scares me is that I'm coming to realise something else.

I love her enough to do what's right for her, and not for me. I love her enough to save her from the destruction my love will cause in her life.

"I'll get you that drink before you wither into dust, huh?"

She chuckles, pulling the sheet up over herself as I slide off the side of the bed. "We could order in and spend the rest of the day in bed, you know?"

"As tempting as that sounds…."

"Go on." Her eyes crinkle with her happiness. I want

to bottle it to save for later.

She'll need it.

"Maybe next time, huh?" Only there won't be a next time. Not if John does what he threatened when he phoned.

Yeah, her father called looking for her, but I only told Belle half the story. I said she wasn't here, but he knew. He always knows; he's my best friend.

"If she shows up, you call me. You hear?"

He knew she'd be here eventually. He'd had that coffee, pieced those parts of the puzzle together. He was getting warmer, and when John reaches hot... yeah.

"I don't know what the fuck Cerise thought she was doing last night, but you tell me man to man, best mate to best mate, Zeus: do I have anything to worry about?"

Of course I said no.

I tug my rugby shorts on and head out to the kitchen while Belle stretches her sore muscles out. Her satisfied moan follows me down the hallway as I scrub a hand over my face.

How did I let things get this far? How can I contemplate letting her go? *What the fuck is wrong with me?* You work to get the things you love, and once they're yours, you keep them. People don't willingly give up what makes them feel good—sane people anyway.

I pull a bottle of water from the fridge for Belle and then down what's left of my PowerAde. The bottle pops as the air rushes back in, the rattle of knuckles on the door almost lost in the noise.

Every cell in my body freezes as I stand with the empty bottle in hand and listen. Sure enough, another three raps on the door.

I set the trash down and head for the entrance. John doesn't know where I live—I made it a point not to tell him the exact address for the reason that one day I might have his daughter here without him knowing— like now. The only other person who knows where I live is….

"Jodie."

She looks up as I open the door, her brow knitted together as she rubs her forefinger and thumb together in that way I learnt over our years together meant anxiety. "Can I come in?"

"I guess. Wait here for a minute though, okay?"

"Sure." She steps inside the entrance and shuts the door behind herself as I head for Belle. "She probably needs to hear this too."

I freeze at the end of the hallway and slowly turn back to her. "Hear what?"

"Just bring the poor girl out, Z."

I step into the bedroom to find Belle half-dressed already. "I heard her voice." Worry etches the lines of her brow. "What does she want?"

"I don't know. But I'm placing bets on it being about the fact your mother's car is in my driveway."

"Shit." She tugs her jeans on and heads out to meet Jodie, sans shoes.

My girl isn't ready to leave. An almost insignificant sign, but one that I shouldn't overlook either. She's willing to fight for this.

I wish I could be confident that I can do the same. My loyalty is torn in two directions, and right now, I can't tell which is the stronger.

"Hey," Jodie greets as Belle walks into the living room, me in tow. "I came straight over."

"Why?" I ask.

"Cerise called this morning. Gave me hell about last night, wanted to know why I was backing you up." Her eyes soften as she looks to Belle. "She wouldn't let up. John caught wind, snatched the phone off her and apologised before he hung up. That's when the messaging started."

I stand stock-still, watching as my ex pulls her phone out and swipes the screen a few times before handing it to Belle.

Her gaze shifts to me as Belle drops onto a seat to read the thread. "Cerise is on the war path, Z. She's determined to destroy everything and everyone in her stupid crusade to make the damn girl pay for things that aren't her fault."

"She blames me for my twin dying, doesn't she?"

The two of us look across at Belle as she sets the phone in her lap and lifts her chin to search our expressions for the answer I'm sure she already knows.

"Cerise told her this morning," I explain.

"Yes," Jodie whispers to Belle. "I think she does

blame you."

Shit. I knew Cerise didn't handle the death well, that she struggled with motherhood at the start. John reached out after the midwife's duty of care ended and found a not-for-profit that could help with counselling for postnatal depression. Eight weeks he thought she went before he found out the truth: she'd drop Belle with Jodie and frequent the mall alone, killing time until she was due home again.

It pissed me off at the time because all that burden did to Jodie was fuel her own jealousy over the fact she didn't have a kid of her own. But I never once thought that Cerise would actually lump the blame squarely on Belle.

As if a baby has any control over what happens in the womb.

"So, what do we do?" Belle asks of Jodie as she hands me the phone to read.

I scroll back to the top of today's thread and read while the other two wait.

C: I will make damn sure you go down for this as well you sick bitch.

J: There's nothing sick about it. She's of legal age to consent.

C: Now. But how long has he groomed her? Sick fuck probably started before he went to

prison.

My gut tightens in a knot, acid burning as I realize the extent of how Belle and my relationship is viewed from the outside.

J: **Which would mean he started while we were still together. I can tell you that is NOT the case. Stop being such a bitter cow.**

C: **She's my daughter.**

J: **A fact you conveniently forgot when some big dick with an even bigger bank account bought your affection.**

C: **At least he sympathised with me. John never did.**

J: **Because you were wrong, Cerise. You were wrong to take this out on Belle.**

C: **What's changed with you? You used to hate her.**

J: **And I admit to that. But unlike you, I realised she had no part to play in my own misfortune. Unlike you, I noticed that she was happy for once. Do you know how many times that girl has been truly happy in her life?**

C: What is this? Some motherhood test?

J: Twice. And both times they related somehow to Zeus.

C: Sick arsehole is going back to prison. I'll make damn sure of it.

J: Good luck. You realise they haven't done anything illegal.

C: You realise he's out on parole? Be a shame if he fucked that up.

"She hasn't got a fucking thing on me." I put the phone to sleep and hand it back to Jodie.

"Not yet, but you better make sure you keep your nose clean. She's out for blood."

Fuck. Belle watches me intently. "It's okay, Dove. I'm doing everything I'm supposed to: check-ins, reporting change of address, staying within the area… I'm fine."

"She would do that, though."

"Without a doubt."

Jodie sighs and backs toward the door. "I'll leave you two alone to talk this out, but you need to come clean before this gets out of hand. You need John on your side, and the longer you lie to him, the more fuel you add to Cerise's fire."

"Thank you." My chest warms as Belle gives her thanks and then steps forward to take Jodie in her embrace.

The two women hug it out, Jodie murmuring her support before she lets Belle go. Who would have thought things could change this drastically in the space of a few months?

"I better go," Jodie says with a thumb pointed toward the door. "Eric is expecting me for lunch."

I cringe at the mention of that fucker's name. Guess not every wound heals that quickly.

"Let me know how you get on. Message me, Z."

"Yeah, of course." I lean my arse into the back of the sofa, arms folded, as Belle sees Jodie out.

I walked into prison after my sentencing with my head held high, convinced I had done the right thing. The officers stripped me of my possessions, but the one thing they couldn't take away was my pride. I held on to that golden key the whole two years that I flew under the radar, behaving myself, and making sure I'd get early release.

Never once, no matter what any of the more seasoned guys said to me, was I afraid.

Yet as I stand here now watching the girl I love walk toward me with a mournful smile, not only am I terrified of what's to come, I'm ashamed.

Grown men who bore tattoos that told of a life spent on the wrong side of the law couldn't break me. Nope. Turns out all it would take was an eighteen-year-old girl. A girl, and the words that fall from her rose-tinted lips as she slips her hands around my waist and lays her head on my chest.

"I love you, no matter what happens."

THIRTY-THREE

Belle

Crickets sing on the front lawn as I step out of Cerise's car. I spent the rest of the day with Zeus, pretending, denying. The two of us seemed content to reject the idea that life would continue after sunset, living in a kind of time-suspended bliss until the room grew dark and we were forced to face the inevitable.

I didn't want to leave. I reverted back to the spoilt brat of not so many years ago and tossed out my bottom lip as I refused to go. The only thing that made me give in was the hurt in Zeus's eyes as his patience wore thin. I wasn't making the whole deal any easier on him by whining about the inevitable.

I was selfish. I still am.

His car idles to a stop on the roadside as I head out to wait for him. I made him come, adamant that today is the day. D-day. The day everything implodes and we find out where the pieces lie after all is said and done. My gut tells me that there would never be a right time to do this. Hell, my shaking hands do too. But as I pointed out to Zeus when he brought up the idea of waiting until I've moved out again, continuing to lie when Dad knows something is going on would be simply insulting his intelligence.

If I want to prove I'm the adult I hope they see me as, then I need to act like one. I need to own up to my faults and face the consequences of my actions.

I need to come clean.

"Are you ready to do this?" Zeus offers his hand as he rounds the car to where I wait on the sidewalk.

"As I'll ever be." I slip my hand in his, and for a fleeting second, I'm bombarded by a slew of conflicting emotions.

His hand brings memories of comfort in recent weeks, of the thrill of a lover's kiss. But it also brings the security of a person I look up to, the man who would guide the child across a busy road, or keep her within reach while in a busy public place.

It's a strange juxtaposition. One I don't welcome in this moment.

"Are you sure this is the right thing to do?" He frowns, the conflict clear in his eyes.

"Positive."

He seems unconvinced, sighing out his nose as he looks toward the front door. "I just... I think it would be better to let things settle."

"What's really on your mind?"

He looks across at me with apprehension. "Do you ever wonder if they can see something we can't? I mean if everyone thinks this is wrong, maybe we are going about it the wrong way?"

"Don't give in to the bullshit," I snap, frustrated that last night's fiasco has got to his head. "You love me, right?"

"Always."

"So do this for me." I tug him toward the house. "Trust me."

I honestly can't pick what Dad's reaction will be. I hope for understanding, for tolerance, but damn... his daughter and his best friend. I'd be a fool not to understand the implications of that.

I give the nod, my nerves a fluttering moth against the burning light of my heart as Zeus pushes the door open.

Conversation stops within the house, the tail end of my father's words lost as I step into the doorway, Zeus close behind.

"You decided to come back." He frowns, eyes darting between the two of us.

Cerise reclines in her seat, wine in hand. "And you brought company. Goodie."

Holy shit. How the hell did I think I could do this? My stomach clenches painfully, my hands hot and clammy as I rub them over the hips of my shorts. The keys rattle in my left, reminding me they're hooked on my middle finger.

I step into the room, slowly, and set them down on the coffee table as though giving a peace offering. Cerise eyes me as I back to where Zeus remains, her shoulders rising with a deep breath.

Dad can't even look at us.

"Should we begin?" Zeus asks, eying Dad.

"Begin what?" he bites back.

"They're clearly here to tell us something," Cerise remarks with a little too much glee in her tone.

"Yeah, we are." Zeus places a hand to the back of my shoulder and guides me to a seat. "And we're going to talk about it like four adults."

"Strange," Cerise snorts. "I only see three."

And I see my hands wrapped around your neck.

"Cut it out," Dad snaps as he turns to face the group.

Zeus settles on the sofa beside me, leaving Cerise and Dad in their individual armchairs like a couple of judges presiding over our case. *Fitting.*

"I really don't know where I should begin," I admit.

"How about with the punch line," Cerise quips.

Zeus stiffens beside me. "If you aren't going to be helpful, you can fuck off."

"Watch how you talk to my wife," Dad warns.

I frown as Zeus voices my exact thought. "You're divorced, remember; she's not your wife."

The two of them stare each other down, the air thick and hot in the room.

"Zeus and I have been seeing each other," I word-vomit before I chicken out. "Romantically."

Cerise bursts into a fit of laughter, wine sloshing out of her glass as she leans forward to catch a breath. My cheeks burn, my neck hot as I focus on not letting the tears win.

"Romantically? Is that what you call it?"

Dad sits deathly quiet, head buried in his hand as he massages the bridge of his nose. "You've touched my daughter?"

He asks as though to confirm his assumption rather than to accuse.

"Yes," Zeus says.

He reaches for my hand, bringing it to his thigh. I grip that lifeline as though it's my only assurance of air, my only promise that I'll get out the other side of this intact.

Dad doesn't miss the contact. His eyes zero in on the possessive hold Zeus has on me as his face grows redder. The veins around his temples show as he grinds his jaw. "How long?"

"Four weeks?" I think. It feels like a lifetime since I stole that first kiss in the kitchen.

"So, since you were under my roof." The barely contained rage is clear in his words.

Zeus takes a deep breath before answering. "Yes."

"You touched my daughter, under my goddamn roof?" he roars.

"I wanted him to," I protest. "*I* started this."

"He knew better!" Dad hollers, making Cerise jump as he thrusts a finger at Zeus. "Jesus, Belle." His voice cracks as he shakes his head, face screwed up in disbelief. "We talked about this."

Zeus's hold on my hand loosens. He looks at me with a confused frown, yet stays resolute in our plan to discuss this plainly without deviating into a slinging match.

"Neither of us planned this." He returns his gaze to Dad. "Fuck, John. I tried to deny it."

"But these things happen, right?"

"Exactly," I say.

Dad scowls at me, shaking his head. "No, they don't, Belle. If Zeus couldn't help himself, he should have walked away."

"Why?" I yell, "Because I'm young? I'm not a goddamn minor. I'm old enough to decide who I want to be with."

"He's like a fucking uncle to you," Dad protests. "He's family."

"Maybe," I level, "but he's not blood. And that right there is why you have no right to be against this."

"I have every goddamn right."

"He's nothing but a predator, Belle," Cerise chimes in.

"You shut your goddamn mouth." Zeus damn near vibrates with pent-up frustration beside me as he exchanges glares with my mother. "Belle is not a child. Not anymore. You don't get to decide who she falls in love with."

"Love?" Dad scoffs. "Is that what you call this... this infatuation she has?" He eyeballs Zeus, chest heaving. "How far *has* this gone?"

"We don't need to discuss that," Zeus says. "The details don't change the outcome."

"Tell me, you backstabbing cunt. What have you

done with her?"

I push back into the seat as Dad rises to his feet. Zeus drops my hand, standing to meet Dad halfway. "Calm your shit, John."

"You tell me to calm my shit, and yet you won't tell me if you've fucked my baby girl. Is this how you repay friends? You take advantage of their kids?"

"She's not a child," Zeus hollers. "Get that through your fucking head."

"She's inexperienced," Dad counters, pushing up against his best friend.

"I'm right here," I yell, trying to tear their focus off killing each other. "Stop talking about me as though I'm incapable of making my own decisions."

Dad's gaze shifts to me as Cerise kicks back in her seat, a smile on her face. "You tell me then, Belle. How bad is this? Were those morning-after pills really for this Scott kid?"

"Yes!"

"You're telling me you're sexually active then?"

"Jesus, Dad," I shout, pushing to my feet. "Why the Spanish Inquisition? Yes, I'm sexually active. Yes, I'm of legal age to be so. And yes"—I pull a deep breath before setting fire to the world—"I've fucked Zeus, and I loved every goddamn second of it."

Cerise pulls in a sharp breath as Zeus groans. "Shit, Belle," she murmurs. "You've done it now."

Dad lets loose an animal growl as he arcs his elbow back and then swings at Zeus. I duck on instinct, watching as Zeus twists out of the way and Dad's fist grazes his jaw. He shunts Dad in the shoulder as he stands straight again, knocking him off balance while I retreat to the safety of the sofa.

"I get you're angry—"

"You've got no fucking idea how far past angry I am." Dad throws another punch as he recovers, this time connecting with Zeus's jaw.

His head snaps back, and blood springs forth from his split lip as he staggers his feet to get a more secure stance.

"Stop it!" I lunge forward to intervene, yet Zeus holds out a hand to halt me.

"Leave it, Belle."

I admit it—I took my statement a touch too far. But shit, is it so hard to believe that at eighteen I can enter into a sexual relationship with a man of my own free will? Why the fuck did Dad have to grill me as though Zeus blackmailed me into it, brainwashed me?

"Got anything to say, big guy?" Dad taunts, staging as though he's some prize fighter.

"Nothing you want to hear," Zeus replies.

By the look on Cerise's face this isn't anything unusual, at least for their younger selves.

I've never seen them argue past the point of a heated discussion. My heart aches at what I've done. I knew I risked a lot when I took matters into my own hands and kissed Zeus, forced him to admit the truth of his feelings for me. But never in my wildest dreams could I have imagined how it would feel to actually be in this moment, watching my world fall apart right before my very eyes.

I did this.

I drove my lonely father back into the arms of the woman who broke his heart by stealing away his time, never allowing him his own to pursue another relationship.

I ruined Zeus's future by selfishly wanting him for myself, damn the consequences.

And who do I have to turn to once I've lost them all? Nobody.

I allowed the distance to grow between Kate and I, because I thought I was so much more mature than her. How wrong was I? The way I dealt with this proves how juvenile I still am. I can view the world any which way I please, but nothing changes the fact I don't have the experience to make sound decisions when it comes to relationships.

I love Zeus. I love my father. I hate that they're fighting, and I hate even more that it's over me.

"You're dead to me." Dad spits, actually spits, on Zeus.

My lungs constrict, my heart in my throat as Zeus calmly wipes it off his arm and nods. "Fine. I deserve that."

"You don't see my daughter anymore," Dad yells. "You don't touch her. You don't come within a fucking inch of her."

"That I can't accept."

My love for Zeus grows as I witness him stand up for what he wants: me. He refuses to back down, even after having lost his oldest and best friend. I mean that much to him. We mean that much to him.

"Are you fucking with me?" Dad asks. "This isn't up for debate."

"Neither is the status of my and Belle's relationship." He squares his shoulders. "Choose your next words carefully, John, otherwise you may lose more than your best friend by the end of this."

He opts not to say a thing, instead driving a hard jab with his right into Zeus's cheek before Zeus catches his left by the wrist mid-strike. Dad roars his frustration as he prepares to go again with his right, yet one carefully placed hook to the jaw by Zeus has my father folding at the knees like a newborn deer.

"Holy shit." I drop beside Dad to check his breathing as Cerise launches her own attack on Zeus. "What the fuck did you do?"

Dad's breaths come even, yet fast, as his eyes roll about in his head. Zeus knocked him the fuck out.

"You'll be okay," I reassure Dad, coaxing him to lie back. "Just rest a moment."

He makes an incomprehensible moan and shuts his eyes, giving in to the black.

"You arsehole," Cerise screams, palms swinging in a futile attempt to harm Zeus.

He holds her off, using his forearms to block her

blows as he looks my way. "Is he okay?"

"What the fuck do you think?" I take Dad's hand, resting my other on his chest to monitor his breathing while I shoot daggers at Zeus. "What the fuck happened to talking about it like adults?"

When it comes to matters of the heart, though, are we ever mature enough to set emotions aside and look at the problem with a purely critical eye?

"Get out of this house," Cerise demands. "Get out before I find something to fucking hit you with."

Zeus backs up, worry in his eyes as he lifts his palms. "I didn't mean to hit him that hard, honest."

What hurts the most is I believe him. Still, punches like that kill people. "Go," I murmur. "I'll talk to you later."

He retreats toward the door, looking between Cerise and me. "Let me know how he is later, okay?"

"Sure," I mutter, watching Dad as he drifts with the fairies.

The front door clicks shut behind Zeus, the distant sound of his V8 starting soon after. I shift to my hip, getting comfortable next to Dad while I wait on him to come around. The soft scuff of Cerise's feet alerts me to her movements as she comes to stand on the far side of Dad.

"He won't forgive him for this." Her eyes narrow as she meets mine. "Or you."

"Of course he will." Although, given how angry he got, I'm not so sure.

Never, not once in my life, have I seen my father take a swing at somebody. Manhandle a guy out of a party after he'd had too many? Sure. But brawl like a couple of idiots at the pub? Nope.

I finally faced my fear and laid all my cards on the table. Where has it left me? I'm no less confused than I was going in to this conversation. All that's changed is that Dad now hates his best friend.

Zeus and I are still frowned upon, my mother still hates me, and I'm still at a loss as to what to do from here.

So much for honesty being the best option.

THIRTY-FOUR

Zeus

Nobody makes contact until the next day, and even worse is it's not Belle who calls me, but Jodie.

"That was a stupid fucking thing to do, Z."

"You aren't telling me anything I don't already know." I've replayed the scene over and over in my mind, coming up with a dozen other ways I could have steered John.

What else did I expect? Of course he'd be angry.

"I'm heading over later to try and throw some water over this goddamn volcano. Cerise is going off her rocker, and Belle is struggling to deal with it."

"Why the fuck hasn't she told me?" I ask.

"She doesn't know what to say to you, Z. She's got one hell of a case of the guilts."

Fuck. None of this is her fault. *I* was the one who gave in, who overstepped the boundaries. Maybe what we have isn't legally wrong, but I seriously ignored some moral standards by taking Belle as my own.

"Tell her to call me," I beg. "I need to talk to her."

The insomnia last night caused gave me time to

think. I should have waited. I should have let Belle set down roots, move out of John's and become a woman in her own time. I should have listened to my gut and let her go, let her experience life before she decided she really does want forever with me.

But the selfish fucker inside of me threw caution to the wind when he thought of the possibility of some other jackass coming along and stealing her away in the meantime. I went against my better instincts and threw fuel on an already uncontrollable fire, all because of a little jealousy.

"And here I thought I was the one who caused all the drama after our split." Jodie chuckles, reminding me she's still on the phone.

"Yeah, nah." I chuckle also. "Couldn't let you have the spotlight to yourself, could I?"

She makes a small "hmph," letting the call hang.

"I'm sorry, Jodie."

"What the fuck are you apologising for? I'm the one who was unfaithful."

"For holding you back." I rise out of my chair and head to the kitchen for a beer; this conversation calls for it. "We were over years ago, but I didn't let you go when I should have."

"You always were the optimist."

"Maybe."

"Don't go changing that," she says. "It's a good thing to have, Zeus."

"Even so, I don't think optimism is going to save me

this time."

"Time will tell. I'll let you know the outcome after I've been over there."

"Sure thing." I disconnect and stand at the kitchen island as I take the first swallow of my lager.

I can't look at this house now without thinking of Belle. My brain hurts every time I try to make heads or tails of the situation. My gut screams at me to let her go, to walk away from the damage I've done and let Belle and her old man sort things out between them. But the stubborn arsehole inside of me who never did care much for doing what's right is determined to see this through to the end.

My gut says no. My heart says yes. And my conscience? Fuck—it's rocking in the corner crying out for the room to stop spinning.

The condensation on the bottle makes a circle on the counter where I set my drink down. I snatch up my phone again and tap through to Belle's number. Fuck waiting. I need to know where she stands. I need to hear her voice to help me make up my goddamn mind on this.

Do I push forward and risk hurting her in the process by alienating her from John? Or do I do what any real man should and admit when he's fucked up and back off?

"Now isn't the best time," Belle whispers down the line.

"Who are you talking to?" Cerise's nasally voice cuts in from the background.

"Kate." *Pause.* "What time do you want to hit the shops? I thought if we got there…" The muted sounds of doors closing, and the wind as it cuts across the mouthpiece tell me she changes locations while she rambles. "Sorry. She's on me like a goddamn hawk."

"I'm so sorry, dove."

"In all fairness, he did start it. But shit… you knocked him the hell out."

"I know. It's been a while."

"You mean to tell me you've done that before?" She doesn't sound the slightest bit amused.

"Once or twice." I turn the beer in my hand, watching the condensation morph on the counter. "How are you?"

"Fucking confused." *That* she sounds amused by.

"Makes two of us."

"He's never going to allow it. He came to and was still spitting tacks until he realised you'd left. Then he started into lecturing me about the logistics of it all, how you'd hold me back, and how I'd be giving up on my dreams. Blah, blah, blah."

My conscience sits up and takes notice as my gut makes a "I told you so" gesture. John will never let it happen. He'll make my life hell, in turn wrecking hers.

Take the sign for what it is, Zeus. I need to listen to my gut instinct on this. I need to let her go before I wreck things further. I should never have let her convince me to admit shit to John last night—I wasn't ready. The resulting fallout just proves every doubt that I've ignored the past week.

Now isn't the time for us. Just because you want something, doesn't mean it's right.

"He's got a point." I hold my breath, waiting on her reply.

"No, he hasn't." Her tone makes me think of her, fists at her side, as she stamps one foot.

I smile even though my heart dies. "He does. You want to travel—"

"I don't have to."

"*And*," I say, cutting back in. "Despite the fact I can't travel with you because of my parole conditions, we never fully discussed the whole 'not being able to have kids' thing."

"I can deal with that."

"You say now. But what about in five years? Ten?"

She falls silent, allowing the echo of my heart beating in my ears to take over. "Why are you doing this?"

Because it's right. "I'm setting you free."

"I'm not trapped."

"You are," I say. "You can't see it, is all." I wish that I couldn't, either.

She expels a heavy breath, reminding me of John in that moment as her anger grows. "What about the studio next to your garage?"

"It's not going anywhere."

"Fuck, Zeus. Don't do this over the phone."

"Trust me, dove, I wish I wasn't." But I know I'd never be able to do it in person.

One look at her beautiful eyes, one glimpse of the

pain I put there…

I give in and set the beer down, turning to slide down the cabinets and sit on the floor. Everything is Belle. Always Belle. "Maybe it's not clear now, but trust me when I say that you'll see that I'm doing the right thing in time."

"Trust you," she scoffs. "I trusted you not to break my heart, and yet here we are."

"I haven't stopped loving you."

"But you don't want me anymore. Why?"

"Because I'm no good for you. I'm a fucking ex-convict with no future other than laying bitumen, dove. I can't offer you anything. All I can do is take and take until there's only half of you left." I sigh, frustrated that I can't find the right words. "I've already driven a wedge between you and your dad. I'm not going to be responsible for ripping your family apart. What I want doesn't matter, not when it means it'd ruin your life in the process. Go and be yourself for a while, find who you are when you're not John's daughter. Find your niche in the world, and then come back and show me what I invested in."

"You aren't investing in me though," she sobs. "You're tossing me aside."

"I'm not. I'm making the ultimate sacrifice so that you won't look back on this in years to come and resent me for smothering your dreams. I'm not doing this for me— I'm doing it for you."

"How?"

"What will you do if I came over there and got your shit to move you in here?"

She sighs. "I don't know. Get a job somewhere, anywhere."

"And your dad? You're willing to accept that he'd probably stop talking to you?"

She meets me with silence. I'm finally getting through.

"Letting you go will kill me, babe, but if it means you get to achieve everything you want in life, it'll be worth it. Carrying this on? It'll just hold you back."

"You're killing me too," she whispers.

I have nothing. So instead I listen to the woman I love cry as she faces the harsh reality of our situation. Maybe this shit works out in movies, but this is real life. People have been hurt, trust has been broken. You don't come back from that and watch a beautiful sunset as it casts a warm glow over the world you've created. You shiver in the cold while the battle fires still rage, the casualties of your selfish campaign strewn around like reminders of every bad decision you made.

"I love you, dove. I've always loved you and I don't think that'll ever change."

"You just don't love me enough," she sniffles.

"I love you too much, and that's why I have to walk away before I hurt anyone else."

THIRTY-FIVE

Belle

Zeus disconnects, leaving me shattered and hollow. I stare at the device in my hand as though it could somehow erase the past week of my life and yet leave me the clarity to do this all again, better, right.

This can't be the end. It can't be that simple.

"There you are." My father's whispered statement cuts at me like a notched dagger straight to the heart.

Through it all, he still loves me. And yet I'd give that up to keep Zeus's love instead.

What kind of daughter am I?

"What's wrong?" He lowers himself to sit beside me on the back step. "Your mum said you were talking to Kate."

I turn to face him, letting Dad take a good look at my tear-strewn face.

"Oh." He frowns, looping his elbows around his knees. "What did he have to say?"

"That he's had enough of hurting everyone, and so he has to let me go." I choke the last words out, the reality a sucker punch to the gut when I voice it out loud.

"Ssh." Dad slings an arm around my shoulders and pulls me in to his side. "It'll be okay."

"It won't."

"It will. It'll take time is all."

I snort a bitter laugh. "Do you remember the first time you told me that?"

He sighs. "You were fifteen. It was after that barbecue he organised to cheer me up." Dad stares off across the back yard, a small frown pinching his brow. "I watched you with him, watched the way he pulled the smiles from you without even knowing he did it, and I knew."

"That I had a crush on him."

"Yeah." He places a kiss to my head. "I told you that it was just your hormones doing a number on you and that it would pass."

"It never did."

"I see that now." Dad's hand tightens on my shoulder, tugging me against him before relaxing again. "I'm not angry that you feel that way, Belle. I'm angry at him for betraying my trust."

"I know."

"He could have talked to me about it."

I twist against his side and look up at him, noting the new age lines around his eyes. "Could he have, though?"

Dad chuckles, his lips pressed tight in a knowing smile. "No."

I pull free to get a proper look at him. "What exactly is it about us that makes you so apprehensive?"

"Without sounding like a right arsehole?"

I nod.

"You're young, sweetheart. You have so much ahead of you, so many things you're yet to experience, and I don't want you to turn anything down because you feel obligated to be here with Zeus."

"That's pretty much what he said," I mumble, staring down at my feet.

"So? Maybe there's an ounce of truth to it?" Dad knocks his leg into mine. "Sleep on it, sweetheart. Give things time to settle."

My lip quivers as I pick at the loose threads on the hem of my jeans. "It hurts, Dad."

"I know," he coos, pulling me into his side again. "I know."

••••

I sleep on it... for three days. What's the point of leaving my bed when there's nothing to get up for? Dad goes to work at night, stopping in each time to give me words of reassurance before he leaves.

I know what he says makes sense, but it doesn't stop me from messaging Zeus like a fool several times a day.

I miss you.

What are you doing?

How was the sunset in your room tonight?

Talk to me.

Tell me I'm not the only one hurting.

Zeus?

Silence. Cold, isolating silence.

"Belle?"

Somebody's here. Cerise never calls my name that sweetly when we're alone. "Yeah?"

"You have a visitor."

I bolt out of bed and rush to my closet, ripping the first outfit that makes sense off the hanger. Deep down I know it can't be Zeus; Cerise wouldn't be that welcoming if it was. But that one per cent, that slim chance, has me tearing my hairbrush through my matted mess before I give up and yank it back into a ponytail.

I head out to the living room to find Kate seated in one of the armchairs. "Hey."

"Hi."

"I didn't mean to get you up."

I chuckle, shaking my head as I take a seat in the other chair. "It's past two in the afternoon—I should be up and about anyway."

She frowns. "Why aren't you?"

I glance about but fail to see Cerise anywhere. "Zeus and I split up."

Kate schools her surprise well; only a slight twitch in

her perfectly poised hands gives it away. "You were a thing?"

I nod.

"Wow." Her whole body relaxes as she slumps against the back of the seat. "That makes things different."

"Different?" I haven't seen her in weeks. Haven't heard a thing from her since she stopped responding to my messages. "Why are you here?"

"I wanted to see my friend. Is that unusual?" She pushes off the cushions to sit straighter again.

"It is for us. Yeah."

The stones roll in my gut, giving me that sinking feeling again. Her jaw is tense, her eye movements jerky. She flits her gaze to the door repeatedly as we talk, almost as though she can't wait for this conversation to be over.

"So, things with Brock and me didn't turn out."

"I know," I say, tucking my legs up beside me.

"We tried reconciling, but it didn't happen. So I went out last weekend with Trent. He wanted to get my mind off things."

"And?" Speed it along, good buddy.

"And I came across Scott."

Oh. I band my arm around my legs, flicking my fingernails. "What happened?"

"He's really sorry about what he did, especially when I told him how reckless it was."

"You talked about me while I wasn't there?" Good to

see I turned out useful for something.

"I didn't bring it up—he did."

"So much better," I drone as I turn away.

I catch the telltale sounds of the back door as Cerise lets herself in after presumably having a cigarette. She appears at the edge of the kitchen seconds later, smile firmly in place. "Would you girls like a drink?"

"No thank you." Kate smiles equally sweetly.

To my horror, Cerise decides that gives her licence to join us in the living room. She takes a seat on the sofa and continues to smile widely at the two of us.

I'm trapped in the music video for Soundgarden's "Black Hole Sun."

"Would you like to continue this in my room, Kate?" I jerk my head toward the hall.

She looks towards Cerise briefly, and then nods. "Sure."

I lead Kate to the far end of the house and take a seat on the edge of my bed as she pushes my door to.

"Truth is," I admit, "I was over what Scott did pretty much right after it happened."

Kate frowns as she takes up residence on the opposite end of my bed. "I admire that, you know?"

"What?"

"How you always manage to keep going, no matter what shit gets thrown your way." She smiles, her chin tucked down. "I guess I was envious of that confidence."

I laugh, drawing her focus. "Confident? Nope. Hardly. I just put up a good show. If they think they can't hurt you, they won't keep trying to do it, right?"

"I guess." She smiles. "I miss us hanging out."

I stare at her, aware this is the part where I'm supposed to say I do too. Yet the words don't come. The sentiment doesn't feel right. I regret losing her, sure, but it surprises me to realise I haven't missed her.

"Anyway," Kate continues when I fail to respond. "I came over because I wanted you to hear it from me."

Whatever it is, I know I already don't like it.

"Scott and I talked for quite a while that night. He's changed since school got out. I guess because he doesn't have the pressure of the others to upkeep an image."

Gee—that must have been so hard on him. *Ugh.* "Really?"

"He, um, asked to see me again this week, and I said yes."

"You don't need my permission to hang out with him," I deadpan.

"I know. I've already seen him." She giggles. "Twice."

She's infatuated with the guy. I could see it in the way her face changed when she thought about seeing him already this week. *Disgusting.* The guy makes a simple apology for being a douche, and suddenly he's a saint in her eyes.

Leopards don't change their spots. And big cats don't stop feeding on weak prey.

"Be careful with him," I warn. "He's a smooth talker until he gets what he wants."

She chuckles nervously.

"Kate?" I cock an eyebrow, suddenly pissed at this traitor sullying my safe space.

"That's the thing. We've slept together already." She holds both hands up, halting my reply. "I know, it's so soon. But he's so genuine."

"How do you know?"

"I just do, okay?" Her lips press in a thin smile as she drops a sympathetic shoulder. "I'm sorry, Belle. I didn't mean for it to happen...."

"It just did?"

"Yeah." Kate drops her gaze to the comforter between us. "I wanted you to hear it from me, anyway. I hope you can understand."

"Thanks for stopping by." I remain impassive.

If they can't see that they hurt you, they won't keep doing it.

"Belle."

"You seem busy. I'll let you get back to the rest of your day."

She blows out a heavy breath when she realises I'm not going to keep this conversation going, and stands. "See you around. Maybe."

I focus on the brilliant white clouds that pepper the sky out my window as I listen to her make small talk with Cerise, and then leave. A car starts on the roadside, and to my horror, I slide across to the window side of my bed to find Scott behind the wheel as they pull away.

The silence afterward is poignant. I don't have a mother who thinks to ask if I'm okay, let alone one who senses that Kate's visit wasn't all that friendly. I don't have a lover to talk to, to seek comfort in.

Instead, I have the empty ache of the theme of my life: everyone always leaves.

I guess Zeus achieved one thing he wanted to without even realising it—I have nothing left to stay here for.

Nothing to tie me down other than the weight of a thousand regrets strung across my shoulders.

Time to lighten that load.

THIRTY-SIX

Zeus

Two questions run through my mind as John steps inside my house and looks around: Why is he here? Is Belle okay?

"You've made quite the home out of it," he appraises as he stops in the middle of the living room.

"I try." Be more of a home if it had Belle in it, but beggars can't be choosers. "What brings you around?"

He sighs, hands on hips as he looks to the floor. "Look, mate. I don't begrudge you for what you did in hitting me." He lifts his chin to look me dead in the eye. "I acted like a jerk, and I got what I deserved."

"I don't think anyone else saw it that way."

He huffs a bitter laugh. "Yeah."

I gesture toward the seats, and he nods.

"Cerise wanted me to report it."

"Of course she did." I roll my eyes as I drop into the solo armchair.

"You know why?" John makes himself comfortable on the sofa. You'd almost think we'd never come to blows over his daughter.

Except, I'll never forget. "I violate my parole conditions if I'm reported for assault again."

He nods, eyes averted. "I can't believe she wants you back in prison, mate."

"What part is unbelievable?" I ask. "That she'd go to that extreme to get rid of me, or that she's that much of a cold-hearted bitch?"

I expect protest, in the very least a lame warning about watching what I say. I get nothing. The way John's mouth turns down as he nods tells me he understands. *Finally.*

"Why did you let her come back?" I ask. "She's no good for Belle, and she's taking you for a ride as well."

He shrugs. "I don't know. I guess I was sick and fucking tired of coming home from work to nothing."

"You had something," I point out. "A daughter who worshipped the ground you walked on."

"Past tense?" he points out.

I tip my head to the side. "You'd have to ask her. All I know is that you lost more than a part of her respect when you let Cerise come back. You lost trust."

"She talked to you a bit, huh?" His eyes narrow as he digs the fingers of his right hand into the arm of the sofa.

"Despite what you might have imagined, we did have more to our relationship than a few hot and heavy moments."

He doesn't take my dry humour well, a scowl pulling his face in. "Easy."

"Why are you here, John? Really?"

He taps his fingers on the upholstery, watching them as he does. "Belle isn't coping well with this split."

He may as well have punched me in the face again. "A risk I took."

"I guess I don't understand why you did it." He tilts his head to one side, eyes narrow as he studies me. "Why go to all that trouble to tell me what was going on if you were just going to end it anyway?"

"Because I wasn't going to end it." At least not consciously. "I wanted her for myself. I still want her for myself. But I guess that was the wake-up call I needed."

"To see what?"

"That she deserves so much more." I sigh, slamming my forearms down on the arms of the chair. "Fuck, mate. My life is all but over. I'm a deadbeat ex-con with nothing in his future but menial labour and weekends spent finding ways to pass the time. I don't have career options, a life to build; this is it. But Belle...."

"She has all of that yet to come."

"Exactly. Her staying with me? That would just hurt her, and I'm tired of hurting everyone." I sigh, over thinking about it already, over the burden of who I am. "All I've done is hurt people, mate, and I'm tired of it. I'm tired of being the bad guy. I can only take so much."

John drags a palm over his mouth and chin, hard eyes watching me as he thinks things over. He taps the tip of his thumb against his bottom lip, the intense scrutiny he has me under making me uncomfortable in my own house.

"If she came in here now," he asks, "and announced that she'd give it all up for you: her dreams, her plans, her options… what would you do?"

"Same thing I did the first time she told me that, I guess."

"Which is?"

"Remind her that she's young and that her view on things will change."

He nods with a low hum. "And what if they don't?"

"Then I guess we reassess the situation when we know that for sure." My pulse beats thick and heavy in my neck, agitation building the more he pushes me to analyse this with him.

I've been over every facet of this fucking situation a thousand times in the last few days. A hundred more in the weeks before. I've thought about it, changed my mind more than my fucking underwear, and always ended up at the same damn conclusion: this is how it had to end.

Early.

"As weird as it is for me to say it to you, J, I love your daughter. Belle…." I pause, crinkling my nose up while I search for the right fucking words. "I've never felt so comfortable with somebody before that they make me forget that I *have* company. Does that make sense?"

"She's an extension of you," he muses.

"Exactly." I point a finger at him. "I don't have to second-guess what she thinks about me."

"About your history, you mean?"

I frown, unsure where he's going with this.

"Mate, I've told you before and I'll say it again. Most of us don't give a fuck that you did time. Most of us would have done the same thing if the roles were reversed. Sefina was an amazing woman, one who didn't deserve even an ounce of what that cunt dealt out to her." He chuckles. "Shit, Z. If you'd told me what you were off to do that day, I probably would have joined you."

"I know," I say with a smile. "Which is why I didn't tell you. You had Belle. You still have Belle to think about. I couldn't take you from her." I glance to the floor and frown. "I can't take her from you now, either."

The humour slides from his face as he leans forward in his seat. "I don't like the idea of it all, but shit, you made her happy." He shakes his head, eyes down as he clasps his hands where they hang between his knees. "I can't do that. Not like you do."

"Why do you have to make this even harder than it is?" I murmur. "Don't kick a dying dog, mate."

"All I'm going to say, is, I hope you understand you're doing the right thing."

"I'm not sure." My mood bounces daily between staying the course in letting my dove fly free, and clipping her wings so that she has no choice but to stay caged with me.

I know which choice suits us both, but I also know which choice is the best for her.

"Hopefully in time she'll understand that, too," I

murmur.

John shakes his head. "She won't leave the house, mate."

Fuck, baby girl. "Then we make her."

Because the sooner she moves on, the sooner I will too.

THIRTY-SEVEN

Belle

The faint smell of German sausage drifts on the breeze from the food trucks parked around the outskirts of the oval. Cars come and go for the monthly get-together; kids squeal and laugh as they make the most of the bouncy castles made available by the organisers as a special treat for Christmas.

"I can't remember the last time we came to this," I muse as Dad locks the work truck.

He pockets the keys and holds his hand out for mine. "Two and a half years ago."

Cerise wanted to come, but Dad shot her down, demanding one on one time with me. I could have hugged and kissed him when he did that, but instead I remained composed in front of her and saved my thanks for the car ride here.

"I thought it might cheer you up," he explains as we head for the first row of shiny classics lined up for admiration. "I have something I want to talk to you about, anyway."

"And you had to bring me here to do it?" I smile as we

walk hand in hand.

Dad ducks his chin, his lips tilted up at the corners. "Well... I have a confession."

"I'm listening."

We stop next to the end of the row, a Camaro polished within an inch of its life gleaming under the massive floodlights while one of many Santas here tonight chats with another man beside it.

"I'm not the only one who wants to talk to you about this." Dad gives my hand a tug and leads me along the row.

I vaguely pay attention to the cars we pass while I study Dad, trying to pick what he's up to, when one sleeper catches my eye. One sleeper that's had a new matte finish since I saw it last.

"What are you doing?" I stop walking, tugging back on Dad's hand.

He tightens his grip so I can't escape as Zeus climbs out of the driver seat.

"Sorry we're late," Dad calls, as though I'm not being trapped into a conversation I don't want to have. "This one couldn't decide what she wanted to wear."

Kill me now. I can't look at him. *Don't look at him.*

I look at him. *Fuck.*

"Hi."

"Hey, dove."

Is he trying to hurt me?

"You know what?" Dad says, fooling no one. "I think that coffee I had before we left is working. I'll be back soon."

Arsehole takes off across the grounds before I can say a damn thing. Zeus takes a step forward to get out of the way of a guy who takes a picture of the car. He's close enough to touch. My hands ache with the need to reach out and pat him, just to make sure this is real.

For weeks he's avoided me. For weeks he's ignored every message I sent. The arsehole has even been radio silent on social media, not posting a damn thing.

"So…." I nod toward the car. "Keeping occupied?"

"Got to do something to keep my mind off other things."

Huh. "I might keep walking. Tell Dad to catch up when he gets back." I take two steps and halt when his strong hand wraps around my upper arm.

"Belle, wait."

"Let me go, please."

He does as I ask, looking like a child who's been caught with their hand in the cookie jar. Maybe I was simply a sweet treat for him? Who would know, considering he doesn't tell me a damn thing.

"I'll walk with you."

Great. "Whatever, Zeus."

He ghosts me in silence, keeping slightly behind me and off to my right as I do my best to appear interested in the cars. It's no use. Ask me what colours there were, what makes and models, and I couldn't tell you a damn thing.

Ask me how he smells tonight, what he does with his

hands when we stop, and how many times he's run his thumb across his bottom lip, and I could recount that in vivid detail.

I'm ruined. Completely ruined.

"How has the job hunting been going?"

I glare at him, pissed he thinks he can slip his way back into my good books with idle conversation. "Why don't you ask me what you really want to know?"

He looks around us, seeming to check if anyone takes notice of us as we stand face to face, before slaying me with those blue eyes I love so much. "Is it getting any easier?" He chews his bottom lip before continuing. "Because I think every day is harder than the last for me."

"Why are you doing this to us?" I whisper. *Don't cry. Don't show him how he hurts you.*

"Because it's the right thing to do."

"Fuck what's right," I snap. "Did you care about what the right thing to do was when you kissed me? Did you give two shits about what was right when you fucked me, Z?"

"Belle." He tugs me along, eyes darting all around.

"Oh, please. As if anyone around here cares." He says nothing, fist tangled in the side of my black sweater as he pulls me toward the fence line. "Where are we going?"

"Somewhere private."

Somewhere without boundaries. "Don't." I dig my heels in, twisting around his wrist as he tries to keep us going. "I want to stay where there's other people."

"Why?" He releases my top, frowning. "Don't you trust me?"

"I don't trust myself."

He swallows hard, the same battle I struggle with clear in his eyes. "This is why I ignored you, dove."

"Don't—"

"Because I knew if I came to see you, if I talked to you, I couldn't keep my resolve." He smirks. "I stayed on my feet, head up and proud when the guys who ran my wing in prison thought they'd try to break me on my first week. Nothing they did brought me down, but babe, one look at you and I want to fall to my knees and beg you to forgive me." His brow knits as he lifts a hand to touch me and then thinks better of it. "If I give in, you'll regret it in the future."

"Don't tell me what I will and won't regret." I take myself by surprise, shoving him hard in the chest.

The release feels good. Too good.

I shove again, and Zeus takes a step back, yet he doesn't lift a finger to defend himself. He takes everything I have as I push again and again, my palms slapping hard enough against his firm chest to make my hands sting.

"You don't get to make decisions about my future for me," I growl as I push him backward. "You don't get to tell me who I can and can't love. You don't get to tell me anything."

"Belle…." He lifts his hand and catches one of my

wrists as he loses his footing, regaining balance before he takes us both down. "Stop."

"I hate you," I yell. "I hate you for loving me. I hate you for showing me what I can't have."

He expels a single heavy breath, his brow furrowed, before he winds his hand in my hair and yanks my head to his. Zeus's lips crush mine; his other hand presses my hips hard against his as he kisses me with all the pain that I've felt in the past weeks.

How can he understand and yet keep telling me that staying apart is what's right? How can he believe the lies he repeats as though they're his gospel?

I cling to his shoulders as I pull free from his kiss and rest my forehead against his lips. "Don't do this if nothing will change."

"Nothing *has* changed," he murmurs against my head. "I still love you, dove."

His face is warm against my palm, the feel of his cheekbones, his jaw under my hand so familiar it soothes the ache that spreads from my heart through my limbs, crippling me from being able to walk away.

"You're everything to me, and if you make me do this thing called life without you, it'll never be complete."

"Sometimes you have to have pieces missing to ensure you never lose focus." He mirrors my actions, tracing the lines of my face with his thumb as he pulls me away. "Stay alert, Belle. Don't settle. Always look for more."

The salt of my tears mingles with the sweet taste of

his kiss as he gives me the most bittersweet goodbye I'll ever know. I lose myself in the moment, blocking out the people and the racket around us. His gentle lips pull me into this lie, this taste of what I could have had if only I was older, more experienced.

"Hey!" Pain lances through my shoulder as Dad jerks us apart. "This is not what I fucking brought her here for." He steps between Zeus and me, his rage directed at his former best friend.

"Dad, don't." Don't ruin the memory. Don't sully the moment.

"I've got nothing," Zeus says as he steps back, hands raised. "No excuse. No regrets. Nothing."

"You even tell her the news yet?"

"What news?" I ask.

"I was getting there," Zeus says with a shrug.

"Real fucking hard to explain it all with your tongue down her throat." Dad makes a disgusted sound. "Fuck it. I'll tell her myself. We can do this without you two having to see each other again."

"Do what?" I cry.

Why the fuck won't anyone fill me in on what so obviously relates to me?

"Come on, Belle." Dad jerks his head toward the car park. "We'll discuss it on our way out of here."

"John—"

"You," Dad growls, whirling on Zeus with his finger jabbed angrily in his direction, "can shut the fuck up and let her go without this having to get physical again. I gave you one shot, one last chance to make things right, and you've just fucked them up all over again."

My focus stays on the man I love as my father pulls me through the gathering crowd. I expect to find my pain mirrored back at me, regret tainting his features.

What I don't expect is blank resignation.

He holds my gaze as I stumble along beside Dad, and then turns away, quickly blending into the crowd and taking the last working piece of my heart with him.

Never settle. All I'll do from here on out is settle, because there isn't a man in this world that will ever compare to him.

I'll damn well prove it.

THIRTY-EIGHT

Belle

"Are you going to talk to me like you said you would?" I lean against my door, wiping away what remains of my tears with the backs of my hands.

"I'm trying to decide what exactly to say."

Awesome. This should be good then.

"Do you think that helped?" he finally asks. "After how you've been the past few weeks?"

"You're giving me the third degree like I'm ten."

"Well, I'm sorry," he snaps. "But unlike some people, I still look at you as my daughter."

"Nice," I deadpan. "Going for the low blow there, Dad."

"Fucker promised he'd keep it civil," he mutters as he stares out the side window.

"I heard that."

"I wasn't trying to keep it from you." He sighs, squeezing his hands around the wheel. "I just…. He surprised me, you know? We've been friends for such a long time, but put you between us and he's a completely different guy."

"You don't exactly help in the whole 'staying friends' department, you know."

"It's difficult." Silence ensues as he navigates an intersection. "I went to see him the other week and the two of us put a bit of a thing into action for you; something to cheer you up."

"Right." About the only thing that could supercharge me with any emotion other than melancholy right now would be the news I'm moving in with Zeus.

Somehow, I don't think that's it.

"Zeus showed me how to use Instagram," Dad announces as though he's proud his Generation X arse managed to tackle a new platform. "I found your profile and did some digging."

My heart seizes in my chest before smashing itself against the confines of my ribcage. *What the hell did he find?* I mentally catalogue all of the shit I post on there, trying to pre-empt what he'll say next.

"I looked at who you follow, and found this Chris Ellerhope guy."

"Okay?" I'm lost. So damn lost I can't remember how we started out on this topic anymore. "And?" Chris is one of the best tattooists alive in my opinion. His work is epic.

"I sent him a D... what is it is?"

"DM?"

"Yeah." Dad snaps his fingers. "That's it."

"I can't believe how technologically challenged you are," I say with a chuckle. "You're not that old."

DESIRE

"Maybe." He smiles. "But I've never been into that whole scene."

"Anyway. What did you say to him?" I press the side of my finger under my eyes, frustrated they'll be a puffy mess tomorrow.

"Told him I had a daughter who needs an apprentice-ship."

I want to die. My father has officially shamed me with an ink god. I purposefully didn't contact him myself because there's no way my talent could ever measure up to his.

"He asked to see your art."

"Really?" What the hell would I send him? Which pictures would I choose?

"So I sent him a shot of those sketches you have above the desk in your room."

"They're not finished," I cry. "Oh my God, Dad, no."

He laughs, reaching across to pat my knee. "It's okay. He liked them."

"He did?" This isn't my life.

"He doesn't have space to work under him, but he got you a position with a friend of his at a shop nearby so he could still oversee your learning."

"Are you fucking with me?" I can't believe how far the spectrum of emotion has gone for me in the past half hour. From feeling at absolute rock bottom when he dragged me away from Zeus, to being on a high at this unreal news.

"I'm not pranking you, Belle. I'm being real here."

351

"So why involve Zeus?" I ask the question that burns as hot as the searing pain in my bones the further and further away we drive from the man I want.

My legs itch to jump from the truck and run back to him, yet this revelation from Dad keeps me rooted to the seat as we wait at a red light.

"Well," Dad says, lifting his eyebrows. "When I sent the message to the guy, I didn't realise he's in Colorado."

"Dad...."

"You know I can't afford that."

"Cerise can."

"I'm not asking her for help," he snaps.

"Why?"

He swallows hard, glancing across at me as we start to move again. "She hasn't wanted to do a damn thing to help you this far, I'm not letting her have this. We'll figure it out on our own, like we always have." He hesitates, his thoughts clearly elsewhere as he gazes out the window. "I thought I could make a go of things with her for your sake, fix the problems from before, but...." He seems to choke on the next words, a frown pulling his brow down. "She hasn't changed, sweetheart. I'm sorry."

"Don't be." I sigh. "She hates me. Always has."

He looks across at me, the concern clear in his eyes.

"It's okay," I reassure him. "I've made peace with it." And I have. I didn't need her for the last ten years. Didn't need her for the milestone moments in my life. She can take a long jump off a tall cliff for all I care. "Why Zeus?"

I ask again.

"Zeus is going to pay for you to fly there."

My jaw drops. "What?"

"He knows as well as I do that if we wait until you've got a job, saved enough, too much time will pass. He wants you to go there and grab the opportunity with both hands. So do I." Dad smiles across at me. "This guy is talented, Belle. Not just in his artwork, but as a businessman; you could learn a lot from him." He reaches out and takes my hand in his. "Spend a few years there. Chris will help you do the paperwork to get in on a work visa. He seems excited to take you on. Do the work and come back with the base you need to start your own shop."

I can't comprehend. I can't deal.

I hang on to Dad's hand and stare out the window at the world as it passes us by, oblivious to the emotional torment being in the cab of this truck brings.

I'd be leaving Zeus, but he's paying for me to go. What's his end game? Does he want this for me so I can come back to him and start the shop out of his studio like we talked about? Would he wait for me?

He's made no indication he would, but a girl has to hope.

"I'm speechless, Dad. I really don't know what to say."

"How about, 'Thanks, Dad'?" he teases.

"Thanks, Dad." I lean across and place a kiss to his cheek.

"You're welcome, sweetheart. Now go knock the world on its arse."

••••

My hand shakes as I hold my phone over my head, laid out on my bed while I debate whether I should send a thank you message to Zeus or not. It would be the polite thing to do, but Dad seemed pretty adamant when he reminded me as we got out of the truck that he doesn't want me to deal with Zeus; he would do it all.

Fuck it. You only live once.

B: Thank you. I'm still thinking about it, but the offer is generous.

His dots dance immediately, making my heart skip a beat.

Z: What is there to think about? Take the opportunity, Belle.

B: Are you sure you can afford this? You sunk all your money into the house.

I ignore his obvious neglect of my nickname.

Z: Not your concern.

B: You aren't jacking cars again to pay for it, are you?

Z: Ha ha. Close, but no.

B: What have you done? *taps foot*

Z: Sold the GTO.

B: What? You're pulling my leg.

Z: I had it there tonight to meet the guy and go through the paperwork. He wanted one last look at it before he signed. I had plans, but I can spare some cash for you.

B: Zeus...

Fuck my tears. Fuck him and his ability to make me all mushy.

Z: Goodnight, Belle. And good luck.

I give up trying to reply when I lose focus of my phone. He signed off with the damn heart and the dove.

Damn him. Damn everyone and everything.

I throw my arms over my eyes and sob as my heart is tugged in multiple directions. Why does life have to be so hard? Is this what people talk about when they say teenagers have no idea what it's like to be an adult? Because if this is adulting, I quit.

"Everything okay?" Dad asks, breaking me out of my pity party for one.

I throw a thumb in the air, my other arm still over my

eyes.

"Can I do anything?" he asks from the relative safety of my doorway.

"Message Chris, and Zeus," I say, taking a moment to regain myself after choking on his name, "and let them know I'll do it. I'll go to the States."

Colorado, here I come.

THIRTY-NINE

Belle

I've lived in a constant state of anxiety the past six months. Life has been turned on its head since I walked out the school gates and entered my new life as a so-called adult. In such a short space of time, I've managed to love, lose, and learn.

Each achievement as painful as the other.

Dad delivered an ultimatum to Cerise the week after I saw Zeus at the car show: on New Year's Eve. He made me proud, standing up to her like he should have done years ago, and telling her that if she didn't put in real effort when it came to fitting in to what is *his* life, then she could move out.

In true Cerise style, she stormed out declaring that she wouldn't stay where she wasn't wanted, and holed up in a motel for a few days before returning with her tail between her legs. He told her she either puts in a real effort to change her ways, or the next time she'll find the door locked.

Standing up for himself was the best resolution Dad ever made.

I don't understand the woman; I don't think I ever will. But we've come to a kind of truce: I've stopped expecting her to act like my mother, and she's stopped trying to be one. It's better that way—at least, for now.

Kate and Scott still date, making it Facebook official on New Year's Day. I keep track of their progress on social media, as much as I know I shouldn't. It's like watching a car travel down the highway with a buckled wheel, waiting to see if it'll fall off and cause an accident or somehow manage to reach its destination without creating carnage for everyone around it. She seems content though, so I have to give her that.

It's more than I can say for myself.

My American work visa came through seventy days after I applied and after two rounds of interviews. Dad seems to think they wanted to be thorough given my age, and I guess I have to agree. How many nineteen-year-olds travel overseas for work rather than play?

My sketchbook is filled with ideas I can't wait to present to Chris after he meets me in Colorado. The idea that I'm to travel to another country to work in the same city as one of my idols... yeah, I still can't get over that. How does this even happen?

Simple: Zeus.

He's stayed silent since saying goodbye to me the night of the car show. I managed a week before I wanted to cave and send him a message, but to my initial shock I discovered he's blocked me on Facebook. I guess we all deal with our heartache in different ways. All I hope is that wherever he is, whoever he may be with—as much as the thought makes me nauseous—he's happy.

Dad doesn't mention anything about him. I don't even know if they still talk after everything that happened. To be honest, I don't think Cerise would allow it. I should feel bad, but I regret nothing. I love Zeus—that hasn't changed. I'll always love Zeus, and I know that I'll never meet anybody who makes me feel complete like he did.

Maybe that sets me up for a life of disappointment? I don't know. All I do know is that I wouldn't trade the time we had for anything. I only wish for more.

Two years in another country, and then I'll come back and do whatever it takes to fulfil my dream. I'll have a shop, even if it's only me in it to begin with, and I'll make him proud.

I only hope that by then he's ready to talk, ready to see me. It's all that keeps me hanging on as I stand in the middle of the international lounge at the airport, my sketchbook under my arm, and my heart in my throat.

This is it. Today is the day.

"Got your passport handy?" Dad asks, checking the zipper on my carry-on for the millionth time.

"Yep."

"And you have water and snacks for the flight? That airline food is sketchy at times."

"Yes, Dad." I frown, frustrated to admit that I feel let down. "Why didn't Cerise come?"

He chews his bottom lip as he grimaces. "She's busy

moving her shit out of the house."

"What?" My jaw hangs slack.

"Mmm." He shrugs. "I guess it's a new beginning for both of us."

"I'm so proud of you." He deserves better than her—always has.

Dad smiles, patting his hands on his thighs as he looks me over. "You've grown, sweetheart, and I don't mean in height."

"I know."

I look back at pictures of myself six months ago in my final weeks at school, and I wonder how I ever could have expected the world to take me seriously when I so obviously reflected my age. I've changed since then, and I think it was all a part of the process of finding myself.

Shit things happened to me: I was bullied, taken advantage of sexually by Scott, and I had my heart broken by the one person I truly want in this world.

But each of those experiences taught me something about myself. Love, relationships, heartache, and suffering: they're all facets of who we are. If you don't love deeply, then you don't feel deeply. And if you don't feel deeply, then how can you expect to truly understand the complexity of the world in such a way that it shows in your art, your actions, and your values?

I learnt acceptance. I learnt sacrifice. And I learnt that sometimes we give up the things we love the most for the people we love the most. And we do it without a second thought, because those people are what we live for.

"I better go through security and board, Dad." I check the time on my phone. "They opened it five minutes ago."

"Yes." If I didn't know better, I would think they're tears in his eyes.

"Are you going to cry?"

"No." He chuckles. "I'm going to leak happiness."

"You dork." I throw my arms around him, my sketchbook slapping his back. "I'll call when I arrive, okay?"

"I'll be waiting." He gives me a tight squeeze and then releases me. "Now get."

I push down my own emotions at leaving the man who's given tirelessly to make sure I had the best start in life, and grip my carry-on with white knuckles as I head up the escalator.

The security personnel let me through without issue—after I'm asked to remove my studded boots. I slip them back on and gather my things, my quickened pulse vibrating throughout my entire body as I head for the gate.

I've never been on a plane before. Never left the country. This is huge for a homebody like me, but the opportunity at the other end is more than I'll ever get again in my lifetime. Too much for me to pass up because of an irrational fear of flying, that's for sure.

The hostess scans my boarding pass and welcomes me with a wide smile. If she can recognise my fear, she doesn't show it. But then again, she probably sees people like me a hundred times a week. My skin burns as I stow my luggage in the overhead compartment, my panic rising the more it dawns on me I'm going to be trapped in this metal tube for almost an entire day.

"First time to the US?" A friendly voice asks from beneath me.

I glance down as I give my bag the last shove and see my row-mate stow a book in the seat pocket before him. Kind eyes meet mine, and he smiles as he waits on an answer.

"First time flying."

"Wow. Quite a way to break the ice, isn't it?"

Something about the man draws me in, something that makes me want to scoot closer and pick him apart to find out what's so unique inside.

"I'm known for causing a bit of drama," I tease, "so I apologise now if I'm an anxious heap the whole way there."

He chuckles, dimples showing as he runs a hand through his blond hair to push it back. "Well, I'm known for my patience. So, you're in luck."

I take my seat on the aisle, and reach across the empty middle one to offer my hand. "Belle."

"Damien." He takes my hand and pumps it firmly in his.

I gesture to the empty seat between us. "Do you have a companion?"

His lips curl up on one side as he cocks an eyebrow.

"I take it you don't then?"

"Nope. Completely solo over here." I'm pretty sure I just broke some safe-travelling rule by sharing that, but it's not exactly a secret when I'm going to spend the next twenty-two hours not uttering a word to anyone.

Except maybe Damien.

"What are you reading?" I jerk my chin at the book before him.

"A thriller," he says, touching the top of the cover. "Murder, mystery, shady characters doing even shadier things. You know the sort."

"Sounds interesting."

He shrugs, eye on the book as he states, "I can read it anytime." Damien turns his head and smiles. "You, however, I only get to discover your story right here, right now. So, tell me, Belle, what makes you such a troublemaker?"

Maybe I'm going to enjoy this flight after all.

"Well, it's a bit of a long story, but...."

FIND CLOSURE IN

Break the rules,
then set your own.

REGRET

BOOK TWO IN THE TWISTED HEARTS DUET

MAX HENRY

Thank you for reading the start of Belle and Zeus's story!

I hope you enjoyed the tale of forbidden love as much as I enjoyed writing it.

If I could ask one wee favour now that you're done?

Please take just a couple of minutes to leave a review. It doesn't have to be long: one or two sentences with a star rating is perfect.

Reviews not only help your favourite books be seen amongst the millions in the store, but it helps other readers decide if they'd like to experience the same magic.

Until next time, happy reading!

Want to hang out with like-minded chicks?

Then jump into **Max's Minxes** on Facebook!

www.facebook.com/groups/346994535466425/

Sign on for exclusive content with

www.maxhenryauthor.com/newsletter

THE MUSIC

Listen to the songs that inspired the book here:
http://spoti.fi/2Dbs2Fr

"Angel" – Massive Attack
"Crawl Inside" – Evans Blue
"Crazy" – ICEHOUSE
"Huggin' & Kissin'" – Big Black Delta
"Judas" – Fozzy
"Not Just A Girl" – She Wants Revenge
"Paradise Circus" – Massive Attack
"Perpetual" – VNV Nation
"Song #3" – Stone Sour
"Sorry" – Meg Myers
"Tear You Apart" – She Wants Revenge
"Teardrop" – Massive Attack
"These Things" – She Wants Revenge
"Undisclosed Desires" – Muse
"Until It's Gone" – Linkin Park
"Waking Lions" – Pop Evil
"You & Me" – Disclosure, ELIZA, Flume

ABOUT THE AUTHOR

Check out a full up-to-date list of titles at:
www.maxhenryauthor.com/the-books

Born and raised in Canterbury, New Zealand, Max now resides with her family in beautiful and sunny Queensland, Australia.

Life with two young children can be hectic at times, and although she may not write as often as she would like, Max wouldn't change a thing.

An avid lover of stories from a young age, she enjoys nothing more than to get lost in the pages while the characters dictate what direction she takes. Her favourite genre to write is young/new adult and the events in her stories may or may not be related to real life experiences (only she will ever know for sure).

In her down time, Max can be found at her local gym, brainstorming through a session with the weights. If not, she's probably out drooling over one of many classic cars on show that she wishes she owned.

FOLLOW MAX

AMAZON
http://amazon.com/author/maxhenry

TIKTOK & INSTAGRAM
@maxhenryauthor

FACEBOOK
www.facebook.com/MaxHenryAuthor

BOOKBUB
www.bookbub.com/authors/max-henry

GOODREADS
www.goodreads.com/author/show/
7555353.Max_Henry

www.ingramcontent.com/pod-product-compliance
Lightning Source LLC
Chambersburg PA
CBHW061512020726
47502CB00006B/2032